Secret Fires

Candace Camp

Anastasia Hopcus

Clutch Books LLC Edition

Other titles by Candace Camp

Heartwood
Cutter's Lady
Satan's Angel
Before the Dawn
A Perfect Gentleman
A Momentary Marriage
The Rainbow Season
The Rainbow Promise
Mad Morelands series
Mesmerized
Beyond Compare
Winterset
An Unexpected Pleasure
His Sinful Touch
His Wicked Charm
Her Scandalous Pursuit
Lost Heirs Series
A Stolen Heart
Promise Me Tomorrow
No Other Love
Matchmaker Series
The Marriage Wager
The Bridal Quest
The Wedding Challenge
The Courtship Dance
St. Dwynwen Series
A Winter Scandal
A Summer Seduction
The Marrying Season
Secrets of the Loch Series
Treasured
Pleasured
Enraptured
Willowmere Series
A Lady Never Tells
A Gentleman Always Remembers
An Affair Without End

Prologue

Stephanie looked at the posters of various eye maladies on the wall without really seeing them. The doctors had thought Ty's problem had something to do with his eyes when they first admitted him to the hospital. When they'd realized it wasn't his eyes but still didn't know what it was, they simply left Ty in that wing. The neurologist had asked to speak to her alone and shuttled Stephanie off to this empty exam room twenty minutes ago. She wished she'd brought her jacket from Ty's room—it was freezing cold in here. Or maybe that was just her.

Stephanie had sat on a padded stool with wheels, which left Dr. McIlhenny only the examination chair to perch on when he came in. He looked both foolish and grave. Stephanie felt nothing but icy terror.

"Mrs. Tyler, I ordered a PET scan on your husband. I wasn't satisfied with CT scan." He spoke with the detached manner of a frequent observer of grieving. "Mr. Tyler has a very fast-growing brain tumor."

Stephanie just stared, unable to absorb the news, while he went on with his clinical analysis of the tumor in Ty's brain. Ty's brain. This man was talking as if it were an inanimate object. But it was Ty he was talking about. Ty's brain that was being destroyed. The neurologist must have seen the sudden, confused panic in her face. He came off the exam chair quickly and reached down to touch her arm. "Mrs. Tyler, is there someone you can call? Someone to be with you? Your parents? Mr. Tyler's?"

"No, they live in California. My parents. Ty's mother is in Florida. She's—I—we hadn't told her Ty was ill. We didn't want to worry her. Ty's father died just a year ago…" Stephanie's voice trailed off.

"A friend?" he suggested.

"Yes. Neil. I'd like to call Neil."

"I could have one of the nurses call him for you."

"No. I'd rather do it." She rose, feeling strangely disconnected from herself, and went to Ty's room. He lay in the bed, a long, silent mass beneath the sheets. Tubes ran into his arms and nose. His eyes were closed, his face lifeless. He didn't look like Ty at all, except for the mockery of his bright golden hair against the pillow. Stephanie took her cell phone out of her jacket and headed into the hall. She didn't want to make the call from Ty's room, no matter how unconscious he looked. She dialed Neil Moran's number. Neil had been at the hospital almost every day since Ty entered—helping Stephanie, taking her down to the cafeteria and forcing her to eat, talking to Ty as if Ty could respond to him. It was ironic that he hadn't been there when the doctor chose to tell her about Ty's brain tumor.

A lump filled her throat when Neil's familiar voice answered the phone, and for a moment she couldn't speak. Finally she whispered, "Neil?"

"Stephanie? What's wrong?"

She cleared her throat. "Could you come to the hospital?"

"Has something happened to Ty?"

"No. Well, yes. Nothing's happened, exactly, but they—Dr. McIlhenny told me he has a brain tumor." There was a stunned silence at the other end, and she went on tremulously, "Neil, I need you."

"I'll be right there."

He must have driven down from his hill like a maniac, for it was only minutes later that he charged out of the elevator. Jaw set, hands clenched at his sides, his face stamped with cold determination, he looked for all the world as if he were running onto the field to turn the game around, except that there was a white touch of fear around his eyes that Stephanie had never seen there before. She jumped to her feet and ran toward him and let him engulf her in his hard arms.

She clutched at his shirt and buried her face against his chest, sobbing out broken incoherent words. His long, supple fingers smoothed her hair. His cheek caressed the top of her head as he murmured her name. For a brief moment she felt protected. Then reality returned and she pulled away shakily. "The doctor's still here. Do you want to talk to him?"

Neil nodded, then impatiently shoved back the thick black hair that fell over his forehead when he did so. They returned to the exam room, but this time the neurologist didn't sit down. Neil remained standing, already towering over the doctor, and it was obvious that Dr. McIlhenny didn't want to add to his disadvantage by having to look up at Neil from a chair. The doctor explained again about the tumor. Neil, unconsciously positioning himself between the doctor and Stephanie, snapped, "What are you going to do about it?"

McIlhenny sighed. "Mr. Moran, this is a very difficult tumor to treat. It has spread, and—well, I'd like a neurosurgeon to see him before I give you a definite answer, but my suspicion is that it's inoperable. It's—"

"Oh, my God!" Stephanie burst out, raising her hands to her mouth. She felt suddenly sick.

Neil knelt down beside her, one arm going around her shoulders. "Maybe the doctor and I better talk alone. Do you want to go to Ty's room?"

"No. I have to hear it." She smiled weakly at Neil. "I can handle it."

Neil squeezed her shoulders and stood. "When do you plan to consult with the neurosurgeon?"

"I think we should transfer Mr. Tyler to Barrow Neurological Institute at St. Joseph's. The neurosurgeon I want him to see is on staff there. He's the best in the state."

"Considering Arizona's size, I'm not sure that's saying a whole hell of a lot," Neil countered.

"I'd put him up against anyone. Barrow is one of the top neurological facilities in the country. If the surgeon thinks he can operate, Mr. Tyler will be in the best hands. I don't want to hold out any false hopes, but Mr. Tyler is a very healthy man, and young. A much better candidate for surgery than most."

Neil strode to the door and back, his hands clenching and unclenching. Stephanie knew the look. Like Ty, he wasn't good at accepting things. He was accustomed to competing, to fighting and winning. Neil found it hard to deal with something he couldn't beat himself. His thick black brows drew together, and his tan face was tight with suppressed anger. The black stare was flat and grim, unfocused. He was struggling to control his rage.

"What I want to know," he began softly, his voice building, "is why the hell it took you so long to figure this out. A man comes in here with a tumor and you're testing him for eye diseases, stroke, diabetes—you thought it was a sinus infection at first, for God's sake!"

"I wasn't called in until this morning," Dr. McIlhenny interjected, understandably nervous at the fierce anger coming from the other, much larger man.

"Why not?" Neil thundered. "I've watched you doctors run around here for a week, doing test after test and not coming up with a scrap of information. Why didn't they call you in earlier?"

"Brain tumors have many, very variable symptoms. Because they affect both the brain and the central nervous system, it may seem to the patient that the pain is in the stomach, a leg, or some other completely unrelated area. That's why it can take a while before doctors realize they need to call in the neurologist."

Stephanie rose with a weary sigh. "Come on, Neil, it's no good blaming the hospital. The team doctor thought it was football-related, too. You guys spend half your life in pain. Everybody was looking for something they could trace back to an injury—sinus problems from his broken nose, a pinched nerve, a hit to the head. Who'd expect Ty to have a brain tumor?" Her voice caught on the words.

Neil's face softened. "Stringer, I'm sorry." His calling her by the nickname he'd given her when they'd first met made Stephanie smile through her tears. She'd always thought it was a cute name for a freelance journalist—though it hadn't given her the thrill that Ty's calling her Red had. "I just wanted to lash out at somebody. But it doesn't make it any better, does it? I feel useless."

"I know. Me too."

The doctor interrupted gravely. "This tumor is exceptionally fast growing. That's why it didn't show up on the CT scan they did at the beginning. I'm not sure it would even have shown up on a PET scan back then."

The doctor left soon after that, and Neil and Stephanie returned to Ty's room to sit numbly by his bed and stare at him. Ty didn't open his eyes or speak, and finally, hours later, Neil talked Stephanie into going home to rest. They drove in silence to the huge, echoing mansion where she and Ty lived. Neil walked her to the door, and she turned to him with huge eyes. "Will you stay with me for a while? I—I'm scared to be alone."

"Of course." He smiled, but his bleary eyes showed he was just as exhausted as she was. Stephanie fixed coffee for them and they talked about the past, the days before the three of them knew each other, and gradually worked their way back to Ty. Stephanie and Neil laughed about their respective first introductions to the force of nature that was Kenneth Tyler. Stephanie's laughter suddenly turned to tears. "I don't know what I'm going to do! Neil, what if he dies?"

"He won't. Ty can't die. Don't worry, Steph, I'll be right here with you. All the way."

Chapter One

Stephanie Tyler stretched her legs out on the lounger and settled back to enjoy her morning coffee. Heat waves shimmered in front of Camelback Mountain, the most distinctive of the barren mountains surrounding Phoenix. Although it was the middle of June, the first gentle month of summer in other places, it was already blazing in Phoenix. That was why she had scheduled her appointment with Howard Perry for 9:30 in the morning; she liked to get trips outside the house done before the afternoon.

Thinking of Perry, she sighed and for the hundredth time wondered what he wanted to say to her. An overlooked team-owned insurance policy or pension plan for Ty? A paper releasing the team from responsibility for his death? A lawsuit was something Perry's conniving mind might conceive of as a threat. He would cover all the angles. Ty had said the first rule to remember in dealing with Howard Perry was to distrust him. Howard was the vice-president in charge of Player Personnel, and at the time Ty had been embroiled in bitter contract negotiations with him. Howard Perry was all business and practicality; Ty all talent and fire. They didn't mix well.

Stephanie herself had had a few tussles with Howard Perry years ago when she was cowriting a book with Mel Williams. It had been about Mel's life as a former Olympic volleyball player and football wife to Jalyn Williams, the best cornerback the Pumas had, but Howard had demanded approval rights on the manuscript so he could remove anything unflattering about the Puma organization or its players. Stephanie had told him there was no way he'd have any sort of control over what she wrote. She'd had ample access to everyone on the team through Mel and Ty; she didn't need Howard's help.

Stephanie shook her head, dismissing the thoughts. She wasn't going to let Howard Perry spoil the precious morning peace of her garden. Her eyes turned to the high oleander hedge that shaded her back yard and separated it from her neighbor's. In front of it several hardy irises bloomed in a graceful, nodding arrangement. The pint-sized pool was a fresh blue rectangle, and the fragrant lemon and lime trees made a splash of waxy green against the white wall of her office.

Her office. That was a joke. It had been weeks since she'd done any work. Stephanie swung her legs off the lounge chair. If such disagreeable thoughts were going to intrude on her morning contemplation, she might as well go to Howard's office. She stood up and went into the house to get ready for her appointment.

Her house was smaller than the sprawling wood-and-glass home in which she and Ty had lived, but it suited her. She hadn't been able to stay in Ty's house after his death, and the settled charm of this older neighborhood appealed to her. There was something comforting about the white stucco, red-roofed house. The last family had lived there for almost thirty years, and the love seemed to have settled into the walls. That had been what Stephanie needed at the time, a place to curl up and be comforted. And the one-room guesthouse in the rear, perfect for a freelance writer's office, had completely sold her on the house.

Stephanie put on light make-up and swept her long red-brown hair into a knot so it wouldn't straggle and cling to her face in the heat. She had chosen a light linen sundress with blue stripes that brought out the color of her eyes. She knew that her eyes were her best feature. They were large and an unusual blue-gray color that glowed or darkened with whatever she was feeling, and they were strongly accented by the slash of dark brows above them. Looking her best always bolstered Stephanie's confidence. As Ty had said, you couldn't let Howard Perry see you sweat. She didn't know what Howard was after, but their conversations had a tendency to turn into arguments.

The business offices of the Phoenix Pumas lay beside the stadium and practice field south of Tempe on Interstate 10. The closer she drew to the familiar gold-glass building and the looming stadium beyond it, the tighter her stomach knotted. She hadn't been here since Ty died, and it was a jolt to face Ty's home ground again.

But by the time Stephanie got past security at the gate and parked, she had shoved aside the sadness and the nerves—or, at least, locked them away well enough they didn't show. She lifted her chin and strode through the front doors. Just inside, she had to pass through a metal detector. That was new since she'd been here last. And she didn't recognize either of the guards. Everything moved on.

The halls were carpeted in dull gold to match the no-longer-trendy gold glass of the exterior, and the walls were decorated with large paintings featuring famous players and scenes from their games. Stephanie didn't look at the one of Ty leaping through the air to catch the game-winning touchdown of the Super Bowl. No expense had been spared on this dream-child of the Ingram brothers back in the 90s, but, while they kept everything in immaculate shape, the design of the place was now rather dated.

The Ingram brothers had taken a family fortune and parlayed it into a staggering multibillion-dollar enterprise dedicated to real estate and entertainment. The centerpiece of their empire was the Phoenix Pumas. They'd hired the best of the best to make their fledgling team competitive and profitable. The result was a team that had won the championship of their division multiple times and even one Super Bowl.

Stephanie took the elevator to the top floor, where the executive offices lay. Howard's secretary—who looked like she'd probably marched in the first women's suffragist parade in 1913—took her name and ushered her into the spacious corner office. Howard Perry rose to greet her, flinging his arms out wide and smiling like she'd just made his day.

"Stephanie! Damn, but you look good, girl!" Perry always laid his Texas accent on for all that it was worth when he was trying to be charming. Stephanie thought it just sounded like he was imitating Matthew McConaughey. That was where any resemblance ended though. Howard was as short and rotund as the actor was tall and lean. "Come in, come in. How are you?"

Stephanie answered, but her words were drowned out by the wild yapping that erupted behind her.

She turned to see a small white dog that looked like two cotton balls glued together with spindly legs and a tail emerging from the fluff like a Q-tip. The dog was standing on a pink satin pillow and barking so hard its entire body lifted off the pillow with each yap.

"Well, who is this?" Stephanie started toward the animal, hand stretched out for the dog to sniff, but she stopped when the little dog flew into such a paroxysm of barking that she was afraid it might tumble off the couch entirely.

"Princess Fleek! Shut up!" The dog stopped barking, whirled around a few times and dropped back to its cushion, heaving an enormous sigh. Howard's sigh was just as loud. "Jeez..." Howard, who was not exactly a big man, looked like he could hold the puffy dog in one hand—though Stephanie could tell by his expression he had less than zero interest in doing that. "Her name is Princess Fleek. And don't even ask me what that means. My youngest daughter who named her tried to explain it to me. I had to wash down six aspirins with a scotch afterward and I still don't have the slightest clue."

"And she stays at your office?" Stephanie asked. "It's certainly a different look."

"Ha!" Howard gave one of his loud short laughs and gestured toward the chair nearest his desk. "Sit down, sit down. Not on the couch; it'll set the fluffball off again. Princess was 'diagnosed' with separation anxiety, and my wife started her on some kind of doggie Xanax, but it hasn't kicked in yet. She'd bark at her own shadow if it was big enough to notice—though, nothing could compare to the pure terror that is our Roomba." Howard glared at the dog. "Little rat should be scared I'm gonna tie her leash to a park bench and never return."

Stephanie suppressed a smile as she sat down in the chair he indicated. Maybe Howard wasn't as bad as she thought. Anyone who would put up with that yapping—even if complaining about it—had to have some kindness in him. Not to mention nerves of steel.

"Where's your wife?" Stephanie asked.

"She took my middle daughter—you know Kailee, she's a writer like you—to New York City. Kailee can't get a single agent to read her ten-page opus about an anthropomorphic toilet brush that moves to Hollywood on a mission to become a street sweeper. Did you know how hard it is to find an agent?"

"I have some idea," Stephanie responded drily.

"But according to her mother, just finishing the thing entitles Kailee to a vacation in the publishing capital of the world."

"Well, I'm sure they'll enjoy it."

"Let me get straight to the point, Stephanie." Howard sat back down in his chair, placing his forearms on the desk and forming a careful steeple with his fingers. He stared intently at his hands for a moment before turning his gaze back to her. "We're involved in a project that I think will please you a great deal."

"Please me?" Stephanie repeated, already lost.

"Yes. The Pumas Wives' Association has been raising funds for the past year to set up the Kenneth R. Tyler Cancer Foundation."

"A foundation in Ty's memory?" Had Perry summoned her to his office to brag about someone else's hard work? Stephanie had seen in the past how quickly Perry made a break for the bar at any of the Wives' Association's charities—she couldn't imagine him getting personally involved.

"They've raised a tidy sum. Karen Randall was the chairwoman, and you know what a go-getter she is. They sold a cookbook and had some kind of crazy auction and I don't know what all. Anyway, they came up with a bunch of money, which Russell and Winslow Ingram doubled."

"Mel said something to me about their raising money for Ty, but I didn't know the details. That's so good of them. And very kind of the Ingrams."

"The Ingrams are always generous where their players are concerned. And they were very fond of Kenneth. They were saddened by his loss."

It was on the tip of Stephanie's tongue to remark that the Ingrams were primarily saddened by the loss of Ty's talent, but she bit back the words. However cynical she might be in regard to the owners of football teams and their loyalty to their players, it was a very generous gesture, and she was grateful. She would have to call Karen to thank her and write a note to the Ingrams.

"But it gets better," Perry went on, making a sweeping gesture. "Kimberly Gates—you know Kimberly, don't you? She's the V.P. of Branding."

"Branding?" Stephanie asked warily. She did know Kimberly, the woman who was in charge of making the organization look good. Kimberly had been the one who convinced Howard that letting Stephanie have access to the facilities and personnel would make them look open and honest in her book rather than secretive and sketchy. "What does branding have to do with this foundation? The team is going to publicize it?"

"Oh, better than that." Perry beamed. "Kim's connected with the NFL Foundation, and they're going to add it as one of their charities. We're going to have a ceremony during halftime of the first exhibition game, the first weekend in August. Now, that's where you come in. It seems appropriate, since it's in Kenneth's name, to present you with a plaque commemorating the fund. His profile will be etched on the metal plate, and below that will be the 'Kenneth R. Tyler Cancer Foundation' and the date."

"I see," Stephanie responded flatly. She did indeed. This was an opportunity to get some good press. Typical.

"Maria Hernández, the head of the Wives, is coordinating the ceremony. Her office will get in touch with you closer to the date. I just wanted—"

"Wait a minute. I haven't agreed to attend."

Howard blinked. "Pardon?"

"I said, I haven't agreed to attend. Frankly, I find your trading on Ty's premature death more than a little macabre."

"Where did you get the idea we're 'trading' on Kenneth's death? We're simply—"

"You're simply using this fund to obtain more publicity for the Pumas," Stephanie replied.

"Stephanie!" He appeared shocked. "I… I never dreamed you'd fight a foundation in your husband's memory."

"I have nothing against the foundation. It's great."

"Then what's the problem? Look, I talked to Scott about this."

"Scott? Ty's agent? What does he have to do with this?"

"Sales for his jersey and memorabilia will go way up. It'll all go to you. And, not to speak ill of the dead, but we both know Tyler was never one to hang on to money. I'm sure you could use it—how good could that writing stuff pay?"

"You think I'm interested in the money?" Stephanie jumped to her feet. "What I'm interested in is not using Ty's death and the Wives' Association's charitable efforts to make the Pumas organization look good. It's blatantly transactional—and disgusting."

Perry stared at her as if she were a rare form of animal life, interesting but bizarre. "Kenneth and I had our differences, but I hope you aren't holding that against me or the company. It was only natural. We were on the opposite sides of the bargaining table. That didn't mean I didn't respect him as a man and a talent."

"As a talent, perhaps. But you didn't know him as a man. If you did, you wouldn't call him Kenneth. He hated his first name. His friends called him Ty." Old anger and submerged pain flooded her. "You don't know any of those players as human beings. To you they're machines, something you buy and sell, something you squeeze every last ounce of energy, talent and courage out of, then toss aside when they can't perform for you. It's profit to you and vicarious enjoyment to others, but to those men on the field it's broken bones and torn ligaments and an incredible amount of mental anguish."

"It's also quite a few dollars to them."

"That's always your argument, isn't it? If they don't want to play, they don't have to. But this is what they've been trained to do their whole lives. Football is worshipped by their towns, their parents, and they're just kids dazzled by visions of fame and money."

"A lot of them love the game," Howard interjected mildly.

"You use that against them too. That's why they tape themselves up and take painkillers and go out to play with injuries that aren't allowed enough time to heal completely. I've met fifty-five-year-old ex-football players who shuffle along like old men because their knees will hardly bend! And that's not even getting into CTE and concussions and—"

"Hey! We're working on that. We've got a protocol now."

Stephanie rolled her eyes. “Only because you were forced into it by all the negative publicity. You know, the sort of thing you want to counter by having some big ceremony where people can praise the organization for how generous it is.”

“Okay, okay. I get it.” Perry held up a hand like a traffic cop. “Look. I realize you’ve interviewed a lot of malcontents for that book you wrote with Jalyn Williams’ wife—what’s her name?”

“Mel,” Stephanie supplied tightly. “I have a little more personal experience than that. I was married to a football player for almost three years.”

“Kenneth—Ty—was the best wide receiver this team had—maybe the best playing in this country at that time. He was talented, likable, outrageous, but he wasn’t typical. He was a freak of nature.”

“I think I know my husband better than you!” Stephanie struggled to get the volume of her voice under control. “What’s the purpose of this lecture on Ty?”

“I’m just saying that you can’t judge football based on one man. Ty lived for drama. Most men couldn’t keep up his lifestyle, especially the life he led before he married you. And he was a bundle of nerves who spent most of the time before a big game hanging over the toilet vomiting. Ty could tell a good story. He enjoyed talking about the hard things in football, but I bet he didn’t tell you about how much crap Coach Davis and the Ingrams and this organization took because of him.”

Stephanie closed her eyes and drew in a calming breath. She had trouble controlling her temper, a problem that had gotten worse since Ty’s death. “I’m sorry, Howard. I know Ty wasn’t all sweetness and light. Nor is the game of football all bad. And this discussion has gotten way off track. We were talking about the ceremony at halftime. I don’t like it. It’s commercializing something that began as a noble impulse, and it’s using Ty’s death to promote your product. It’s the Wives’ Association’s and the Ingrams’ money, and they’re free to give it to whomever they want in any manner they choose. But I won’t be a part of it.”

“That’s your final word?”

“That’s it.” Stephanie gave him a brittle grin. “I’m sorry to have blown off steam in front of you.”

A genuine laugh burst from Howard's throat. "Kid, your little tirade was a dream compared to some of the things that have been said in this office. I hope you change your mind."

"I won't."

Stephanie turned and walked out of the room. Her knees trembled, part of the aftermath of her anger. She couldn't remember how many times she'd blown up like that in the last year and a half. She'd always had strong feelings about things, was full of opinions, and had a tendency to be blunt. But in the past Stephanie's emotions had been more likely to spill over in loud laughter in a crowded theater or tears at a sad scene in one of her favorite TV shows—she didn't just yell at someone. But Ty's death had brought her anger to the surface, and it seemed that she hadn't yet recovered.

Apparently her departure was as displeasing to Princess Fleek as her entrance had been, for the dog jumped up and began to bark as soon as Stephanie started out the door. As she walked down the hall, she heard Howard Perry shout, "Shut up, you little furball from hell!"

Even in her present mood, Stephanie couldn't help but smile. However much her refusal had displeased Howard, she was sure it was nothing compared to dealing with that yapping day in and day out.

As she walked to her car, she glanced toward the mountains. For a moment she considered driving out to Neil's house but decided not to. He was a great friend—the best—but she couldn't take advantage of that. For the past few months she'd managed on her own, and she needed to continue rebuilding her life.

Stephanie turned her car toward home. Poor Neil. His grief had hit him almost as hard as hers. Probably because he'd believed up to the bitter end that Ty would beat cancer. No matter what the doctors told him, Neil thought Ty couldn't die. Stephanie had wanted to believe it, too, and Neil's determination had almost convinced her sometimes. But deep down she'd realized Ty could die—that Ty *was* dying—long before Neil did.

The neurosurgeon at Barrow Neurological Institute had immediately agreed that the tumor was inoperable. Russell Ingram had flown in an expert from California at his own expense, but even he had agreed with the two prior diagnoses. The treatments the doctors prescribed allowed Ty to live almost three more weeks. Stephanie was able to take him out of the hospital, with round-the-clock RNs at home. He was asleep most of the time, and when he was awake he was confused and often mistook Stephanie for his mother or his sister. Ty died quietly, with a funny little sigh. Stephanie was standing at his side, holding his hand, and she had felt the life slip out of him.

Neil had been there too, sitting in an armchair on the other side of the bed. He had kept his word to Stephanie to see her through everything. Even on the weekends, even with the night-shift nurse on duty, he had slept at their house, his long frame stretched out uncomfortably on the living room sofa so that he would be near in case Stephanie called for help.

Neil and Ty had been so different, but despite that—or maybe because of it—they were as close as brothers. Ty was always joking and laughing, a brash, controversial guy who had trouble living by the rules. He was flashy, charming, and enormously talented. Neil called him a "natural," a player who was so skillful that his success was inevitable, and she'd heard him referred to as 'a freak of nature' many times before Howard had today.

Neil, on the other hand, was not as naturally talented but far more hardworking. He succeeded on drive, mental ability and his ice-cool nerve, surpassing other quarterbacks in the league who had more powerful arms. Neil's personality, though he showed frequent flashes of humor, was quieter and calmer than Ty's. He was good-looking, but not a player. He was steady, intense and deep. He was reliable, a "team guy" who could always be counted on to pull everyone together.

Neil had stuck with Ty through everything, even those horrible days before anyone realized he was ill, when Ty had changed personality, becoming sarcastic, moody, and even violently angry. Ty had actually taken a swing at Neil once, but Neil, the stronger of the two, had merely wrestled him to the ground and restrained him until Ty's anger passed.

After Ty's death, Neil had continued to help Stephanie, taking care of the funeral arrangements and managing to keep away most of the press. He'd listened patiently to Stephanie's litany of what-ifs, always reassuring her that she had done everything she could have to save Ty. Most of all he had given her a shoulder to cry on. Numb with shock, it wasn't until several months later that Stephanie realized how hard that must have been for Neil when he himself was grieving the loss of his best friend. But that was just Neil.

Stephanie drove home mechanically, her mind occupied with the past. She barely noticed anything until she turned onto her street. She put her car in park in her driveway and rested her forehead against the steering wheel. The sharp pain of losing Ty had long since passed, and she no longer cried at the slightest bit of sadness in a book or movie. But her talk with Howard Perry had dredged up the sorrow-laden memories.

She thought of Ty as he had looked when she first met him—golden hair, golden skin, bright blue eyes, a smile as mischievous and winning as a boy's. She had come to his house to interview him for the book she was cowriting with Mel Williams. When she rang his doorbell and he opened the door, a spontaneous grin had split his face. "I never expected you to look like this," he'd teased, "or I'd have agreed to talk to you weeks ago, Red."

Stephanie had been unable to resist smiling back at him. She had gone inside for the interview and had emerged an hour later after accepting a dinner invitation from him for that evening. The quality of the notes she had taken during the interview was poor, but it didn't matter. By the end of the evening she was sure she was in love with him, and two months later they were married.

Tears filled Stephanie's eyes and plopped onto the lower rim of the steering wheel. She thought of Ty, and she cried for all that had been lost.

Chapter Two

Neil Moran sat on the padded bench with his legs splayed wide enough to lower the weight between his legs until his arm was at full extension, then he carefully squeezed the dumbbell back up to shoulder level, holding the last rep for a long, burning few seconds. He let out a short burst of breath before lowering the weight again slowly, placing it on the floor of his workout room. Neil let his head droop forward, perspiration dripping from his black hair as he used the end of the small towel draped around his neck to wipe the sweat from his face.

The careful workouts had been paying off. His elbow hadn't felt any more strain than the rest of his arm. The surgery had frightened him, and the long month and a half when he couldn't use his arm for anything strenuous had been even worse. He could almost see his muscles atrophying. But then he had begun a programmed schedule of 'rehab' workouts beneath the watchful gaze of Chris Garcia, the team's head trainer.

Neil had had to be patient, but that was his forte. His ability to exercise control over his body and emotions was one of his most powerful weapons as a quarterback. It was a rare day indeed when pain, fatigue or anxiety was allowed to shadow Neil Moran's game.

He had applied his control to rehabbing his injured elbow, and it was beginning to look as if he'd succeeded. Of course, he wouldn't know for sure until the arm was put to the stress and strain of an actual game, but at least Neil was in a much better spot than he'd been last season, when he'd started out with a partially immobilized throwing arm.

He rose and strode out of the workout room and opened the sliding-glass door leading onto the wooden deck, and stepped out into the dry heat. He had turned on the whirlpool hot tub before he began his workout, and it was bubbling away, ready for him. He stepped into the sunken tub and positioned himself so that the jetting water massaged his arm.

Finally, when the heat became unbearable, Neil heaved himself out of the tub and dashed across the patio to dive into the large rectangular swimming pool. This was Neil's favorite part of his morning routine, and he swept through the water with powerful strokes, luxuriating in the glide of the cool water over his heated skin. He'd done three laps when his cell phone rang so loudly that he could hear it under the water. He climbed out and padded to the patio table to grab it. "Yes?"

"Neil? This is Howard Perry."

"Howard. How goes it?"

"Not so good at the moment. You were right. She wouldn't go for it."

"Stephanie? You asked her about the ceremony?"

"Yeah, this morning. She hated it, jumped all over me. Accused me of using it for publicity."

"Imagine that," Neil replied blandly. "I told you she wouldn't like it. She's been anti-football since Ty died."

"Football didn't kill him!"

"No, but you have to turn your anger somewhere, I guess. Who's responsible for a brain tumor? Ty? God? There's nobody to blame."

"But why take it out on the team? Seems illogical to me."

A spark of humor glinted in Neil's eyes. "Howard, anything that conflicts with what you want seems illogical to you."

Perry chuckled at the blunt statement. "You're probably right about that. So I'm handing it over to you. Talk to Stephanie and see what you can do with her."

"Me? Are you kidding?"

"No. You're the only one who has a chance. You were Tyler's best friend. She likes you, trusts you. Doesn't she?"

"I guess." Neil's black eyes narrowed as they gazed down at the pool. He didn't see the sparkling aqua water. He saw Stephanie Tyler's face, tear-streaked, tense and white, as she hurried toward him down the hospital corridor, hands stretched out to reach him sooner. Her mouth had been so downturned and vulnerable it had shaken him to the core. He'd pulled her close, wrapping his arms around her tightly as if his very strength could ward off her demons, though there was nothing that could do that. Yes, she trusted him. It was one thing that made the way he felt about her so difficult. "But that doesn't mean I can convince her to come to the ceremony. Why don't you leave her out of it?"

"It wouldn't be as effective. Damn it, Neil, it would reflect badly on the team," Perry uttered the most condemning words in his vocabulary. "It would look as if Tyler's wife was snubbing us, as if she didn't approve."

"Which is the truth."

"It doesn't look good."

"Did you tell her the team's retiring his jersey?"

"Nah. It's gotta be a surprise. If she knows beforehand, she might not cry, and I want that on camera."

"And people say you're insensitive."

"What," Perry tossed back. "You didn't want me to tell her either."

"I know." Neil thought the surprise would bring her more happiness, even if the joy came with a few tears. And God knows, Stephanie could use some happiness.

"Look. All I'm asking is that you talk to her. I'll understand if you can't get through to her. She's a stubborn girl."

"She's a woman who knows her own mind," Neil corrected. "Your sexism is showing again."

"Please, spare me. Females have been kicking my butt all day."

Neil heard a sharp, high yipping on the other end, and Perry obviously turned from the phone to shout, "Shut up, Princess!" Speaking into the receiver again, he went on, "See what I mean?"

Neil grinned. "Keeping the dog again, huh?"

"Yeah, yeah, I hear you laughing." Moving his mouth away again, Perry yelled, "Estelle! Come get this worthless piece of lint and take her outside." After a moment, the high-pitched yips mercifully ended. "Just talk to Stephanie, okay?

"Howard, I'm sorry, but I can't try to change Stephanie's mind. I refuse to use my friendship like that."

His words halted Perry for a moment. It was rare for a player to refuse a request from the powerful director of player personnel, but Neil knew he was indispensable enough to get away with it.

"I'm not sure I understand your point," Howard began cautiously. "You wouldn't be asking her to do anything illegal or immoral."

"I won't trade on my friendship with her dead husband to get to her." Neil's words were clipped and precise.

"Then don't. Go to her as her friend. You've done enough for her to qualify as that. Just tell her what you think. You told me you thought the ceremony would mean something special to her if she'd ever agree to it."

"Yeah. I know." Neil pinched the bridge of his nose and closed his eyes, his thoughts turning inward. He didn't want to prey on Stephanie's emotions, to play on her grief in order to benefit the team. But he didn't have to do that. Neil could simply offer her his opinion. She would listen to him with a more open mind than she would to Perry, whom she disliked to begin with. No pressure, no talk about 'what Ty would have wanted' or 'helping the team.' It would be a simple discussion, and she could make up her mind freely.

He wavered, picturing Stephanie as he had last seen her over a month ago, in a flower-covered sundress. Her straight, spicy red-brown hair had hung unadorned to her shoulders, pushed back behind her ears to reveal dangling earrings that swung softly against her delicate jawline. There was something slightly bohemian about Stephanie, a certain flair and free-spirited attitude, though she never seemed like she was striving for any particular look. She just looked like herself: casual, unique—and utterly devastating to the senses.

It would be great to see her again. It had been a long time since his last visit. He wanted to see her, and Howard's request would make a reasonable excuse.

But, no, he didn't like it. He didn't want to struggle for excuses to see Stephanie: It was too dishonest. And he didn't want to open up the wounds of Ty's death again just to help out Howard Perry. "No." Neil's voice was flat and uncompromising. "If I happen to see her, I'll give her my opinion, but I'm not going to force it. I think a widow has the right to keep the memory of her husband to herself."

"Man, you've gotta lighten up on all that nobility. You were a real pain in the ass that year you were the players' union rep." Perry sighed. "All right. I know when it's pointless to argue with you."

"Good." Neil smiled. "I'll remind you of that next contract."

"Jeez. You're killing me here."

Neil hung up the phone and wandered to the edge of the pool. He was tall and well-built, with lean hips and wide shoulders. His chest was a hard pad of muscle and his arms bulged with strength. His hands were those of a natural quarterback, large, supple and long fingered. His face was angular, the cheekbones broad and high, the jaw wide. It was a tight face, usually impassive, as if the skin had been stretched too tightly across his prominent bones. But fire and sparkle danced in his black eyes, and when Neil was amused, the planes of his face shifted upward and the skin around his eyes crinkled almost boyishly. A small scar bisected one of his thick black eyebrows, cutting it into two distinct pieces, offsetting the cold structure of his features and giving him a slightly rakish look.

Wealthy, famous and handsome, he was one of the most eligible bachelors in Arizona. He knew most people would be amazed, then disbelieving, if they knew that for years Neil had been quietly in love with a woman that just considered him a friend.

But it was the truth. The moment Ty had walked into that bar with Stephanie, every nerve in Neil's body had leaped up in a clamor of desire and certainty that he'd finally encountered that elusive feeling that he'd heard others talk about as love at first sight. And in that same instant he was gripped with the despair of knowing that she was Ty's girl.

As the couple drew closer, Neil had fallen even harder. Stephanie didn't radiate obvious sexuality like the girls Ty usually dated. But her expressive face was filled with a lively curiosity and warmth that made her intriguing, and Neil had curled his hands into fists trying to ignore the impulse to run his fingers through her long, lustrous, cinnamon colored hair. But it was her eyes that went right through him like an arrow to his gut… they were big and beautiful and seemed to shift colors.

Ty had introduced Stephanie, and she had bent forward a little to hear what Neil said and that simple, light smell that was distinctly Stephanie had made him want to grab and kiss her in front of everyone. But Neil had hidden the rush of longing as well as he hid his anger or nerves during a game. It was a skill he would use more and more often around Stephanie.

By the time she married Ty, Neil knew he was hopelessly, irreversibly in love with her.

Most people stopped seeing someone that didn't return their feelings, but Ty was his best friend, so Stephanie became Neil's friend, too. The three of them were together so often that Pete Cherneski, the Pumas' eccentric middle linebacker, often jokingly called them 'the thruple.' Neil had tried to stay away at first—it tore at his heart to see Ty kiss Stephanie—but it was worse to be away from her.

If it had been any other man except Ty, Neil wouldn't have hesitated to try and take her away from him. By nature and long years of training Neil was a predator, a fighter. But it was Ty. He was the one man he couldn't hurt. Ty had been his best friend since their first days in training camp. Neil could no more have betrayed Ty than he could have betrayed his own brother.

Then Ty had developed his tumor. Stephanie had depended on Neil more and more; she trusted him, put her faith in him. He could hardly turn around and tell her that he was not what he seemed to be and never had been.

Neil couldn't forgive himself for that one involuntary leap of hope he'd felt after Stephanie had told him Ty was dying—the thought that now Stephanie would be free. He started to question his own motives until even a comforting hug seemed wrong to him.

He'd gradually cut down on his visits to Stephanie. She needed time alone to come to terms with Ty's death. If Neil were with her constantly, as he had been during Ty's illness, Stephanie might have just slipped into a relationship with him out of sheer convenience or gratitude. That was the last thing Neil wanted.

Every time he saw Stephanie, she was a little bit happier. Soon she might start dating again. If he waited much longer the odds were that another man would snatch her up before he had a chance with her. For the first time since he'd known Stephanie, he had the opportunity to do what he did best—strive and win. He wouldn't go see her for Howard; Neil would go see Stephanie for himself.

* * *

The bout of crying left Stephanie drained, yet curiously at peace. She went into the house and washed the tears from her face. Then she walked out to the guesthouse in back.

The guesthouse consisted of one room and a bath, and it had been easily converted into an office. Stephanie loved the place. Simply being in it made her feel better. There was a big, ugly, incredibly comfortable chair sandwiched between a scuffed end table and a bookcase jammed with books. A desk was piled with more books, notepads, and her computer. The walls were hung with photographs of Stephanie's family and friends. It was not a pretty room, but it was familiar and cozy, filled with the work Stephanie loved.

When Stephanie entered her office she went immediately to the large chair and flopped down, leaning her head against its back. Her eyes were beginning to ache from crying, and she closed them. There had been a difference in her tears today, a letting go of Ty and the memories. It seemed a sort of coda to her grief. She felt… released.

That was odd. She hadn't realized before that she had felt imprisoned by her sorrow. For a time she sat, thinking of Ty, remembering the good times, and she smiled. Perhaps her outburst of resentment against Howard Perry that morning had helped sweep away the remaining dregs of her grief.

There was a knock on the door and Stephanie opened her eyes, surprised. Few people came around back to her office. That was one of the reasons she liked it. She rose and opened the door to find Neil Moran outside, muscularly filling out jeans and a white T-shirt. He was turned away, gazing at her minuscule swimming pool when she opened the door, and he swiveled back to look at her, a smile creasing his face.

"Hi, Stringer."

"Neil!" she exclaimed, her face suddenly glowing. Even though she hardly did any freelance journalist work anymore, she still liked the nickname.

"Am I bothering you?"

"No. Not at all. I wasn't working, just sitting here dreaming." She extended both hands and pulled him inside. "Come sit down. I'm so happy to see you. It's been too long."

He followed her and sat in the large, overstuffed chair she indicated. She sat down in her desk chair and swiveled to face him, curling her legs up under her.

"You must be psychic," Stephanie smiled.

"Why?"

"I almost drove out to see you this morning."

"Really? Why didn't you?"

"For one thing, I wasn't sure my car could make it up your mountain road. It's very possible that my check engine light has been on for several weeks now," she confessed, and was rewarded by the slight lifting of the corners of Neil's mouth. His face was so impassive that Stephanie took every small smile as a big win. "Besides, I figured you deserved a break from my emotional meltdowns."

"Stringer…"

"I know. I know." She held up a hand to stop his words. "You're about to tell me that I'm never a burden and you don't mind. But honestly, Neil, I really feel like I've taken advantage of you." She paused for an instant, then began drolly, "But since you're here…"

Neil's smile returned. "Yes?"

"I wanted to talk to you because I saw Howard Perry today and it stirred up a lot of memories."

"You missed Ty?"

"It was more that it got me thinking about his death. Remembering all that time in the hospitals and everything."

Neil leaned forward to take one of her hands in his. "I'm sorry Howard upset you."

"No, I think it might have been a good thing, actually. I thought about Ty all the way home, and I cried for a while. But it felt different. I mean, I still have a headache and red eyes, but that deep well of sadness felt like it had finally been drained. It didn't hurt in the same way anymore. It's a soft thing, not as painful."

"Then why did you react so strongly to Howard's wanting you to receive the foundation's plaque?"

Her eyebrows vaulted up. "How did you know about that?"

"Howard called me after you left his office. He wanted me to convince you."

"Is that why you came here?" Stephanie frowned. She was surprised that Neil would go along with Howard, but more than that, it hurt a little. "To talk me into going along with Howard Perry's show?"

"No. Of course not. I told him I wouldn't do it. But it made me think of you, and I decided I'd stop by to see you."

"Oh." She sat back, studying him. "But you think I should agree, don't you?"

Neil shrugged. "I don't understand why you don't want to do it or why you've been so anti-football. But it's not up to me or anyone else." He grinned. "And I'm sure as hell not going to get on your bad side by arguing with you about something that doesn't even involve me."

"My temper has been a bit out of control lately." Stephanie let out a snort of laughter. "It's just… if they really want to honor Ty and do a charitable deed, they can accomplish both without the fanfare. I think it's great that they raised the money, and I'm glad that they're establishing a cancer fund in Ty's name. But I don't have to get a plaque on TV and in front of thousands of fans in order for them to set up the foundation. It's a publicity stunt to make the organization look good. Howard's trading on Ty's death, and I refuse to cooperate with him."

"It's the first exhibition game. Hardly anybody will be watching. The stadium won't even be full, and most people will be getting nachos during halftime. They get more publicity on the team's charitable deeds out of the second exhibition game, where all the proceeds go to the children's charity. Of course, Howard wants to wring all the public sympathy from it that he can, but that isn't the major purpose of the ceremony."

"No?" Stephanie asked skeptically. "Then what is?"

"For one thing, you cynic, they actually want to honor Ty. In his bachelor days Ty was pretty good friends with Russell Ingram. Russell invited him up to his ski lodge in Utah a few times. They partied together. Russell flew in that neurological expert, remember?"

"Yeah, I remember. But why does Russell's gesture have to be so public?"

"That's usually the way you pay tribute to someone. That's the purpose of putting it in their name—so the public will remember. What kind of honor is it if nobody hears about it? They also want to give the Wives' Association a little publicity. They've worked hard on the fund drive, especially Mel Williams—she always really liked you. And it'd be nice for the public to hear about the charitable things the Wives' Association does. People think they do nothing but sit around counting their husbands' money."

"I never thought about it being partially for the Wives." Stephanie frowned. Perhaps she'd acted too hastily that morning. Of course Howard hadn't explained why they wanted to do it, but still… she hadn't given him much of a chance. She had to admit that she had been against the idea before she even heard it simply because she and Ty had disliked Howard Perry. "I don't want to taint Ty's memory with commercialism—but I would like the Wives' Association to get some credit."

"Tell me something honestly." Neil leaned toward her, elbows braced on his knees. "What do you think Ty would have said about the whole thing?"

"'Is there going to be an open bar?'" Stephanie answered automatically.

"I can hear exactly how he'd say it, too." Neil laughed.

Stephanie took a deep breath and let it out slowly. "He would have laughed. He didn't care about things like that."

"Right. He wouldn't care either way—as long as he got some free booze out of the deal." Neil gave her a lopsided grin. "Or maybe he would have loved the idea of Howard Perry having to do all this extra work to put on a public ceremony to honor him after all their arguments and everything Ty did to offend Perry."

Stephanie had to chuckle. "You're right." The anger which had been all-consuming in Perry's office seemed to have dissolved in her tears. She really didn't have that much against the actual idea and it meant a lot to a bunch of other people. Ty would have shrugged it off. He never took himself or others too seriously. It occurred to her that her reaction might also come off as more ungrateful than morally upright. She didn't want to do it, of course, but that was simply because she dreaded standing in front of thousands of people to accept the plaque. And fear wasn't a good enough reason to refuse.

Neil's dark eyes twinkled and his dimple had popped into his cheek. He was especially cute when he smiled, Stephanie thought. She cast a rueful glance at him. "For someone who didn't come here to convince me, you've done an awfully good job of it."

He chuckled. "I just said I wouldn't convince you for Howard and the team. I never promised my clear logic and handsome face wouldn't sway you."

Stephanie felt a blush creeping up her cheeks. It was as if Neil somehow knew where her thoughts were going. Which was weird in and of itself; Neil had always been cute, but Stephanie had never thought much about it before. It was more just an obvious thing she knew, like diamonds glittered or candy was sweet. It certainly wasn't something to suddenly be blushing about. But today it seemed different, like there was a feeling attached to that knowledge. Stephanie did her best to shake it off.

"Okay, I'll accept the plaque." She jumped up. "Now let's forget Perry for a while, okay. How about lunch? I can make us something really quick."

Neil rose too. "I'd love that."

Chapter Three

Neil followed Stephanie into the house, his eyes on the sway of her hips, so clearly outlined by the dress she wore. Her cinnamon-brown hair brushed against her bare shoulders, tantalizing him with the thought of his fingers doing the same. Whenever he was away from her for any length of time he forgot precisely how lovely Stephanie was, how desirable. And each time he saw her again he was hit full on in the chest with how much he wanted her. How he longed to reach out and stroke her hair or trace the smooth line of her leg. She stirred everything within him—thoughts, emotions, passions.

He was always able to disguise how he felt about her. By now the suppression of his desire was almost automatic. But inside him the fire still burned. He would never be content without Stephanie. There was no more time for guilt. She'd just said that she was recovering from Ty's death. No matter what the difficulties would be in overcoming their past, Neil had to try.

Stephanie checked her almost entirely empty refrigerator. "Any interest in a mustard sandwich or baking soda soup?"

"And women complain that bachelors never have any food," Neil teased.

Stephanie glared at him playfully. "That's enough from you. My mother didn't raise any housekeepers. We'll just have to stop by the store."

The nearby grocery store was as old as the neighborhood around it and the aisles were narrow. It reminded Stephanie of the kind of store she'd gone to as a child in Los Angeles—the handful of times her real estate entrepreneur mother had cooked something for the family herself.

Stephanie pulled out a cart and they started down the aisle. "What would you like? Something fancy or plain?"

"Do you know how to cook something fancy?"

She shot Neil a thundering look. "As a matter of fact I can cook two—count 'em, two—fancy dishes."

"Consider me corrected, ma'am." Neil gave her a short military-style nod.

"I cannot believe you just "ma'am-ed" me."

"Oh, do you not like that?" Neil did his best surprised face.

"I'm starting to think you want me to make a lunch you hate."

"I promise, I'll be good." He held up his hands in surrender. "Don't make me that gross 'rice cakes layered with pimento cheese tower' you like."

"Perhaps I'll spare you." Stephanie appraised him regally. "What about the fancy dishes? They're good but both take a couple of hours to fix."

"I'd rather not wait. How about sandwiches?"

"That's too plain."

"Well, excuse me and my terribly provincial taste buds." He laughed. "What would fit your, apparently very specific, requirements?" Neil smiled down at her, thoroughly enjoying their banter. It was one of the things that made it impossible to stay away from her.

Even their glib chatter warmed his blood, and he loitered behind her as they walked along the aisles, watching the movement of her rounded ass beneath the thin material of her dress. Her fair skin was lightly tanned, almost apricot-colored, and it beckoned the touch of his fingers. Her shoulders and chest above the top of her dress presented an enticing amount of bare flesh.

Stephanie turned and smiled up at him, and he had to shove his hands into the back pockets of his jeans to keep from jerking her to him and kissing her. She said something, and he nodded, not hearing a word. She stretched forward and up to reach a jar of mayonnaise on the top shelf, balancing on tiptoe. Her skirt slid up, revealing several more inches of her long, slender legs. Neil watched with hooded eyes, his black gaze glittering and hungry. He imagined the feel of her lithe body pressed against his, her legs firm, and her breasts pillowy soft against his chest.

He pictured Stephanie clad in the silver backless dress with thin straps that she'd worn the last time they'd all gone to the ESPY awards together.

In his daydream, she stood smiling at him, her lips barely parted, waiting for his touch. He brushed his hands over her hair, delighting in the silken texture, and lingered over the smooth, golden flesh of her shoulders before he pulled the straps of her dress down with excruciating slowness. The top of her gown fell to her waist, the straps shimmering loops on her wrists, like bracelets. He drank in the sight of her high, taut breasts, rounded and white against the darker skin of her chest. The circles of her nipples were the color of her lips, and in the center of the aureoles the nipples pointed with desire.

Her lids were half closed, her lips soft and full. Her tongue swept out to moisten them, and a hot agony sizzled through him like a fallen wire, sparking and jumping out of control. "Take off your dress," he told her, and, as always in his dreams, she obeyed, eager to turn him on. She skimmed the dress down her slim hips and let it fall, caressing her long thighs as it went. She wore nothing beneath it, and he gazed at the full glory of her body. Passion was thundering in him, swelling, aching. God, he wanted her.

Stephanie glanced back at Neil and halted in mid-motion, "What's the matter?"

"What? Nothing. Why?" What the hell was he doing, letting himself drift into sex fantasies around her? If he wasn't more careful, he'd embarrass himself with his too-evident arousal.

"You looked—I don't know, almost angry."

"Thinking about something else, I guess." He recovered quickly, reforming his expression into a tight smile. "I was just thinking about, uh, the summer camp."

"Training camp?" Stephanie asked.

"No, not the Pumas. Asa and I started a football camp for underprivileged children last summer. Ages six to twelve, so nothing but some basics about football, mostly passing and receiving. And we make sure they get lunch and snacks. Some of the players showed up to help out. It's already over. I just need to put a reminder on my calendar to do something nice to thank the guys that pitched in." Neil pulled his phone out and busied himself with setting an alert.

"That's so good of you and Asa," Stephanie beamed.

Neil shrugged, unsure how to react. Stephanie's approval warmed him, but he normally didn't like to talk about the charitable things he did. That certainly wasn't the reason he did it—but he'd let his guard down and it had been the first thing he could think of to cover. He quickly went on, "Otherwise, I've spent the summer rehabbing my arm."

"How are you recovering from surgery?"

"Pretty well. It's slower than I'd like—the workouts take twice as long because I have to burn the muscles out with high reps instead of using the heavier loads I usually would."

"Where do you get all that willpower?" Stephanie groaned. "I wouldn't last two days."

"I'd hope not, or the program wouldn't get me in playing shape."

Stephanie grinned as she put the jar of mayonnaise into the grocery cart and started forward, reverting to an earlier subject. "I've decided on tuna salad. How does that sound? With a melon salad on the side. Cantaloupe is one thing I actually have at home."

"At least you stock the essentials." They continued through the store, with Stephanie shopping in her usual haphazard way—picking up whatever caught her eye and often backtracking for a missed item. The third time she turned the cart around to search for something Neil burst out laughing. "I can tell you're an expert shopper."

Stephanie batted her lashes as if humbly accepting high praise. "Well, I learned well from my mother. I didn't know the oven could be used as anything but another kitchen cabinet until I was grown."

"I take it your family ate out a lot?"

"Always. That's why I'm a junk-food addict." Her grey-blue eyes gleaming mischievously. "You know all my bad habits. I don't do strength training or play any sports…"

"Or do exercise of any kind."

"My favorite hobby is lying on the couch reading."

"And your second favorite is lying on the couch watching Netflix."

"Neil! I'm not that lazy. My second favorite is eating popcorn in a movie theater."

"So sorry. I didn't mean to malign your character."

Stephanie laughed and unexpectedly slid an arm around his waist, resting her head lightly against his arm. "I like being with you. Why haven't you come by as often lately?"

Neil's pulse speeded up. The skin of his arm was tinglingly aware of her hair brushing against it. She was so warm, so vibrant—even if her gesture was probably platonic. He forced his voice to a lightness he didn't feel. "I didn't want to wear out my welcome."

"Come on, Neil. It's been at least two months since you came by."

"Six weeks," he corrected.

She turned amazed eyes on him. "Good Lord, you are meticulous."

He realized then how much his words had revealed. It was pure luck that Stephanie had interpreted them only as an indication of his precise, detail-oriented mind instead of as the statement of a lovesick man who'd counted each painful day. Damn! After this long you'd think he could control his tongue better. He shrugged, as if unable to excuse his ways, knowing that the less he said about it, the better. "I thought you might need some time alone, that's all."

"I was depending on you too much? You're probably right."

"No, not like that. I figured you might need time to process by yourself some."

"I was afraid you'd gotten tired of me crying on your shoulder."

"You know me better than that." Neil couldn't imagine ever getting tired of being close to Stephanie. "I like you crying on my shoulder."

"I always knew you were warped," she quipped and glanced down at the grocery cart. "I think I have everything we need for lunch. No doubt I've forgotten at least two necessities of life, but I won't remember them until I put away the groceries."

"Now, I don't want to suggest anything too uncomfortable for you, but there are these things some people make called lists. They do them for all kinds of different things, but one of the most popular uses is one known as a grocery list." Neil held up his arms as if warding off an attack from Stephanie, but her soft slapping at him did nothing besides make him want to pull her into a tight embrace and kiss her.

After a tedious check-out, they drove home and brought in the groceries. Neil, with the ease of a longtime friend, casually searched her cupboards and set the table while Stephanie prepared the light lunch. For the first few minutes they said little as they ate, but as they began to fill up, Stephanie inquired casually, "How's your love life?"

Neil shrugged. "Like always, I guess."

"Are you still dating Jill?"

"No. We broke up not long after Ty died." He halted, dismayed. "I mean—oh, hell, Stringer, I'm sorry."

"About what? Mentioning that Ty died? It's okay, I can talk about him now without crying. It's funny. When somebody you love dies, you know you'll eventually reach the point where you can remember them and smile instead of bursting into tears, but you can't imagine how. Finally you realize you've reached it, and it seems almost disloyal that you don't hurt any longer. Has it been that way for you?"

"Yeah. I know what you're talking about." Neil carefully dipped out another portion of melon salad, keeping his eyes on the bowl as he talked. "Does that mean you've started dating again?"

"Dating?" She laughed. "No. My friend Claire very clearly wants to set me up, but I don't think I'm ready quite yet. In fact, she wants me to come to the opening of a community theater she's started, but it'd be so strange going alone; I guess I got used to having someone to force into doing those things with me. I feel guilty because I just lied and told her I couldn't make it—actually…" Stephanie paused and looked at Neil.

He raised his eyes to meet hers. "Actually what?" His stomach churned, part excitement, part apprehension that he thought he knew what was coming. "You thought of someone not named Neil that you can force into watching community theater?"

"Come on, it won't be that bad," Stephanie swatted at him with her napkin.

"It's community theater." Neil gave her a grave look.

"Claire is very talented and a good friend. I'd hate to miss the opening. She's worked so hard on it. And you're such a good friend to me…"

"Which is why you're repaying me with torture that rivals waterboarding?" Neil tried to hold the same serious expression, but he couldn't repress a laugh at the mock-outrage on Stephanie's face.

"I wouldn't even ask if you were dating someone, but since you said you don't have much of a social life right now—Neil, I'd really appreciate it."

"I see: since my love life is so sadly lacking, I can be your date that's not really a date." Neil cocked his eyebrow with the scar running through it. "How could I refuse such a flattering invitation? When is it?"

"Neil, I didn't mean it that way. It's just that you're a friend, and you won't expect… I mean, it wouldn't be like a real date…" She floundered to a stop.

"You're getting in deeper and deeper," he teased, grinning. "Okay, I'll take pity on you. But you better remember this when I need someone to go with me to the opening of a friend's vegan restaurant or something."

"As if you would know anyone opening a vegan restaurant."

"Hey, none of us know what Gramps will do with his life when he finally retires. Kowalski loves philosophy and baby animals—I can see it."

"Poor Kowalski, no one that is thirty-three and has never had kids should be called Gramps." Stephanie shook her head. "I can just see him with his shaved head and leather biker jacket flipping veggie burgers."

"Hey, the guy is an enigma." Neil speared a piece of honey-dew with his fork. "So when is this wild non-date of ours?"

"A week from Friday."

"Why don't we throw caution to the wind, and I'll take you out to dinner before the play?"

"I'm not sure I can stand the excitement. Besides, who knows, you might decide you want 'compensation' if you paid for a meal."

Neil's grin was exaggeratedly wolfish. "You know me. If I pay for dinner, I expect dessert."

"Like ice cream?" Stephanie opened her eyes wide in innocence.

"I had something hotter in mind."

"You're such a tease." Stephanie laughed. "Did anybody ever tell you that?"

"Usually people think I'm the epitome of the straight-arrow, All-American jock."

Stephanie stood up to take her plate to the sink. "I don't think I'll ever figure you out."

"Why not? I thought I was pretty simple."

"It seems like you would be Captain America; I mean, you're loyal, steady, honorable."

"You make me sound like a Boy Scout."

"They're very attractive qualities. I'm not downgrading you. There were lots of times when I wished Ty was a bit more down-to-earth. But you also have this wicked sense of humor. People thought Ty perpetrated half of your jokes on other players. And you're the last guy on the team I'd pick as the hold-out bachelor. By all rights you should have a wife, two kids and a home in the suburbs. Yet here you are, thirty years old and still unattached. You haven't even been divorced."

"I know. It's a disgrace I've had a hard time living down."

"Be serious. Aren't you the marrying kind?"

"Of course. In a lot of ways I'm old-fashioned. But I think it's because of that that I haven't married."

"You mean you want a virgin." Stephanie tilted her head to the side, scrunched up her face and nodded like she understood his predicament. "I get it. You and the demons that need them for sacrificial rituals must be having a really hard time nowadays."

Neil laughed. "I said I'm old-fashioned, not delusional. What I mean is I don't fall in love easily. Once I get married, I intend to stay that way the rest of my life, so I have to wait for the right woman. I don't want to get stuck with the wrong one."

"And no one good enough has come along?"

"I didn't say that. But maybe she didn't want to marry me."

"Give me a break. What woman in her right mind would turn you down? You're handsome, wealthy, witty and very, very kind. She'd have to be crazy."

"Not if she was in love with someone else."

"Are you serious? I'm sorry. I didn't mean to dredge up any bad memories." Stephanie frowned. "Let's forget it, okay?"

"Okay." They were skirting far too close to the truth for safety. If he were to have any hope of winning Stephanie's love in the future, he couldn't cloud it with pity. "Why don't you tell me about your work?"

"What work?" Stephanie responded with a sigh. "I haven't done anything in weeks."

"Why? What's wrong?"

"I can't come up with a subject. I've been through all my old articles"—she waved a hand toward her office out back— "to see if there was anything I might expand into a book but nothing appeals to me. It's getting bad. The book I finished after Ty died will be out in a few months, and I don't even have an idea for a new one yet."

He frowned. "Writer's block?"

"I guess so. I've never had it before, so I'm not sure. But I do know that I've filled many virtual recycle bins with the beginnings of three different books. When I couldn't pick a topic for a nonfiction book, I tried my hand at a novel. It was a worse disaster than the rest of my efforts. So now I'm back to nonfiction. But nothing grabs me." She sighed. "I have to find a topic before I start running out of money."

"I'd let you ghostwrite my autobiography, but I'm too boring. Who wants to read about a quarterback who's never dated an actress, been investigated for gambling or gone to rehab?"

"Who indeed." Stephanie laughed. "Maybe you ought to get involved in something scandalous so I can do an exposé."

"Thanks, but I think I'll decline that offer."

"It's such a helpless feeling. It's not like the days when I'm too lazy to write. Then I can talk myself into doing it anyway—threaten, bribe, whatever."

"How do you threaten and bribe yourself?"

"Food and exercise. Or, you know, the reverse."

"Yeah. Even I wouldn't bribe myself with exercise."

"Do you think I just lost my self-discipline?" Stephanie rested her chin on her fist and looked up at Neil.

"You're very disciplined when it comes to your writing."

"That's what I always thought—until recently. Now I'm beginning to wonder. What seems really strange is that when I was so torn up after Ty died, I was able to finish that book. I made myself do it. One time I was writing about the death of that person's youngest child, and tears were running down my face while I typed. But I kept on. I told myself I had to, and I did."

"Maybe that's why you can't now."

"You mean I burned myself out? It's a possibility. Maybe I used up all my discipline and power then; I drained myself."

"Those things replenish themselves. All you need is rest, and they'll rebuild. Why don't you give yourself a week off without worrying about it?"

"You think that'll work?"

"Yes. If there's one thing I'm an expert on, it's waiting patiently. I sat around for weeks after my elbow operation, not using it. I wanted to test it out. It was like the urge to scratch a mosquito bite, you know? But I knew it'd do more harm than good. Your body needs time to heal. Why not your mind and emotions? You spent every last reserve during Ty's illness and afterwards finishing that book. Now you need a chance to relax."

"I might as well. That's all I'm doing anyway, but I'm making myself miserable worrying about it."

"Right."

Stephanie flashed him a smile. "Want to do it with me?"

"What?" Longing coiled in his abdomen, and his hand tightened around his glass.

"Relax."

"Sure. What did you have in mind?"

"Well, we could swim."

"In that outdoor bathtub you call a pool? No way. You want to go back to my place?"

"Then I'd have to actually swim. Too strenuous." Stephanie shook her head.

Neil wanted to suggest they just sit in his hot tub, but he'd already come too close to letting his true feelings for her show today. Stephanie in a bathing suit at his house might be more temptation than he was prepared to handle. Neil knew that for now whatever they did would only be as friends. But every moment they spent together was another chance to change that. Another chance to win Stephanie's heart.

Chapter Four

They decided on an afternoon excursion to Sedona, about two-hours from Phoenix. Backed by the red cliffs of Oak Creek Canyon, it was a scenic location for small boutiques and art galleries. Stephanie leaned her head back against the passenger seat of Neil's 1965 Corvette Stingray as he roared up I-17. The aftermarket A/C system that Ty had helped Neil install may have made a true vintage car lover cringe, but Stephanie welcomed the cold breeze even in her thin sundress.

Funny, she thought, how much she had missed male companionship the past few months. It was odd to have Neil's masculine presence looming beside her, to smell the faint trace of aftershave and hear the deep rumble of his voice, to see the corded muscles of his forearm move beneath his skin as he shifted gears. Yet it was also comforting—no, not comforting exactly. There was a tinge of excitement to it, and the pleasure was more distinct than simply comfort.

She'd hardly been around a man since Ty's death. At first Neil had been with her a lot, but the past few months even he had stopped coming by. As much as she liked her female friends, there was something nice about having a guy around. She wasn't totally sure why, but she was enjoying hanging out with Neil today more than she'd enjoyed anything in a long time.

Stephanie smiled, her eyes on Neil's hand, resting lightly on the gearshift. She noticed the fine sprinkling of black hairs across the backs of his hands and above his knuckles, and the sight brought a peculiar little ache to her abdomen. Stephanie glanced up a little guiltily at his face. She had felt a flash of desire. Was she finally thawing after all this time? She'd have to keep a tighter leash on her feelings—it wasn't a bad sensation, certainly, but she definitely should not be feeling it for Neil. He'd been Ty's best friend. He was so kind and helpful after Ty's death, and they'd developed such a close friendship of their own. It seemed almost a betrayal of those relationships to feel anything but friendship for him.

Neil was watching the road, not her, and she was grateful, for she was afraid he might have been able to read her thoughts on her face. Stephanie had never been good at hiding the emotions behind her eyes. She studied him for a moment, taking in the smooth, sculpted structure of his face, the prominent cheekbones and thickly lashed eyes, the ink-black hair. He was handsome, there was no doubt about that. And there was a sensual undertone to his carefully controlled face, a suggestion of a passionate nature kept ruthlessly banked. The hot black eyes…strong, sensitive fingers…magnificently well-toned body…yes, Neil was unquestionably sexy as well as handsome.

Stephanie was sure that Neil had had his share of women over the years. Had he really been in love with a woman who hadn't loved him? Maybe it had just been a joking way to slide away from a subject he didn't want to discuss. It was hard to tell with Neil sometimes. Ty had been an open book: volatile, emotional, never hiding anything. But Neil was different. He was deep and silent, easily hiding his emotions with barbed remarks and humor. Stephanie suspected that there were more twists and turns to him than anyone expected.

Had the woman actually existed? Had he really loved her that much? Why hadn't she reciprocated? Stephanie had trouble imagining that even a woman with feelings for another man wouldn't have had any for Neil as well—maybe she was already married when he met her. Stephanie wondered if she had ever met her. Whoever it was, Neil had certainly kept her identity from Stephanie. She felt a small pang of jealousy. She had thought she was Neil's good friend. Why wouldn't he have told her about it? Confided in her like she had confided in him? But that was stupid. It wasn't like she'd confided in Neil when she had problems with Ty. And Ty would have been the one that Neil would have discussed it with, if he had talked to anyone about it. Knowing Neil, he had kept it locked within him.

Besides, Neil's interest in some other woman was not Stephanie's problem. What she should be concerned about was the spark of physical attraction she'd felt for a man she'd once regarded as a brother. It seemed unfaithful to Ty—and no doubt Neil would think it was less than loyal of his best friend's widow to be fantasizing about him.

Stephanie turned away to gaze out the side window at the stark desert beauty. This feeling probably wasn't really about Neil, anyway. Her senses had been frozen by Ty's death, but she'd noticed a big shift in them today. Being alone with any man right now probably would have inspired the rush of reawakened emotions. It just happened to be Neil, which was a good thing—if it had been someone else she might have mistaken her feelings for more than they were.

Soon they reached Sedona. The beauty of the red sandstone buttes flanking the town was breathtaking. The sun slashed across the jagged rock formations, throwing them into a magical pattern of light and shadow. They spent the remainder of the afternoon browsing among the shops and galleries.

Stephanie lingered over a jewelry display, entranced by a necklace, bracelet and earring set. They were an artistic mix of delicate chains and thin bars of rose gold, her favorite type of metal, and Stephanie fell in love immediately but forced herself to turn away from the case. Ty had made a lot of money but had spent it carelessly, and after his debts had been paid, there had been a relatively small amount left. It had been enough for Stephanie to purchase her house, an important thing for someone with an uncertain freelance career. But she hadn't been joking when she said that soon she would be entirely dependent on what she could make writing. And since that hadn't been going too well, she'd better not make any unnecessary purchases.

They spent the rest of the day in the same lazy, pleasant manner, strolling around and shopping, having a meal in one of the many restaurants. Neil was recognized only a few times and had to stop to sign autographs and take pictures with fans only twice. But Stephanie was well-accustomed to that—and at least none of the women had asked him to sign any body parts like they sometimes did with Ty.

It was a happy day, a bright spot in the hollow sameness of her life. Thank God Neil had dropped by and eased her into this small re-entry to the world. When they returned that evening and Neil walked her to her front door—trust Neil to follow the old-fashioned courtesies—Stephanie impulsively hugged him and said, "Thank you so much. I needed this afternoon."

His arms went around her loosely, the embrace of an old friend, but suddenly she remembered her earlier thoughts about him, which had been anything but those of an old friend, and she stepped back quickly, hoping the darkness would hide the blush in her cheeks.

She stood in the open doorway, watching him walk back to his car, and she felt a pang of loneliness. But that was silly; she would see him again in a little more than a week, when they'd attend the opening of Claire's theater. With a final wave to him as he backed out, she closed the door and started toward her bedroom, thinking about what she would wear.

* * *

Stephanie decided to try Neil's suggestion not even try to write the next day, and she spent the morning cleaning her house. Afterward she sat down to read but was unaccountably restless. She considered visiting a friend; she had really let her friendships slide after Ty's death. But most of them worked during the day, and Claire was busy preparing for the opening of the theater. Mel Williams came into her mind, and Stephanie grinned.

Mel might be home. She had spent her entire life training to be an Olympic volleyball player, and she often lamented the fact that for more than a decade she'd had a full-time job in which she didn't get paid, as well as a part time job at In-N-Out—when her training didn't even allow her to eat the food. Now Mel was the full-time mother of three boys and did copious amounts of volunteer work. She'd confided in Stephanie that some of the wives had given her back-handed compliments about 'the freedom in not having a traditional career,' but Mel was quick to point out she'd done enough thankless work for a lifetime and wanted to enjoy her time with her kids, thank you very much.

Stephanie dialed her number and was happy to hear Mel's voice answer the phone. When Mel realized who was calling, she burst into an excited babble of conversation. It was several minutes before Stephanie was able to ask if it was okay to drop by. "I'd love that!" Mel exclaimed. "Darren's down for his nap, and the other two are in summer camp, thank God. We can have some peace and quiet for a change."

A few minutes later Stephanie was on her way to Mel's North Scottsdale home. The house was long and low, a modernistic design of stone, wood and glass which opened across the back to give an unspoiled view of the McDowell Mountains. Stephanie parked and by the time she'd made it up the drive, Mel burst out her front door and hurried to meet her, her arms outstretched.

"Stephanie! I was beginning to think you'd forgotten me." Mel pulled her into a hug. "It's so good to see you. You look marvelous, as always."

Mel was a tall, gorgeous Black woman who had also done some modeling at the height of her Olympic fame. Even though she swore she'd never play volleyball again, she was still just as athletic as her husband Jalyn, spending much of her time in the gym, their pool or on the tennis court. She was dressed in her usual attire of yoga pants and a tank top and her brown eyes sparkled. Stephanie was always impressed with how much energy Mel managed to have despite taking care of three rowdy boys.

Stephanie had met Mel before any of the other wives. Mel had loved an article of Stephanie's and had emailed her to convince Stephanie to cowrite a book with her about Mel's experiences as both a former Olympian and a current football wife. Her bubbly enthusiasm had been persuasive even in written form and Stephanie had liked her immediately. After Mel set up the interview with Ty, Stephanie had liked her even better. In fact, if she'd never met Mel, she wouldn't have married Ty. By the time they finished working together on the book, Mel was Stephanie's favorite Puma wife. She still was, but since Ty's death they had barely seen each other—it was Stephanie's doing, though. She'd found it hard to be with the people she associated with Ty. Well, everyone but Neil.

Today, however, Stephanie didn't experience the usual painful reminder of Ty, and she smiled with genuine pleasure. "Mel, I'm sorry I've been so awful at keeping in touch."

"Don't worry. I understand. Come in. Darren's still asleep, thankfully. I fixed coffee, and we can have some delicious, gooey coffee cake I got yesterday."

"I'd love that." Stephanie strolled into the cold A/C of the house and settled on the couch. Mel went into the kitchen and returned with two mugs and slices of cake. Mel flopped down on the chair opposite Stephanie, turning sideways to throw her long legs over the arm of the chair. She popped a piece of cake into her mouth and closed her eyes in a pantomime of ecstasy. "Delicious. So much better than the green apples my coach used to call dessert."

"The only green apples I ate in high school were sour straws or Jolly Ranchers." Stephanie laughed.

"I'm not sure what nutritionist you had, but neither one of those are actual fruit."

"I guess that's what happens when your 'nutritionist' is a busy working mom with a candy addiction."

"Your family must have good genes then—I've heard you refer to climbing the stadium steps to get to the Wives' seats 'exercise.'" Mel teased.

"So tell me what's been going on in your life," Stephanie prompted. Part of her wanted to ask about Neil but she didn't want to come off as having an ulterior motive for coming to visit her friend, so she held back.

"Let's see. What's been going on that you'd find interesting... I know the politics of football are not your favorite." Mel tapped her fork against her bottom lip. Stephanie had always liked how clear-eyed she was about the sport. Mel loved football, but she had her issues with sports careers as well; she wasn't the complete fangirl type of wife that Stephanie just didn't connect with. "Oh, for almost the whole past year the Pumas have had an unofficial mascot living under the bleachers."

"Wait? There's an actual puma living under the bleachers?"

"No." Mel laughed. "I didn't mean that. A stray house cat gave birth to a whole bunch of kittens, and they were all living under the bleachers at the practice field, but the mom and the rest left this little white one behind. It was the runt of the litter, I guess."

"Oh that's so sad." Stephanie could feel tears welling up already.

"Don't cry! It's a sweet story. Gramps apparently spent an entire day crawling around on his hands and knees under there, trying to get close enough to the kitten to bottle feed it. Of course, the little thing kept running away from him."

Stephanie's tears halted at the thought of the large offensive lineman crawling around under the bleachers with a tiny baby bottle. "You're kidding."

"Nope. I guess the kitten finally realized Gramps was a lot more stubborn than she was, and she let him feed her. After that she apparently decided Gramps was her new mama and started shadowing him at every practice. Hiding under anything close enough to keep an eye on him. She apparently doesn't understand that an all-white kitten can't hide in a bright desert landscape."

"That is adorable."

"Gramps named her Sugar but his Louisiana accent always comes out on his Rs so now she is officially known by the whole team as 'Sugah.' She still won't let anyone but Gramps come near her, but the team considers her an honorary Puma anyway."

"That is too cute. Ty always liked Gramps a lot."

"How could anyone on that team not?" Mel took another big bite of cake, shielding her mouth with her hand so she could keep talking while she chewed. "They're lucky that he still bails them out. When Jalyn got mature enough to stop getting into trouble himself, we were already so busy with our boys that he certainly didn't have time for their shenanigans. Gramps is the reason half of that team has been able to stay out of gossip blogs."

"Speaking of gossip…" Stephanie really wanted to find out more about the woman Neil had talked about being in love with, but she wasn't sure how to broach the subject without being obvious. Still, it didn't look like the conversation was going to head that way naturally so she decided to give it a push. "What about Neil and Jill Byerly? He told me the other day that they'd broken up."

"Oh, yeah. A long time ago. Well, she was the kind who couldn't take being second best."

"Second best?" Stephanie's insides felt all jittery. Was she about to learn the other woman's identity? "What do you mean by that?"

An almost guilty look flashed into Mel's hazel eyes, but it was gone as quickly as it had come. "Oh, you know. Football's his first love."

Stephanie sensed that Mel's response wasn't what she had originally meant, and she was puzzled by Mel's unusual attempt to hide something.

Did Mel know this other woman Neil claimed to have loved? If so, she apparently wasn't going to reveal it, even to a friend. "Who's he been dating since?"

Mel crinkled up her eyes thoughtfully. "Nobody. I mean, no one particular girl. For a long time he avoided all the parties. He was real torn up when—" She paused uncertainly, sneaking a glance at Stephanie.

"When Ty died," Stephanie finished for her. "It's okay to talk about it."

"For months Neil was moody. He avoided people. Last season he had a lot of trouble with his game too. You know he injured his elbow again."

"Yeah, and it hadn't been good to begin with," Stephanie added.

"Well, he also had difficulty adjusting to the other receivers. I mean, he was used to Troy and Asa, but he used Troy only in short situations, and he just didn't have that almost psychic connection with Asa like he did with Ty. You know how it was. He and Ty understood each other so well I think Ty could have run the right route without even being in the huddle."

Stephanie smiled fondly. "Probably."

"Anyway, Neil stayed away from social gatherings. When he did attend, he was by himself or with a different girl each time."

"When you said Jill couldn't take being second best, it sounded like she broke up with him."

"I think so. At least, that's what I heard."

"Do you suppose he was really upset by it? I mean, was that the reason he dated a bunch of different girls?"

"I don't think so. He never seemed that crazy about Jill, if you ask me. I think he just likes to be alone when he's troubled." Mel paused. "I take it you've seen him recently?"

"Yeah. Yesterday, in fact." Stephanie went on to relate Howard Perry's request and her initial refusal, then Neil's visit.

"Then you'll be at the ceremony?" Mel beamed, confirming what Neil had said about it meaning a lot to the Wives' Association. "I'm so glad."

"Well, when Neil pointed out how hard you'd worked, I realized I couldn't refuse."

"We really did. Maria Hernández put me in charge of assembling the recipes for the cookbook, and I was glad to be able to do a little something for Ty." She paused, her face sad. "Everyone liked Ty a lot. We wanted to do something special."

Tears burned in Stephanie's eyes. "Thanks, Mel. It was a wonderful thing to do, and I appreciate it."

Mel, who was unable to stay on any sad topic for long, moved on. "Listen, I'm having a lunch next week for a bunch of the wives. Why don't you come? I know everyone would love to see you."

"Oh, no. I'm not part of the group anymore."

"It's not an official Wives' function, just a bunch of us getting together to talk. You know."

"It's so sweet of you to try to get me involved, but I'm not one of you any longer. It would be awkward."

"We're still the same people. We can be friends, can't we?"

"You and I can. But we worked on the book together before I even met Ty. We were actually good friends. Most of the other wives were acquaintances. And not even ones I had much in common with. You know I was never as into football as the other wives. How many of them would be friends if their husbands didn't play on the same team? I was never a very active member to begin with, and now…"

Mel sighed. "Maybe you have a point. But you won't stop seeing me, right?"

"Of course not."

"Good. Training camp starts in a few weeks, so Jalyn will be gone, and the kids don't return from their summer camp until August the eighth. I can get a babysitter for Darren and you and I can go to dinner and a movie."

"That sounds great. Just text me when it gets closer and we can work out an exact date. Now, tell me all about the boys."

Mel proceeded to recall their various accomplishments over the past few months. Darren was his usual vigorous two-year-old self, and he promised to grow into his father's size and skill. As if on cue, he awakened from his nap and came bounding into the room. He turned a little shy when he saw Stephanie but was soon bringing her toys to examine. Stephanie dutifully admired what he brought her, smiling at the sturdy boy. He was larger and stronger than most boys his age, and his flashing grin was irresistible. There was a painful tug at Stephanie's heart. Once she had dreamed of having Ty's son. She had imagined him being like Darren, athletic and charming even as a child. Now it would never be. At least not with Ty.

Stephanie looked away, and Mel must have caught the sudden flash of sorrow in her eyes because she quickly ordered, "Darren, that's enough for now. Why don't you go play in your room for a bit?"

Darren began to protest, and Stephanie interrupted. "No, please, it's all right. I actually need to go."

Mel frowned. "Promise you won't disappear again?"

"I promise. Text me about dinner and a movie."

Stephanie tried all the way home and for the entire rest of the week to forget about the little 'at least not with Ty' thought she'd had at Mel's house, but she couldn't stop picking it apart. Obviously, she could still have kids someday. Obviously, she might meet someone else and love again. But it had seemed like more than that. Like maybe she might still have an athletic, charming, little pee-wee football playing kid. And that kid wasn't going to get those attributes from her side of the family. When anyone in Stephanie's family saw a ball coming their way, they instinctively ducked like they were involved in a life-long game of dodgeball.

And Stephanie hadn't been imagining some random kid with reddish hair like hers, or blond like Ty would have had. No, that little kid she'd pictured had black hair and gleamingly dark eyes. Just like Neil.

Chapter Five

Neil jumped into his vintage Stingray and started the engine. He was so nervous that you'd think he was a kid going on his first date. His palms were sweating on the steering wheel and there was an icy block in his stomach. It was absurd.

It was also a lot of pressure. Even though Stephanie had asked him only because she considered him safe—God, that hurt like a knife—it was the perfect opportunity to give her a taste of how much more they could have together. But he couldn't push. The whole night would be like walking a tightrope.

The past week had been one of the worst since he'd known Stephanie, comparable only to those first few aching weeks after he met her. She was never far from his mind, no matter what he was doing. She invaded his sleep, his workouts, his business dealings, his conversations. He thought of her constantly, envisioning her in a bathing suit, dressed in that backless silver gown from the ESPYs, or, more often, completely naked. He dreamed of the body he had yearned for, for so long, yet never actually seen, and imagined her opening her arms to him, beckoning, welcoming…

Neil ground his teeth as he pulled to a stop at the traffic light. There he was again, daydreaming about Stephanie and getting himself all wound up. It wouldn't be an easy evening if he started out this way already. He drew three deep breaths, then turned right and headed for the expressway. As he drove, he concentrated on the Pumas' play book, which he had been studying recently in preparation for training camp. If anything could vanquish his desire, surely it would be thinking about "off S 3Ps" and "X gold 67 jumps."

Neil was reasonably calm by the time he reached Stephanie's house, but when she opened the door at his knock, he was once again shaken by the force of his feeling for her. She was beautiful and infinitely desirable, with that long-legged slim build that made him ache. Neil was agonizingly aware of the warmth flushing his neck and jaw.

"Come in," she greeted him, extending both her hands to him as she would to any close friend. He clasped her hands briefly and hoped she didn't notice the blazing heat of his skin. She turned and led him down the short hall into the living room. Entranced, he followed, watching the movement of her legs and ass beneath the long skirt.

She wore a sheath dress that skimmed gracefully down her body to her ankles. It was an odd color, sort of a muted teal, that reflected the always changing blue-gray of Stephanie's expressive eyes. The thin spaghetti straps made it obvious that she wasn't wearing a bra and the straps looked like the type that would be slipping off her smooth shoulders all evening. It was going to be a night of exquisite torture if that turned out to be true.

It was a simple dress, and not overtly sexy. But her hair was swept up in a knot and just the sight of her bare shoulders and throat was inflammatory to Neil's over-sensitized nerves. As he followed her, he was aware of an almost overpowering urge to hook a hand in the back of her dress and pop a fragile strap from its anchor.

He closed his eyes briefly; her effect on him was staggering. She chatted as she strolled into the living room, blissfully unaware of his torment. "Would you like a drink before we go?"

"No, thank you." His voice came out raw and hoarse.

She turned, brows drawing together in concern. "Are you all right?"

He cleared his throat. "Of course. You took my breath away, that's all."

Her silvery laughter bubbled out. "Neil, when did you get so smooth?"

"And here I thought I always was."

Stephanie picked up her purse and a dark grey moto jacket. He took it from her and held it open for her to slip her arms inside. His fingertips grazed the satiny flesh of her collarbone. He could see the clear outline of the bone beneath her skin, and the vulnerable hollow of her throat, faintly pulsing. It was a contrast of softness and rigidity as subtly arousing as the hovering scent of her perfume.

"Where are we going?" Stephanie asked as he escorted her out of the house to his car.

"How about Le Pur?" He named a restaurant famed for both its elegance and its French cuisine.

"Really? I've been wanting to go there. How did you know?"

"I didn't," Neil confessed. "But that's where Pete Cherneski took his girlfriend for Valentine's last year.

"And you trust Pete for food recommendations?" Stephanie raised an eyebrow.

"God, no. For weeks Pete kept bringing it up, complaining about how he couldn't read a damn thing on the menu and wound up eating snails. As I remember, he and that girl broke up not long after that. But the girlfriend loved the place, and Asa Jackson said the building is very cool—practically all glass—and the view is amazing."

"Clearly, the most important part of any restaurant." Stephanie teased. "How'd Asa like the food?"

Neil grinned. "He said they brought out giant plates with tiny portions. He stopped at In-N-Out on the way home and got a Double-Double. But he said what little food they did bring him was good."

Stephanie laughed. "Well, you are very sweet, risking all that for me."

Neil loved watching her laugh. Fancy French food was a small price to pay. "You mean I'm not tough and dangerous?" He cast her a wounded look. "Next time I'll have to make us a reservation at that Brazilian Steakhouse that serves nothing but meat skewered on swords."

Their meal was delicious, though Neil had no interest in telling the team nutritionist about it. It was definitely not part of his high protein, good fat, low carb regimen. Le Pur was also not the kind of place where Neil had to worry about anyone asking for an autograph, which, even after all this time, he found a little embarrassing if it wasn't a kid. There were some whispers and stares, but both he and Stephanie had long ago become adept at ignoring that. They talked as they always did: bantering, perfectly at ease. But underlying it all, there was a low throb of desire deep in Neil that made it difficult to maintain his just-a-friend persona.

Even the smallest of things were hard to ignore—he'd almost reached over to take her hand as they walked into the restaurant. Without noticing, when he'd opened the door for her, he laid his hand lightly on her back as he ushered her in before him. It wasn't anything unusual; it meant nothing, it was just something he did because his mother had instilled 'acting like a gentleman' in both her sons. But when the tips of Neil's fingers touched Stephanie's back, heat pulsed through him, and he'd had to fight the urge to slide his hand over and curl it possessively around the side of her waist.

The whole romantic, candle-lit aura of the restaurant didn't help any. Everything was soft and dim and private, with small curving booths designed for sitting close together. It was difficult to keep a friend's width apart from her. Worse, his legs were long and so were hers—better not to let his mind dwell on that—and frequently they brushed one another. Each time it sent an electric jolt through him.

He hoped the flickering candle light was weak enough to conceal the heat that he knew must come into his eyes as he gazed at her. How could he watch her lips close around a bite of food and not think of those lips on him? Or hear her 'mmm' at the taste of the crème brulee and not imagine it longer and louder and aroused by his hand?

Neil thought the heat would subside when they left the restaurant, but he discovered he was wrong. Le Pur was located at the top of one of Phoenix's many luxury hotels. This level was shared by an elegant bar, and there was only a single elevator that went up to it and so there were a number of people waiting.

In the close confines of the elevator, Stephanie was pushed back against Neil. The sweet curve of her ass pressed into him; the high heels she wore augmented the length of her legs—putting her at a very problematic part of his body. He went for the all-jocks-everywhere position, hands linked in front of his crotch, but that meant his hand was tight against her. He hoped she realized it was inadvertent... even though touching the soft roundness of her ass was something he'd fantasized about for years. Of course, in his fantasies the elevator wasn't crowded. *It was empty. Maybe stuck between floors as he yanked her skirt up...Stephanie's hands pushing against random floor numbers as Neil...* he had to stop thinking this way or he was going to have a problem on his hands. Neil took a steadying breath.

There was some general shifting among the group as the elevator started down, so that Stephanie moved closer against him. Her body was pressed to his all the way up and down now; he couldn't breathe without taking in her perfume; the knot of her hair brushed against him when she turned her head. He felt as if he were drowning in her. He couldn't stop thinking about turning his hands around to cup her deliciously firm butt—and how the hell did she achieve that with the way she hated exercise—or sliding them around her waist, pulling her tighter to him. It would be so easy to bend down and nuzzle into her hair, kiss her bare neck. The ride down was interminable, but when the doors opened, he wished it had gone on longer.

The rest of the evening was more of the same. Neil loved having Stephanie beside him, but her nearness added to the fire inside him. He watched the play without really seeing it, his mind more occupied with the lascivious images in his head. Neil's fingers tingled, he wanted to glide them over Stephanie's back, down her ass and thighs. He yearned to bury himself in her and lose himself in oblivion. He ground his teeth together trying to repress the thoughts that were taking over.

It was like he had the self-control of a fourteen-year-old boy. It was embarrassing. And when the couple on stage kissed in the second act, desire flooded him. Neil ached to kiss Stephanie—wildly, deeply, his tongue filling her mouth and tasting her sweetness. He wanted to taste and touch her everywhere, to rip away her dress and view the reality of her nakedness about which he'd dreamed so often. He could almost feel her breast in his hand, soft and full, her nipple prickling into a delicious bud beneath his circling thumb. *She would lean against him, moaning with pleasure, lips sultry and moist from his kisses, and she would slide up and down, rubbing herself against him, seeking fulfillment as he teased her to a frenzy, taking his time.*

Neil closed his eyes. This was crazy. He adjusted his program to hide his lap. Thank God for the darkness. He'd intended to take Stephanie to a quiet bar after the play for leisurely drinks. But that was out of the question. Alcohol was the last thing he needed—his famed control was already nonexistent right now. Neil had to take Stephanie straight home and leave immediately. He simply couldn't trust himself around her tonight.

But how could he walk her to her door and leave her without a kiss? All he could think of was pulling her to him and kissing her until she was breathless and begging for his touch. But that was something he couldn't do. Not yet.

Stephanie would be shocked; she'd only asked him to go with her tonight because she trusted him; he was safe. He needed to stay that way in her eyes. He had to go slow; she'd said she wasn't ready to date. But how could he go slow when everything that happened, every glimpse of her, drove him half insane?

* * *

When the play ended and the lights went up in the theater, Stephanie busied herself with picking up her purse and program, avoiding Neil's gaze for fear he would see on her face all the things she'd been thinking and feeling all evening.

From the moment she opened the door tonight and saw him standing there, smiling and handsome in his suit, this evening had felt so different, so much like... a date. Was it a date? Did he think of it that way? It seemed absurd. This was Neil, Ty's best friend, doing her a favor.

But what about the romantic atmosphere of the restaurant? That screamed date, didn't it? On the other hand, Neil had never been to Le Pur so he wouldn't have known about the candlelit intimacy.

Still... a French restaurant carried some expectation of romance. And he'd known it was the kind of place you took a woman to on Valentine's Day. And why had he gone to that much trouble to choose a special restaurant? He was thoughtful, but that seemed like something more than thoughtful. Suddenly the kind of light banter they'd always exchanged felt very close to flirtation.

Then there was that ride down from the restaurant. Shoved back against Neil in the elevator, Stephanie had been heart-stoppingly aware of the warmth and power of his long, muscular body. His lapel had brushed her bare arm, sending goosebumps up it, and his breath ruffled the sleek updo of her hair. She had breathed in the spicy scent of cologne and warm flesh that was Neil's alone, and she'd wanted to melt back against him.

But perhaps all this interpretation was only on her side. Maybe to him this was nothing more than an evening with a friend. It was impossible to tell what Neil was thinking. He was always so cool and in control—in life just like he was on the field. It was wonderful; you knew you could turn to him in any emergency. It was also kind of maddening. What did he really feel?

Throughout the play, she'd been all too aware of Neil sitting beside her. His shoulders were too wide for the small theater seats, so that his arm brushed hers, and he'd had to angle his long legs into her space. Stephanie hoped Claire didn't ask her anything specific about the play because Stephanie could remember nothing about it.

As they filed out of the theater with the rest of audience, Neil's hand was on the small of her back, his touch light and almost nonexistent, but she felt it all through her. She wasn't sure what to do, how to talk to him. Should she pretend everything was normal? Should she flirt? Should she invite him in for drinks when they got back to her house? Normally she would, but now everything seemed to have hidden meaning. She didn't want to send the wrong signals; the last thing she wanted was to spoil their friendship.

As they emerged into the lobby, Stephanie glanced around and was relieved to spot Claire, giving Stephanie an easy conversational opening. "Look. There's Claire Webner. I want to introduce you to her."

"The friend we came to support?" Neil asked as they made their way through the crowd. "Is she the same Claire that Ty told me about?"

"Definitely. She makes an impression—once you meet her, you'll know what I mean." She waved to Claire, who stood with the cast and director, greeting well-wishers.

Her friend was stunning in a slinky gold dress that perfectly complimented her golden tan skin and whippet thin figure. Her make-up was, as always, perfect, and her platinum blond hair was cut in a sleek chin length bob. She'd always reminded Stephanie of a glamorous thirties movie star.

"All she needs is long black cigarette holder," Neil murmured, obviously thinking along the same lines, and Stephanie laughed.

"Stephanie!" Claire exclaimed as they approached, her face alight with opening-night euphoria. She reached out and took both Stephanie's hands in hers. "It's great that you came!"

"What a success! I am so, so happy for you!" Stephanie hugged her. When she'd first met Claire almost four years ago she'd been unhappily married to a wealthy dermatologist and not long after that they'd gone through a nasty divorce. Claire had the kind of spirit that was hard to keep down, but even with money from the healthy divorce settlement and a trust fund established by her grandparents, she'd been bored just doing nothing. Eventually she'd turned to a girlhood interest, the theater. It was wonderful to see the project doing well.

Stephanie introduced Neil to Claire, and with a spark of humor she noticed the way the other woman's eyes swept over him, assessing and approving. A waiter carrying flutes of champagne came by offering them glasses. Stephanie grabbed one, hoping it might help her relax and get out of her head a bit, but Neil shook his head. Claire, however, grabbed two and tried to hand one to Neil.

"I'm driving."

"You're also a solid two hundred pounds of muscle, I'd guess. You could probably have four of these and pass a breathalyzer." Claire held it out again, wiggling it back and forth as if to entice him.

"Fine." Neil took the drink.

Claire, her eyes twinkling, leaned in close to Stephanie and whispered in her ear, "I should have said two hundred pounds of *yum*."

Claire had been trying to get Stephanie to date again for months now. Stephanie knew that Claire would probably call her tomorrow, full of eager questions about Neil. Knowing Claire and her distinct disinterest in sports, she probably didn't even recognize him, though.

"Oh! There's Grace!" Claire waved at her leading lady who was winding her way through the crowd over to them. Then Claire unhooked a very un-Claire like necklace that she was wearing and pulled it from around her throat. She leaned in and clasped one of Stephanie's hands, transferring it to her. "I need you to stash this for me."

Neil glanced down at the women's clasped hands, raising his eyebrows. "Strange time to be passing contraband, isn't it?"

Claire laughed. "Like I'd ever walk around with drugs in my hand. A girl always has a place to stash such things. Even girls that don't wear bras." She added with a wink.

Neil's eyebrows shot up further.

"She's kidding." Stephanie looked at her hand, which now held the gold locket. "But I have no idea why I'm hiding a piece of jewelry. You're not actually carrying drugs in this are you?" She joked.

"As if that would hold enough to even be worth bothering." Claire rolled her eyes. "No, I stole it from Grace during the play to help her work up a little more emotion for her big scene in act three. I was gonna slip it back into her bag after curtains, but she's been clutching the thing like a life-preserver!" Claire motioned with her champagne glass at Grace, who'd been intercepted by a regal looking couple that Stephanie was pretty sure were relatives of Claire's. "Talk about someone who probably has drugs."

"I don't want to be caught holding her stolen property!" Stephanie yelped, shoving it back at Claire.

"It's not Her Majesty's Tiara." Claire rolled her eyes but took it back. "It's not even that sentimental. She didn't get it from her dead mother. It was some 'forgive me' jewelry from her estranged husband. And not even good 'forgive me' jewelry at that. At least I got several carats out of my ex-husband's infidelity."

"Well, I'm glad to hear her mom's not dead." Stephanie said. "This play would've hit a bit close to home if she was."

"Oh, no, she is. Which is why I would never steal her stuff." Claire remained completely solemn for half a second. "I am kidding! Her mother is alive and well. Or alive, at least. I don't know that you can say she's well. She's a personal assistant to some celebrity in LA. Doing bitch work for professional narcissists is about the worst job I can imagine. It's like being someone's mistress without all the sugar daddy perks and scrumptious illicit sex."

Neil, who had just taken a small sip of champagne, covered his mouth with his fist. After a moment his Adam's apple bobbed and then he coughed.

"Didn't mean to make you choke, darling." Claire laughed. "But if that shocks you, you might refrain from drinking while I talk. No one is ever quite sure what I might say. Least of all me."

"It's true." Stephanie nodded. "All part of her fun."

"Thank you." Claire tilted her head, looking at Stephanie with affection. "Almost four years later and I'm still so happy for that day I ran into you."

"How did you two meet?" Neil asked.

"I feel like what you're actually asking is how could someone as sane as Stephanie be friends with someone as wonderfully eccentric as I am," Claire teased. "But to be polite, I'll answer your 'cover' question."

"You're the picture of decorum." Stephanie shook her head. "She actually rear-ended me in traffic."

"You literally ran into her?" Neil repeated.

"There's a whole story that goes along with it." Stephanie assured him.

"No doubt."

"Yes, well, my husband had very obviously been cheating on me, and I was trying to tail his car without him noticing, so I was wearing this large hat and huge sunglasses so my vision was obstructed."

"Didn't it occur to you that he still might recognize your car?" Neil broke in.

"That is exactly what Stephanie said when I got out to exchange insurance and phone numbers with her!"

"Imagine that." Neil smirked.

"But, of course. he didn't recognize me, which I should have known because he hadn't noticed me in almost a year at that point, if you know what I mean."

Neil nodded.

"And then this one," Claire gave Stephanie a playful push on her shoulder, "Comes to an abrupt halt and her taillights aren't working."

"I obviously take great care of my car." Stephanie added.

"Oh, I'm aware of the way you take care of your car. That's why I always insist on driving." Neil laughed.

"So we're in this strip mall parking lot and I get out of my car dressed like the shifty vixen in an old movie, and I just started bawling." Claire threw her head back in demonstration. "Most people would've gotten out of there as quickly as possible, but this little empathy machine here immediately wanted to know what was wrong. We must have spent thirty minutes standing there talking." Claire put her arm around Stephanie and squeezed her shoulders. "We met up another time for repair reasons, and then I invited her out to lunch and the rest is history."

Grace, who had finally made it over to them, pulled Claire away from Stephanie, hugging her tightly. "You took my locket! You are an angel!" She snatched the necklace out of Claire's hand. "I was struggling hard in that last scene all through rehearsal, and then you go throw me into a frenzy and I give one of the best performances of my entire life!" The actress fastened her necklace back around her neck. "I just don't know how you are going to keep it up through the full run."

"I'm sure I will think of something." Claire said, her smile cat-like.

"If anyone can!" Grace waved as she melted back into the crowd.

A growing line of theater patrons had been gathering behind them since they'd been talking, all waiting to congratulate Claire, so Stephanie and Neil said their goodbyes and deposited their half-drunk champagne flutes before they headed out to the car.

"So… Claire was—" Neil turned the key in the ignition.

"See! Now you understand why I said you just had to meet her."

"Yes, I have to admit. It is hard to find words adequate to describe her." He pulled out of the spot, a wry smile pulling at his mouth.

"I thought when I first met her that she was a bit unhinged but fun—I figured she'd just be my zany friend that all my best stories would happen with. And, obviously she was."

"Oh, I remember Ty telling the story about the time she did an impromptu 'You're the One that I Want' performance at a carnival you three went to." Neil laughed.

"She loves to be busy so I don't get to introduce her to people as much as I'd like. Half the time she just randomly drops by and drags me out, so there's not a lot of time to plan. But she's good at getting me out of my comfort zone, which, as you know, is notoriously difficult."

"I'm definitely aware of the fact that I can never get you to go rock climbing or geocaching or even to play tennis." Neil agreed.

"See, the common thread there is those are high-intensity activities done under the even more high-intensity Arizona sun. Claire is an 'indoor cat' as she is fond of saying." Stephanie laughed. "She takes me to plays and she's the only person that has ever successfully dragged me up to a karaoke mic. I mean, it was only a duet, but still, I have to admit it was a weird rush."

"Now that sounds exhausting to me."

"It's not when she's there though. Claire's like a kite: if you try to control her, the string's just gonna rip through your hands, but if you just let Claire be Claire and drag you along, it's really freeing. And she can be calmer too. She's actually pretty great in bad times. When I was so emotional this last year and a half she was easy to be around because she doesn't judge and feelings don't bother her; she lives for emotion. I could tell her my blackest thoughts and she would just listen without trying to help. I didn't realize how much I needed that until I got it from her."

"I'm sorry if I tried to fix things too much." Neil kept his eyes on the road, but even without being able to see them Stephanie sensed a shift in his mood.

"I didn't mean that! No, you were great. You kept on Ty's doctors, made sure I ate. It was just I'd leaned on you so much while he was sick that I didn't want to keep doing it even after he was gone. And Claire was kind of perfect when I reached that point because she didn't have to be Miss Responsible or take care of things for me."

"Not her strong suit?"

"Definitely not. But listening and helping me acknowledge how I felt were."

"I'm glad you have her, then. Even if she's a little nuts."

"She's nowhere near as crazy as Pete Cherneski, and you and Ty both loved him. I remember that night we all had too much to drink after the ESPYs and went swimming, and Pete did a naked cannonball even though no one else was skinny dipping." Stephanie laughed. "That was way more than I needed to see."

"You went inside real fast." Neil laughed. "Which was obviously very disappointing. I mean, I'd certainly much rather see you hop out of my pool dripping wet than Cherneski.

Stephanie flushed. "I've never been much of a skinny dipper."

"That's a shame. You'd make a very good one." Neil flashed her a quick lopsided grin. Then he abruptly looked away with a muttered, "Sorry."

Sorry? Why had he said that? He thought what he said was too flirtatious? His words had sent a bolt of heat straight to her core. And that little half-smile certainly sparked something. Stephanie shifted, pressing her thighs together, determined to ignore the sensations. Maybe he'd seen her reaction and was afraid she'd misinterpreted what he'd said. Stephanie crossed her arms over her chest, suddenly self-conscious.

Neil's jaw was tight and the muscle next to his ear stood out. She wondered what it would do if she ran a hand over it? Would it jump? Would he relax into it? Let out a little sound of pleasure? All the feelings she'd been experiencing during the play came back full force. Why couldn't she just ignore the way Neil looked like she used to? She'd hoped the glass of champagne would help her relax, but it had just lowered her inhibitions, and now all she could think about was the large, masculine presence of Neil and how it made her turn to liquid inside.

Stephanie looked down at her arms and saw that her shifting position had pulled the top of her dress lower, exposing far more cleavage than she usually showed. She pulled her dress back up and glanced at Neil. Had he noticed? She couldn't deny that some small part of her hoped he had. If she was going to have these rampant feelings she couldn't control, it would be nice to know she wasn't the only one. But Neil wasn't looking at her; his eyes were glued to the road. His hands gripped the steering wheel tightly, and the fingers of one hand tapped the wheel restlessly. He shifted in his seat.

Maybe it had nothing to do with her or the talk of skinny dipping. Neil had seemed unusually jumpy all evening, Stephanie didn't think it was boredom from being forced to see a play—there had been a glitter in his dark eyes most of the evening. He seemed... charged up. It was the other side of Neil, the part she'd rarely seen except on the playing field, shooting pass after pass to Ty and Asa Jackson, brilliance zinging from his fingertips.

This was the Neil whose fires were barely banked; the one who ran with the ball to make a first down or stood in the pocket with an enormous defensive end rushing him, not throwing until the last second. This was the

Neil who challenged Ty to a race at three o'clock in the morning after a night of partying. Ty had beaten him, of course; even with several beers in him, Ty was one of the fastest players on the team. But Neil, undaunted, had wanted to go again. Fortunately, Asa had jumped in and smoked them both, putting an end to the contest.

The look on Neil's face set off a little spark of uncertainty in Stephanie's stomach and an accompanying leap of excitement. How well did she really know Neil Moran? Sometimes she felt as if she'd known him forever. At other times she sensed something locked away deep inside him, and she knew she didn't understand him at all.

Had he felt any of the spark she had? Had he sensed her own sudden, crazy attraction to him? Was that why he seemed so tense? Stephanie couldn't think of any way to reassure him that she wouldn't try to turn their relationship into a nonplatonic one. Even bringing it up would be highly embarrassing. If she handled it wrong, it could ruin their friendship.

Or was she being paranoid because of how stirred up she'd felt all night? Logically, she wouldn't have been surprised if the air had hummed with sexual tension between them. The night had felt much more like a date than she'd anticipated. But Neil seemed the opposite, more like he was retreating from her. Not looking at her, not talking to her. He'd even moved farther away from her—as far as one could get in a car this small. She could only see his profile, but his jaw was set, his face immobile. Was he angry at her?

Had she made him feel like he was unhelpful or unwanted with her comment about Claire not 'fixing' things? Or did Neil think she'd used him to make her life easier when Ty was sick and then had just forgotten about him after Ty's death?

When they reached her house, Neil walked her to her front door. She unlocked the door and turned to him. Normally she would have asked him in for a drink or just to talk, but she was unsure what to do now, given his mood. "Well." She smiled, her voice tentative. "Thank you for going to the play with me tonight." She looked into his face. The outside light beside the door cast only a little light over his face, leaving his eyes in shadow.

"Yeah. No problem." His voice was clipped, his hands jammed into his pockets.

"Dinner was lovely," she tried again. "Thank you."

He gave her a short nod. "I enjoyed it. I—good night, Stephanie." Abruptly, he turned and walked away.

A little stunned, Stephanie watched him return to his car. He whipped out of the driveway and took off, tires squealing. Well, that certainly answered the question of whether Neil was angry. Tears pricked behind her eyelids, but she pushed them back. She was not going to get all teary-eyed because Neil Moran was upset with her.

She stepped inside, closing and locking the door behind her. Dropping her clutch on the hall table, she jerked off her high heels and tossed them to the floor—well, threw them would be more accurate. If Neil was offended and wouldn't even deign to talk about it, if he wanted to end their years-old friendship, then to hell with him.

It wasn't as if she was in love with him. These new, tumultuous feelings she'd been having about him were merely part of her reawakening from her grief. She was giving her emotions, her desires, a safe outlet in Neil; she could dream about him, knowing that her fantasies would never become a reality. That was all it was, and they would soon vanish.

Aimlessly she wandered through the house. It would be useless to try to sleep. She opened the glass doors to the patio and looked out. The full moon washed the backyard with pale light. Maybe the moon was the reason for her strange emotions. People claimed that a full moon brought out people's wild side. She strolled across the cement patio to the side of the pool, where she slipped off her sandals. Hiking up her skirt above her knees, she sat down and dangled her legs in the cool turquoise water.

Why had she never noticed the sexiness of Neil's smile before? Had his thick black hair always been so inviting? She thought about his broad-shouldered body, arms bulging with tight, hard muscles, so different from Ty's slender runner's frame. He wasn't at all like Ty physically. Ty's coloring had been fair and he'd had a classic look like the prince in a fairy tale. Neil, on the other hand, was dark as a villain. She had seen him swimming often enough to know that his chest was covered with curling black hair, thinning down in a V to his navel. She wondered what it would be like to feel the prickle of his chest hair against her naked breasts.

Something scraped against the gate at the front of the yard, and Stephanie jumped at the noise, jarred from her thoughts. Annoyed at her nerves, she turned and her breath froze in her throat. A dark form stood inside the gate, watching her. She couldn't move, but her heart began to race in her chest. Then she reacted instinctively, swinging around and pulling her legs out of the water. She jumped to her feet to run to the house as the dark shape of a man left the shadows and the moonlight hit his face.

Chapter Six

"Neil! What are you doing? You scared me half to death!"

He said nothing as he strode toward her. His face was unreadable, a mask of shadow and reflected moonlight. A shiver ran through Stephanie, part apprehension, part anticipation. She had no time to think before he stopped inches in front of her. His eyes were dark hollows, his cheekbones slender shards of light. His mouth was dark and full, softened from its usual precise lines. His eyelids drooped and he reached out to grasp her shoulders. "I couldn't do it," he said thickly, pulling her toward him. "I couldn't leave without—"

The words died in his mouth as their lips met. A ball of ice and fire filled her chest. She'd never expected… His mouth moved against hers, digging in greedily, and his breath was a hot blast on her cheek. A tremor ran through Stephanie and her hands stole up around his neck. Neil's hands left their grip on her shoulders to slide around her back, pulling her against the firm muscle of his chest.

Stephanie was dazed, lost in the moment, awash in sensory perceptions. She felt his heat, smelled the tang of his flesh, tasted him on her lips. His mouth widened, pressing her lips apart. They opened readily, and his tongue swept in, hot and fierce, yet velvety smooth. Neil made a noise deep in his throat, and his fingers sank into her waist, grinding her against him. He kissed her desperately, as if he would consume her, moving his mouth only to change the angle of the kiss. His breath was rasping, almost panting, and the sound stirred her unbelievably. She curled her fingers into the cloth of his jacket, wadding it up in her fists. He groaned and moved his body over hers.

Stephanie clung to him, long-slumbering desire bursting through her. She was filled with brilliant, whirling fireworks, spinning her wildly upward. Neil's hands were everywhere on her body, searing her with the heat of his passion. He shoved his fingers into her hair, wrecking the sleek knot and sending the strands tumbling in a cascade through his hands. The pads of his fingertips dug into her scalp, holding her head so that she couldn't have moved even if some part of her wanted to. And she didn't. Stephanie had never experienced such unleashed passion, and the thought of his furious hunger was as exciting as the purely physical sensations his hands and mouth were awakening in her.

"Stephanie," he mumbled, pulling his mouth away and sliding it across her cheek to find her ear. His teeth teased at the soft lobe. She touched his neck and the soft skin of his throat, and his flesh quivered beneath her hand. Neil, mindless, beyond his own command—it was an astonishing idea.

His hands slid between them, and he cupped her breasts through the fabric of her dress, his thumbs pressing against her nipples. Stephanie sucked in her breath. He was nuzzling her neck now, murmuring unrecognizable words as his hands slid down her hips and around to squeeze her ass, thrusting her even harder against his rigid length.

Suddenly the fierceness of his hunger frightened her. The man in her arms was a stranger—hardly calm, controlled Neil. It was unnerving, despite the delicious sensations he was stirring within her. Even the intensity of her own response was frightening. She went stiff in his arms. She wasn't ready for all this. It was overwhelming.

Neil froze, feeling the change in her, and buried his face in her neck. A shudder ran through him and he relaxed his arms. Stephanie slid back to a flat-footed stance. She looked up at Neil, his arms now just encircling her loosely. His eyes were closed, his face covered with a faint sheen of sweat.

"I'm sorry," Neil said through clenched teeth. He opened his eyes and drew a shaky breath. "I shouldn't have. I couldn't help myself. I just..." He shoved one hand back through his hair. "Tell me you're not going to hate me for this."

Still stunned, Stephanie shook her head. "No. I… it's..." She scrambled for words to convey her jumbled feelings.

"It was too sudden. Too fast." He nodded and stepped back. "I'll call you tomorrow."

"Okay." Stephanie smiled. God, he looked good this way, eyes hot, hair a little disheveled. "I'd like that."

"Good." Neil took another step back. "I'll go now." Still he hung there for a long moment before he swung around and walked away.

Silently Stephanie stared after him, shaken and breathless. When he disappeared through the gate, she looked around, as if surprised to find herself outside, and wandered back into her house. She locked the sliding door and mechanically got ready for bed, her mind whirling. She was jittery and jumped-up, too excited to sleep, yet she lay down in bed, her mind retracing the moments by the pool, her blood racing as she recalled Neil's kisses and exploring hands.

Imagine that. Neil Moran was hiding a very passionate nature beneath that layer of cool. She smiled to herself, recalling the heat and urgency of his caresses. Neil, like her, suddenly wanted more. Or had it been a fluke, a combination of a romantic play and a full moon?

Neil had probably been fighting what he felt all night; his moodiness had been from resistance, not anger. Did he think it was too much complication? Football season was about to begin, and he was coming back from an injury after a mediocre season. Neil was a man with such focus and control that he might decide not to get involved with anyone—especially when they had all this baggage attached.

Or maybe he felt too guilty about the idea of being with his best friend's widow. Certainly Stephanie had a nagging little voice in her head telling her she was being unfaithful to Ty. How could she desire another man? Especially Ty's best friend—it seemed a further betrayal. She knew it meant nothing about her love for Ty, but knowing that and acting on it were different.

Neil could decide the whole thing wasn't worth it. He could call her tomorrow to tell her he'd been wrong. Or he might simply avoid her altogether. Her chest went icy at the thought that she might never see him again.

This was crazy. It was all pure speculation, she told herself. She had no idea what Neil wanted. She obviously didn't know the man at all, despite their years of friendship. So how could she hope to guess what he would do? The best thing would be for her to get some sleep. Firmly she turned over and willed her mind to stop running. But her brain stubbornly refused, and it was hours before she finally fell asleep.

The next morning she awakened, not sleepy like usual, but fully alert. She jumped out of bed and hummed as she made a quick breakfast, then sat down with her food and pulled up the local newspaper on her tablet. She clicked on the link to the sports section, something she hadn't done in months. The rookies were already in summer training camp. There was only one more week before quarterback camp.

Neil would leave Phoenix next week. Even if he wanted to pursue what had begun last night, he wouldn't have time. In a few days he'd be in California, and it would be over a month before he returned. What crappy timing. She wondered if he was thinking the same thing. Or was he looking forward to leaving as a way to extricate himself from a complicated situation?

Stephanie frowned and stood up. She had to stop thinking about Neil; obsessing wouldn't change anything. Today she was going to return to writing. Stephanie usually avoided taking her cell phone out back to her office, but she itched to bring it today. What if Neil called? Well, if he wanted to talk to her that badly, he'd stop by. Neil had never been one to give up easily. Resolutely, she left it on the kitchen table.

She refilled her mug of coffee, and, setting her chin, she marched outside to her office. She picked up the notepad where she'd sketched out several brief outlines for stories before her writing break. She had decided to take the pressure off by working on a short article instead of a book. One of these would work even if they weren't perfect. Soon two of the ideas emerged as the most workable, and one was perfect for a blog that she'd sold articles to before. She opted for that one and settled down to work.

After an hour of serious thinking and jotting down questions, she did her preliminary research using her online sources. Once she'd narrowed down who she needed to speak to in person, she went about setting up interview times. Interviewing people was always her favorite part of her job, and as she entered her appointments on her Google calendar she found herself humming happily. Stephanie noticed her stomach rumbling and headed back to the main house for lunch.

Her cellphone was ringing as she came in the door and she grabbed it up from the kitchen table, almost dropping it in her hurry. "Hello?"

"Stringer?"

"Neil!" Her voice came out more excited than she wanted it to. "How are you?"

"Fine." He paused. "Um, I wanted to know if you'd be home this evening. I found something that might interest you."

"Oh? What?" Did he intend to act as if nothing had happened last night? Resume their old friendship? Just slide into dating?

"An idea for a book. It's a physical item, though, so I can't just email it to you. I could send pictures… but it's pretty fascinating. I'd rather you see it in person." Neil sounded more unsure than Stephanie had ever heard him before.

He was nervous; that explained the abrupt beginning. She smiled. It was beyond cute hearing him stumble around for an excuse to see her. And it was somehow also sexy as hell. Of course, it was starting to feel like every single thing Neil did was sexy to her now. "Sure. I'll be here all evening."

"Around seven?"

"Sure. Would you like some dinner?"

"No, don't go to the trouble. I need to stick to my plan. My trainer about choked when I told him what I ate at Le Pur." He hesitated for a beat. "I hope I didn't scare you off last night."

"Oh. No. I…was… just…" Overwhelmed? Overheated? In over my head? "A little surprised."

He chuckled. "Well, I promise not to grab you and kiss you unless you ask really nicely." She could almost see the wicked grin in his voice.

Stephanie relaxed, joining in his laughter. At least they were able to talk about it. Perhaps they could keep their friendship alive even if nothing were to come from their kisses. She wondered if that was Neil's real purpose in coming by. To get things back on their normal track. Her heart sank at the thought.

"We can talk when I get there. All right?"

"Okay."

Stephanie had difficulty concentrating the rest of the day. She kept thinking of what she should wear. It had to be just right—certainly not the baggy T shirt and sweatpants that she wore right now. But she didn't want to come across as trying too hard. It had to be ordinary yet subtly sexy.

She managed to stick to her job until almost five before she left the office and hurried to her closet. She went through her clothes, mixing and matching until finally she settled on a pair of faded old jeans that had rips across the thighs, showcasing a flash of skin from her long legs and a simple white crop top that just barely reached her waistband. It was the kind of outfit that didn't try too hard but was still subtly sexy.

Neil arrived on time, like usual, and Stephanie jumped up to open the front door. She smiled at him a little shyly, remembering his kisses and her response. Her senses were abnormally heightened. She was aware of everything about him, from the strong curve of his jaw to the way his shirt hugged his broad chest. He was familiar, yet unknown at the same time. "Hello, Neil."

"Hi." All six feet, five inches of Neil was practically jumping with joy. He looked like a hugely overgrown kid with his boyish grin and something clasped behind his back like it was both his prize possession and a gift he couldn't wait to give her.

"What do you have that's put that half-crazed look in your eye?" Stephanie couldn't help but laugh, some of her tension at how awkward things might be after their kiss melting away in the wake of Neil's excitement.

"Okay, so I never really told you and Ty, because, frankly, I figured Ty would never stop laughing at me, but my brother and I really like going to those escape room things when he's in town. So I got us both a subscription to an escape room themed monthly crate. It's called True Escape, and each one is based on some real-life stronghold, and they have a little booklet all about the real place in each box."

"That's so cool." Stephanie frowned. "I would have loved to do an escape room with you. I actually wanted to try one for my birthday, but Ty never wanted to go."

"Well, if you ever want to do a True Escapes box, we should do the H.H. Holmes one—I know you were fascinated by that documentary, and they recreated everything from his 'Murder Castle' down to the smallest detail in the map."

"We should definitely do that." She nodded. "But what does this have to do with a book? You know I can't write stuff about serial killers—I'd never sleep again for the rest of my life."

"I remember—we watched that Manson Family series together."

"Ty passed out half-way through the first episode." Stephanie laughed. "If you hadn't stayed up with me, I wouldn't have finished it."

"I know. Then you had to follow it up with a New Girl binge before you could sleep."

"You shouldn't have let me watch it at all; I still think there's some psycho creepy-crawling through my house when it gets cool in the evening and the house starts to settle."

"Hey, don't blame me for your bad ideas." Neil raised his eyebrow with the scar running through it. God, he looked cute when he did that. "We watched that one-hundred-percent on your recommendation. And I promise this new crate has nothing to do with murder." Neil brought the box out from behind his back and handed it to her. "The Fortress" was stamped across it in big letters. "I figured I'd better bring it by because I'm leaving town tomorrow."

"Tomorrow? But I thought the passing camp didn't start until next week."

"It doesn't." A big smile broke out on Neil's face. "I'm surprised you still keep up with when all the camps are. You never seemed like football stuff was that important to you."

Stephanie blushed. Why had she let that slip? Now he was going to think she had his schedule memorized like some kind of stalker.

"I just happened to see it in the sports section today."

"Right." A twinkle in Neil's dark eyes said he didn't believe it was as casual as she was trying to make it seem—but he obviously wasn't bothered by it either.

"So where are you going?"

"Madison, Wisconsin for a week to visit my family. Hannah is getting married next Saturday."

"I always forget you have a sister, too. You talk about your brother more."

"Charles and I have always been closer."

"Well, come in and let's check out this possible story that I owe to your and Charles' escape room habit." They sat down in the living room on opposite sides of the coffee table, and Stephanie opened up the box.

"This month's one is based on a kidnapping from the 2000s. Well, it's partly about the kidnapping, but more about what came after it."

Stephanie pulled out the shiny sheet of paper sitting on top of a heavy folded partition that was probably a game board. The page she held looked like an artistic recreation of an old newspaper article. A faux-headline read, "Cinematic Star Angela Drake's Only Child Kidnapped!"

Stephanie scanned the page quickly before picking up the game's instruction booklet that lay underneath the article.

It stated that they were bringing out "The Fortress" now to celebrate the wedding of Gabrielle Willoughby of Tucson, Arizona to Wesley Hammond of Caulfield, Massachusetts. 'Gabrielle, the once kidnapped daughter of 90s star Angela Drake, is finally getting her own movie-ready happy ending.'

"I remember her kidnapping! I can't believe she's all grown-up and getting married now. She was younger than me."

"I wasn't sure you would have heard of it. It was when you were a kid."

"But it was big news. I was ten, I think. Angela Drake was married to some wealthy guy that wasn't at all involved in Hollywood. Right?"

"The Willoughbys. They were New England, old money, filthy rich. And Angela wasn't exactly poor."

"And the kidnapper asked for a huge amount of money, didn't he?"

"Five million dollars. They paid it and got their daughter back alive. Later the police caught and tried someone for the crime."

Stephanie snapped her fingers. "Rodriguez! The Rodriguez case. It was almost as famous as the kidnapping. They convicted the wrong man. A couple of years later the nanny confessed that she had lied."

"Yeah, Molly Adams," Neil supplied. "It was really her boyfriend who had kidnapped the girl, and when he dumped her, Molly finally went to the police."

"There were a lot of civil rights groups involved because the man that Molly falsely accused, and who was wrongly convicted, was Latino."

Neil nodded. "The hunt for the real kidnapper was equally fascinating. They finally got him years later."

"So what is the 'Fortress' in the game though? I thought he just kept her at some abandoned warehouse in Los Angeles for a few days. Doesn't seem like much of an escape room."

"It's actually based on the Willoughby home in Tucson." Neil leaned forward, placing his elbows on his splayed knees. He was so close Stephanie could smell the woodsy scent of the shampoo he used. A little involuntary shiver ran through her. "Did you notice that there isn't a picture of the happy couple or Gabrielle Willoughby in any of the game sheets?"

Stephanie pulled out all the components of the box and went through them more slowly. There were pictures of the house where Gabrielle had been kidnapped in Los Angeles, the warehouse where she had been held, both of her parents and the outside of the 'Fortress,' but none of Gabrielle.

"Yeah. That does seem strange. The wedding must be a big society event."

"Well, they have a disclaimer with this box saying that even though the outside has been recreated perfectly, and the inside contains all known rooms, the blueprint is laid out 'as imagined based on outer architecture' because no one has ever been allowed in to photograph it. Gabrielle also hasn't been seen in public or in pictures in over fifteen years."

Stephanie's brows went up. "Really? Because they're afraid of another kidnapping?"

"Apparently. Bernard Willoughby bought the 'Fortress' right after they got Gabrielle back, and, after spending millions to make it as secure as possible, he and his daughter moved in. Bernard and Angela split up after the kidnapping, and Bernard's family lawyers were so good he managed to get sole custody of the girl. Gabrielle literally hasn't left the grounds since. They were already terrified that something might happen to her, but after it was discovered that the real kidnapper was still in the wind, it made it even worse."

"Poor girl. She sounds like Sleeping Beauty."

"And now the prince, this Wesley Hammond, is kissing her awake."

"I wonder how she met him. Perhaps he's an old family friend of her father's—this does say he's from New England." Stephanie mused. "I mean, how many men could she have met, living that way?"

"Couldn't have been many. It makes you wonder if she's really in love with the guy or if he's just the only man she's ever been around besides her father and the people that work at the house."

"This one's got everything: wealth, glamour, suspense, even issues of equality and justice." Stephanie felt a rising excitement in her chest, something she hadn't experienced in a long time. "Neil, I think you've brought me a fantastic idea. What else is known about this 'Fortress?'"

Neil unfolded the game board which was a map of the house and grounds. He pointed everything out as he described the details.

"First of all, the place is in the middle of the desert, with nothing around for miles. There's an electrified fence around the estate, with an armed guard at the gate. There are thermal cameras that can track any person on the grounds inside the first gate—as well as the trained attack dogs." He showed her the little dog figurines that could be moved around in the game. "Then there's a second wall, an unscalable ten-foot-high block of cement. Inside that are the yards and the house, which has a roof-top helipad for a quick escape, bulletproof windows, and the latest alarm system with motion sensors and cameras. As far as anyone can tell, all servants are also trained bodyguards—even the chauffeur figurine is a big burly guy." Neil handed Stephanie the tiny plastic muscle man with a limo driver hat on.

"Can you imagine how weird it would be to have a house that was so legendary that someone made a game out of it?" Stephanie shook her head. "Like, do you think the chauffeur got a subscription to this crate just so he could have a figurine of himself?"

"I would have." Neil laughed. "Now, the True Escape people configured the inner rooms of the house in the most likely pattern based on aerial photography and rumors, but they say that this layout is not exact.

Still, they know there are indoor and outdoor swimming pools, stables, a tennis court, and a bowling alley. It's believed that the basement is essentially one huge panic room with its own dedicated generator just in case power to the rest of the house gets cut. There's even supposed to be a small movie theater with a little concession stand."

Stephanie stared. "How bizarre. I can't imagine never leaving your house. She must have had the most peculiar life." She leaned forward, propping her elbows on her knees and resting her chin on her clasped hands as she examined the board carefully. "Neil, this could be the best book I've written yet." She flashed a grin at him.

"I thought you'd like it." He returned her smile. But now that they'd discussed the story idea an awkward silence fell. Neil studied his hands. "Steph, about last night…" She swallowed. Her stomach squeezed itself into a ball. "I hope I didn't come on too strong." Absentmindedly he rubbed one thumb along the opposite forefinger. "I don't want to scare you."

"It's all right. Don't worry."

He faced her squarely. "I'm not saying I'm sorry I did it. I wanted to kiss you." A faint smile eased his tense expression. "In fact, I'd like to do it again."

Stephanie's indrawn breath was shaky. "Why don't you?"

Before she could regret what she'd said, his hands whipped out and latched onto her wrists, knocking the game box onto the ground as he pulled her out of her seat and around the coffee table. She looked up at him, eyes wide, as he settled her sideways on his lap, one arm curling around her shoulders. With the other hand he tilted her chin, and then his mouth came down to fasten on hers.

Chapter Seven

Stephanie was unprepared for the lust that immediately flooded her body. Neil's lips were warm and not as demanding as they had been last night. He was obviously in control of himself as his mouth worked over hers. The tip of his tongue came out to trace the line of her lips, and she opened her mouth to him. The sudden heat of his skin on her cheek was mute testimony to the desire bubbling under the surface of Neil's control. Neil wouldn't rush her, but it wasn't because he was uninterested. He wanted her.

His tongue played in her mouth, sliding against the sharpness of her teeth and curling around her own tongue. His thumb rubbed along her jaw, caressing the smooth skin, and his long fingers wrapped around to tangle in the hair tucked behind her ear. His other hand went to her side, stroking her waist and venturing up until it brushed the underside of her breast. Stephanie shivered and brought her hands up between them, clutching his T-shirt in her fists. Neil's name came from her in a sigh as his lips left hers to press a path to her ear. Carefully he nibbled at the lobe. His arm pulled her closer as he coiled his other hand tighter in her hair, lifting it from her neck. Soft as velvet, his lips explored the gentle skin on the back of her neck, starting a barrage of shivers through her.

Wetness bloomed between Stephanie's legs and she shifted on Neil's lap, seeking answering pressure from him. A groan came from deep in his throat and he moved his mouth lower, biting at her shoulder as he tugged on her hair. Stephanie's lips curled in a smile as she felt him harden under her. Neil suddenly let go of her hair like he was aware of how rough his grasp had become and she took the opportunity to turn so she was straddling him on the couch. Her body was taking over, no longer taking directions from her rational mind. All she knew was that she wanted Neil. Wanted to roll her hips against his rigid length. Wanted to experience the passion only he could give her.

One of his hands stole under her shirt, and he squeezed her breast, running his thumb over the nipple so that it tightened even more. It was almost painful, Stephanie wanted him so much, and she let out a gasp. Neil shoved her shirt up at her involuntary sound and bent his head to capture her nipple through her bra. A long groan was ripped from her body as he sucked harder, lightly teasing her with his teeth. She moved her hips more frantically and Neil responded to her search for release, pressing the seam of her jeans into her with his thumb. He instinctively found exactly the spot she needed, and he rubbed harder. Stephanie's breath was coming out in gasps, and she could feel tension coiling in her, tightening, rising…

"Neil, I… I can't think."

"You don't need to," he leaned back, lowering her zipper and slipping his hand right back to where she wanted it—but this time only her thin panties were separating their skin. Neil watched her with hooded eyes. Stephanie could feel herself so close to the edge. It wouldn't take much more. Neil moved his thumb faster. Between his electric black stare and the magic of his hands she didn't know if she could stop the waves that threatened to roll over her.

She was about to come apart, right here in her living room. With a man that was her good friend. With Ty's best friend. The hazy cloud of lust retreated for a second. Enough for Stephanie to press away from Neil. "Stop."

Neil did so immediately, even though he was breathing heavily and his stare was as hot as anything she'd ever seen in her life. He zipped her jeans back up for her before adjusting his own and Stephanie slid from his lap onto the couch. She leaned her head back against it, still practically panting herself and with the residual tension of her non-orgasm swirling inside of her like a tornado. Pulling down her shirt, she let out a long exhale.

"I'm not sure I can do this right now. With any man. But especially you." She hauled herself up, and stood to face him. She obviously couldn't trust herself around Neil right now so she needed to put some space in between them. He made no effort to pull her back into his arms, just sighed and gazed up at her. Stephanie went on nervously, "Don't you feel funny? I mean, because of Ty?"

"A little," he admitted. "But I still want you."

She tilted her head to one side, studying him. "This seems so strange and sudden. I feel guilty—almost as if I were cheating on Ty."

Wearily Neil closed his eyes and nodded. "I understand. I don't want to push you into anything." When he opened his eyes, his gaze was direct and piercing. "I don't want it to be clouded with doubt. It's got to be right for you." He stood up and took one of her hands in his, lacing his fingers through hers. "We'll move as slow as you want."

She swayed a little toward him. "Neil…"

"Yes?" His black eyes were alert, and she felt a thrill of trepidation. Once Neil set his mind to something he didn't back down. Could he really just turn it off? "I'm not sure when, or if, I'll ever be ready."

"You mean you think you'll just stay—alone?"

"I don't know. I've been drained of emotion for so long."

"I could certainly give you some of mine," he joked dryly. "It's not a tragedy. If things don't work between us, it won't be the first time I've struck out." Neil paused. "All I want to know right now is whether you feel anything. Or is it just me?"

Stephanie's eyes flew open wide. "You've got to be kidding—I feel so much for you it's scary. That's why I cut it off. I don't want to get too involved. Ty's death left such a huge hole in my life, and I don't want to hurt you or me by jumping in and trying to fill it up. Do you understand?"

"You're vulnerable still. You don't want to rush into anything."

"Pretty much." She let out her breath. "I should have known you'd understand."

He bent to place a final kiss on her lips, a quick, hard one, as if he dared nothing more. "I better leave now, before I do anything we might regret. I'm flying straight to quarterback camp from Wisconsin and then two weeks of training camp, so I won't see you until the exhibition game."

"Yeah." Her heart fell into her stomach. Was she really ready to let him go like this—without something more to hold on to?

"I'll call you from camp."

"Really?" Spontaneous pleasure lit her eyes. "Good. I'd like that."

"Count on it, then." He stood staring down at her for a moment, then turned abruptly. "I'll let myself out."

She listened to his steps down the hall. He opened the door and then she heard it close behind him. It would be several weeks before she saw Neil again. The thought brought an ache to her chest.

* * *

Stephanie occupied herself over the next few days by delving further into the story of the Willoughbys and the Rodriguez case. There were pictures of Gabrielle Willoughby from before her kidnapping. She'd been a pale, skinny little girl with a gap-toothed, winning smile. Stephanie's chest contracted painfully. How horrible to think that this child had undergone the terror of kidnapping and then years of isolation following it.

Stephanie dreamed about Gabrielle that night, but her face was a strange shifting void, probably because she had no idea what she looked like now. The next morning Stephanie called her editor in New York to discuss the idea. Her editor loved it, so, feeling more excited than she had about any story in a while, Stephanie decided it was time to get serious about research. She called various LAPD officers who had been involved with the original case and the lawyers from the Rodriguez trial and lined up several in- person interviews for the following week. Running on pure adrenaline, Stephanie packed her suitcase, threw it in her car and drove to Los Angeles. The interviews were fascinating and led to a few more impromptu meet-ups with people from the fringes of the story, too. Before long her brain was swollen with information, and on Saturday she returned to Phoenix to sort it all out and develop her outline of the book.

Stephanie was exhausted by the time she drove into her driveway, and she straggled into the house carrying a suitcase that seemed twice as heavy as it was when she left. As soon as she sank onto the couch, her phone started ringing from her purse in the kitchen. She really wasn't in the mood to talk, but she'd ignored her cell the entire time she was in LA. Her friends were probably starting to wonder if she had been kidnapped herself. She stood back up with a sigh.

"Hi, Claire." Stephanie felt bad as soon as she saw her caller ID. This was definitely not the first time her friend had called since she left town.

"Why have you not been answering your phone?" Claire's voice was almost frantic. "I've been calling you all week."

"I was in Los Angeles researching a story." It had only been a few days, but after not returning any of her calls or texts, Stephanie didn't think she should nitpick. "I barely had a chance to glance at my texts. I'm sorry."

"Well, I suppose I'll forgive you. But it was terrible! I was just bubbling with news about the play—and questions about that gorgeous male specimen you were with last Saturday night—and I couldn't get hold of you to gossip. It was sheer torture!"

"I'd suspect that someone in an iron maiden would probably still trade places with you," Stephanie retorted dryly.

Claire chuckled. "So tell me, who was he?"

"Neil Moran?" Stephanie laughed. "Did you really not recognize him? He's the quarterback for the Pumas. Ty's friend."

"Another football player?"

"Yes. But don't get too excited. He's just a friend." Even as she said it, Stephanie knew it was a lie. She wasn't sure what they were now, but Neil was definitely no longer just a friend.

"You must be crazy! How can you be 'just friends' with a guy that looks like that?"

"Easily. He's a good guy."

"He also has sexy black eyes and an unbelievable body. I could practically see his abs through his dress shirt."

"Claire…" Stephanie closed her eyes, amused despite herself.

"I'm telling you, if you don't try to lock that down, I may have to take you in for a psych evaluation. I'm talking full mandatory 72-hour hold."

"He was Ty's closest friend on the Pumas and the one that helped me the whole time Ty was sick. It would be very... complicated. Plus I don't know that I'd even want to get involved with a quarterback. All the team politics and the Wives Association; it was exhausting the first time around." Stephanie hadn't really laid it out so clearly yet, even to herself, but as soon as she said it, she knew it was at least part of what was holding her back. She had never been very good at the footballer's wife thing—of course she was jumping forward about fifty steps even thinking about marriage. Neil hadn't taken her out on a real, official date yet.

"Why didn't anyone ever tell me jocks were so handsome? I always thought they had necks a yard wide and flattened noses. Think you could introduce me to a player or two—or the whole team?" Claire laughed wickedly.

"As if you need more men in your life." Stephanie chuckled. "The last I heard you were dating three different guys."

"One of them has a boring job, one has a boring hobby, and one has boring friends. I thought maybe all together they'd equal one interesting guy. Turns out I'm just bored three times over." There were several beeps on Claire's end of the line and the slight whirring sound that had been in the background got louder and faster.

"Are you on the treadmill right now?" Stephanie frowned.

"Not all of us can sit on the couch reading and eating junk food and still have tall, dark, handsome men beating down our door."

"That's not how I would describe it."

"Close enough. For the rest of us there is a lot of effort involved. Even so, the only men I meet who seem to have anything going for them are already married and I refuse to stoop to the level of my ex's new wife. I wish I was interested in women, too; I could double my dating pool. But, alas, I'm stuck with men that are dull, snobbish or have absolutely no sense of humor."

"You don't need to tell me. I can guess the quality of the men you know from that guy you were obviously trying to set me up with at the fundraiser last month."

Claire laughed. "I'm sorry. I just thought you needed to get back out there, and he seemed pretty interesting."

"Interesting is one way of putting it. Another way of putting it is that he makes his living selling painted rocks on Etsy and has a pet skunk."

"I've heard that his main source of income is actually the quilts he makes from old jean pockets. And that skunk was descented." Claire was obviously at a full jog now, but she could still manage to make conversation. Sometimes Stephanie admired her various friends' fitness levels, but then she remembered getting there took actual exercise and quickly got over her admiration.

Stephanie smirked. “Someday I’m going to set you up, just to get back at you.”

“Please don’t. I can find enough weirdos on my own. Besides, you need to concentrate on your love life.”

“I’m trying.”

“Really?” Claire countered skeptically. “Not if you consider that luscious quarterback ‘just a friend.’”

“Maybe I’m thinking about reclassifying him.”

“That’s the most intelligent thing I’ve heard you say in months.” There were a few more beeps on Claire’s end, and the treadmill noise dialed back to almost nonexistent.

“How is the play going?”

“Subtle change of topic,” Claire commented but went on to talk about the good reviews and full houses the play had had. Stephanie was happy to hear her friend so proud of herself. Claire hid her pain well with her sense of humor, but Claire’s self-image had taken a hit when her husband left her.

Before hanging up they made plans to meet for lunch the next week. Claire added a playful warning that Stephanie had better come prepared to dish on “the quarterback.”

Stephanie headed back to the couch but hadn’t even made it to the living room before her phone rang again. She made a noise of annoyance and grabbed the cell off her kitchen table without even looking to see who was calling. This time it was Neil’s voice on the other end of the line, and her stomach began to flutter. She hadn’t expected him to call so soon after he’d left. “Hey, Neil, how are you?” She managed to sound far calmer than she felt.

“Fine. I just got back from the wedding reception.”

“How’d it go?”

“Not a single slip-up—unless you call the flower girl’s dumping her entire basket full of red rose petals at the entrance of the aisle so they got ground into the white carpet a slip-up. I’m pretty sure my parents will be paying for the church’s new carpet—and for several pairs of shoes ruined by wading through the red compost pile.”

Stephanie laughed. “I’m pretty sure that’s just how it goes with flower girls. At my wedding my cousin’s little girl took each flower petal out very selectively and dropped it in a specific spot. It took her about thirty minutes to walk down the aisle."

"I remember. Ty and I had to stand there without fidgeting while she sauntered along." Neil said in faux-exasperation. Stephanie felt awkward that they were talking about her wedding to his best friend. This was never going to be as easy and uncomplicated as the beginning of a new relationship should be. "So how was L.A.?" Neil asked after a long beat.

Stephanie told him about her trip and how interested she'd become in Gabrielle, the kidnapping, and the trial and false imprisonment of Julio Rodriguez.

"So that was my week," she finished. "What about you?"

"I've just been visiting relatives and my old friends who still live around Madison. Last night I went to confession at my parents' very strong urging."

"Confession! That must have been the highlight of that priest's week."

He laughed. "It was no worse than the ones I made in high school. Except those didn't cover as long a period of time."

Somehow I can't quite picture you in the confessional booth."

"It's your WASP mind. Every good half-Irish, half-Italian boy goes to confession. Although I have to admit that growing up Mom had to threaten me with the Bad Brown Spoon before I went."

"The what?" Stephanie giggled.

"The Bad Brown Spoon. It was what she used to keep me in line when I was a kid. God, I thought that wooden spoon was a yard long."

"I bet you were a tough one to keep in line."

"What makes you say that?" he asked in an injured tone. "I was a very upright individual."

"Tell that to someone who hadn't heard about all the practical jokes you and Ty played during training camp. I can just see you as a kid, little black eyes gleaming with mischief."

"You have a very distorted picture of me," he assured her gravely.

"Uh-huh." Her voice conveyed supreme disbelief.

"Hey, Stringer," he began, his tone suddenly serious, "I miss you."

Her breath caught in her throat. "I… I miss you too."

"A lot?'

Her breath came out in a little rush of a laugh. "Yeah, a lot. You need to feed your ego?"

"That's not what needs feeding at the moment." He paused. "I have the feeling that camp is going to be worse than ever this year."

Stephanie didn't know what to answer. She had never carried on this kind of conversation with Neil. It warmed her, and she felt silly and giggly, like a teen with a crush. Yet it was strange, too. It wasn't what she was used to with Neil, who had been a rock in her life until now. "I don't—I don't know what to say. This is crazy."

"Yeah. But isn't it fun?"

"Yeah."

Neil cleared his throat. "I have to go now. I'll call you from camp."

"I'd like that."

"Me, too." He paused. "Bye, Stringer."

* * *

Neil disconnected the phone before he started spewing out his love for her. He smiled at the enthusiasm in Stephanie's voice. She was even more beautiful when she was happy. He thought about the sparkle in her gray-blue eyes, the glow that warmed her skin, flushing the gold of her cheeks with an apricot stain. He knew that if he was with her right now he would have to pull her into his arms and kiss her. Just thinking about it made the ache start deep within him.

Neil unfastened the bow tie of his tuxedo with one hand and opened the top button of his shirt, then lay back on the bed, setting the phone on his stomach. He gazed at the familiar water stain above his bed and idly wondered how many times he had lain here as a teenager and spent hours on the phone with the current love of his life. The clutch of eagerness in his chest now wasn't all that different from what he'd felt then. Despite the activities his family had arranged this week, there had been an empty ache inside him during his whole visit. He'd wanted to call Stephanie every day but had managed to hold off, reminding himself he shouldn't rush her. But today at the wedding the empty feeling had been overwhelming. Repeating the responses of the wedding mass, listening to his sister and fiancé say their vows, he had been able to think of nothing but Stephanie.

He wanted her with him. He wanted to see her standing here in his bedroom, looking at the trophies his mother had kept on display. He wanted to stretch out on the old cracked leather sofa in the game-room and hold Stephanie in his arms just like he would have done at one of the high school parties that he and Charles would throw whenever their parents were out of town. They had had to bribe Hannah to keep her mouth shut with multiple pints of Ben and Jerry's, but she always eventually cracked and told on them to their parents and it was back to the confessional again.

He smiled to himself. Stephanie had probably been more serious than that in high school. She was so smart; she would've been studying or off at a weekend debate team trip or something. But he definitely would have invited her and then spent the whole night trying not to be obvious that he was looking for her instead of paying attention to his friends' keg stands.

He wished he had brought Stephanie home with him. They'd tour Madison and then he'd take her to his little neighborhood in the suburbs and show her every spot that held a part of his life—the field where he'd first played pee-wee football, the tree in front of the pizza shop that he and Charles and Hannah would climb on while his parents went in to order alone so they wouldn't overwhelm the patrons with their rambunctious kids. Neil would have even taken her to the small cross they'd put in the clearing where they'd buried their family dog, Rambo. He wanted to see Stephanie in all those important places, so that, in a way, she'd be a part of his past, too. Even though that didn't make any logical sense.

Most of all Neil wished he could have shared with Stephanie the intimacy of the wedding ceremony, and the laughter and high spirits at the reception afterwards. Hell, he'd dreamed through half the mass of marrying Stephanie at the little white chapel he'd gone to every Sunday since he was a kid.

"Hey, big brother." Charles slammed open the door to Neil's room without knocking, like he always had.

Neil pulled the pillow from behind his head and heaved it at his brother's face. "That's for not having any more manners than you did growing up."

Charles caught the pillow right before it hit the floor and threw it back onto the twin bed. "That was a weak-ass throw. Good thing you don't do that for a living."

"And it's those spectacular catches that make me wonder why you didn't go on to be a wide receiver in college, too." Neil swung his legs around and sat up on the bed. "Oh, no, wait—that's because no one recruited you."

"I didn't need a sports scholarship. Besides, NYU's football team wasn't up to my high standards."

"NYU doesn't have a football team."

"And existing is one of the most important requirements I have for a sports team." Charles idly picked up one of his brother's old trophies and pointed it at Neil. "Besides, I didn't want playing football to be the only thing I was good at—like some people I could mention. Being a one trick pony isn't exactly something to brag about."

"I'm sorry—it must be some other brother I got season tickets for…"

"I'm still the one that has to drive in from Vegas every time."

"In a car I bought for you." Neil crossed his arms.

"Do you buy me things just so you can hold them over me?" Charles laughed.

"Yes. Exclusively."

"So how do you feeling knowing our little sister will never need us to beat up another boyfriend?"

"We never beat any of them up." Neil moved over so Charles could sit down next to him on the small bed.

"Yeah, but we always threatened to." Charles grinned. "I think that one sophomore might have ruined his driver's seat when we came up on either side of his car, leaned in his windows and told him we'd seen him chatting with that girl that wasn't Hannah."

Neil laughed. "Yeah. We were kind of dicks."

"Eh," Charles shrugged. "I also thought the girl he was chatting with was cute."

"Oh, yeah. You went out with her the next weekend." Neil shook his head.

"Yup. And he didn't break our little sister's heart. It was a win-win." Charles smiled. "So how's Stephanie?"

"How did you know?"

"Your phone was lying on your chest when I came in and you were staring up at your ceiling like you always did when you were lovesick over some girl. Not to mention I heard you talking in here earlier and I doubt you're still choreographing football plays with stuffed animals you stole from Hannah." Charles gave Neil a side-long glance. "You were one strange kid, you know that?"

"You're one to talk. You used to break Dad's passwords so you could take money out of his bank account and buy stocks for him on Ameritrade."

"His money manager was an idiot," Charles said as if this explained everything. "And I made Dad a lot of money. Besides what was I supposed to do? I couldn't buy stocks for myself at sixteen."

"You can't buy them now."

"Yes." Charles nodded. "But that's only because I don't have any money."

"If you'd get a regular job instead of counting cards, you'd have more money. And you'd be barred from fewer casinos."

"But regular jobs are boring. And how can I resist when it's so easy? I mean, it is Vegas."

"Hmmm…" Neil tapped a finger against his chin. "Perhaps you shouldn't have moved there."

"When you're logical like that, you're a real drag." Charles said. "I am considering moving though."

"Really? Where?"

"I was thinking Phoenix, but I hate the heat."

"Yeah. It'll be a real change coming from the frigid tundra of Nevada."

"But I could probably learn to deal with it." Charles leaned back on his elbows. "I'm definitely okay with the skimpy summer wardrobes the girls wear."

"You should make the move." Neil said seriously. It would be great having Charles around full-time. Part of the reason he'd felt comfortable with Ty right off the bat was because of how similar he'd been to Charles.

Both of them were all gas, no brakes. And completely separate from all the stuff with Stephanie, Neil really missed Ty. Charles couldn't exactly replace his best friend, but his brother had been the only one Neil had actually been able to talk to about Stephanie. Plus, it'd be easier to keep his brother out of trouble if Charles was in the same city as him.

"I'm considering it." Charles looked about as serious as he ever did—which wasn't saying a lot; he often came up with plans only to completely forget about them the next day. But it was a start. "Will you have time to hang out with me now that you're dating Stephanie?"

"We're not dating exactly. At least not yet."

"Well, if I know you, and after twenty-eight years I think I do, you'll get what you want."

"Oh, I intend to." Neil smiled.

Chapter Eight

Stephanie threw herself into her work, setting up interviews with the people involved in her story that no longer lived in LA or hadn't wanted to meet her in person. She had almost zero free time, but she was so grateful to be interested in a story again that she didn't mind the tiredness. And at night she was exhausted enough to fall asleep without lying awake for hours missing Neil and thinking about the future and how he might figure in it.

Still, his frequent calls were always the highlight of her days. When he missed more than two nights in a row, she was disappointed. Stephanie told herself she was lonely just because she was working so much that she hardly saw her friends, but it was obviously more than that. She wanted to see Neil. To feel that little flutter in her stomach when he appeared.

But because of the book, the days didn't drag by. Before long it was the second week of training camp, and the day of the ceremony honoring Ty loomed before her. It was scheduled for Sunday evening, during halftime of the first Pumas exhibition game. The team would fly in for the game but then return immediately to California for the final two weeks of camp, so it would also be her only chance to see Neil.

On Thursday evening Stephanie went to the stadium, where she met Maria Hernández, the head of the Wives Association and coordinator of the program. Maria showed her where the ceremony would take place in the middle of the field. "We'll walk out from the tunnel at half-time, and go to the middle of the field. Don't worry; I'll be right there so you don't have to worry about where to go. There'll be an area for the sideline reporters and local media and photographers."

"Media?" Stephanie's stomach churned. "Reporters?"

"Yeah, but just ignore them. Amber from Media Relations always keeps them in line. They know better than to try to talk to you before the ceremony or else they'll drop to the bottom of the interview list. The Ingrams will walk you out and then you'll be standing between Coach Davis and Neil."

"Thank God. At least I'll have somebody to pick me up when I faint from terror."

Maria laughed. "You're always so funny. Ty, too." Her smile dropped away, and her voice was a little hoarse as she went on, "We all loved him a lot, Stephanie. Even Karen." Stephanie had to chuckle at her remark. Maria went on, "We were really glad to do something in his name."

"It's wonderful. Thank you," Stephanie replied. "You did so much. Please don't think I'm not grateful. It's just... this ceremony."

"I know." Maria squeezed Stephanie's arm. "You never liked publicity. Now..." She pulled a packet out of her purse and held it out. "There's your parking permit; just hang it on your rear-view mirror. And your lanyard and ID badge. It'll get you into the stadium and up to the luxury boxes."

"The luxury boxes?" Stephanie repeated. "I won't be sitting with the wives?"

"No. You didn't know? Russell Ingram wants you to watch the game from their suite."

"Seriously? I have to sit with the Ingrams?"

Maria laughed. "Oh, they're nice—as owners go, I mean. They're in real estate, you know, so they're very friendly. And that suite is gorgeous. I've only seen it once, when I had to get approval for the project from him, and, wow, it really qualifies as luxury. They expect you to arrive about 45 minutes before the game."

"Sure." Stephanie forced a bright smile. They were doing all this to honor Ty, and she couldn't appear ungrateful even if she wished they'd just given her a seat with the players' wives. At least she'd see Neil again even if it was just for a few minutes, and that thought was enough to turn her smile into a real one.

On Sunday afternoon Stephanie laid out the pale-grey linen shift she'd chosen for the occasion. Large buttons closed the slanted opening that ran from the high neck to one shoulder, the only ornamentation on the dress. It was simple and conservative enough for a young widow, yet form-fitting and attractive. She tried to picture the look on Neil's face when he saw her in it.

She drove to the domed stadium, where a security guard inspected her identification and sent her up to the box seats floor. Stephanie didn't really want to spend the whole game here, but Maria had made her curious to see what the fanciest of the private rooms looked like.

At her knock, a casually dressed Russell Ingram opened the door. He smiled and shifted his drink in order to take her hand.

"Stephanie, you're as pretty as ever. Come on, I'll introduce you around." He looped one arm around her shoulders and led her over to the fully-stocked and fully-staffed bar. The box was aggressively luxurious, with wide, butter-soft leather seats, carpet so thick your feet sank into it, a marble-topped bar, and multiple televisions for viewing replays, but it wasn't as garish as she had envisioned from Maria's description. As soon as she had a wine glass in her hand, Russell toured her around the room, introducing her to so many people that she knew she'd never keep all the names straight.

Finally Russell turned Stephanie over to Howard Perry. He wasn't exactly her favorite person, but she was relieved to see someone she knew. Howard smiled at her. "I'm glad to see you reconsidered."

"Neil's very persuasive."

"Yes. Although I don't know that persuasive is the word I'd use. Usually he's more forceful than that." Howard motioned to one of the plush swivel chairs in front of the plate-glass windows "Would you like to sit? The players are coming onto the field."

"I wasn't sure what that flood of men in tights and helmets was. Thanks for the heads-up." Stephanie smiled sweetly as she took a seat.

"I always said the only thing more intoxicating than a tall redhead was a tall redhead with a sharply-honed sense of sarcasm." Howard sat next to her.

"How is it that even your compliments sound like insults?"

"Must be my own sharply-honed sense of sarcasm."

Stephanie had to chuckle. "How's Princess?'

Howard gave his signature loud, short laugh. "Damn dog. Back home with the girls, thank God. I think Estelle was on the verge of quitting."

Stephanie watched the team enter the field and begin warming up. The sight of the familiar white, yellow and orange uniforms sent an ache through her chest. Instinctively she looked for a jersey numbered 86, wondering who was wearing Ty's number now, but she didn't see it. She spotted Neil's number, 14, and leaned forward intently. Howard offered her a pair of binoculars, and she adjusted them until Neil's head popped into focus. His features were clear and unnaturally close. She felt a little guilty, as if she were spying on him. But you could hardly call it spying when he was standing in front of over 80,000 people.

That was something she had never fully understood—Neil's and Ty's ability to play in front of huge, often hostile crowds. Ty had loved attention, and even though he'd been incredibly nervous before a game, once he was on the field, the fans' cheers pumped him up and spurred him to perform. So did the opponents' fans' boos. That was easier to comprehend. But Neil wasn't the showman Ty had been. He didn't play to the crowd or use its excitement to drive up his own adrenaline. Rather, he played as if the stands didn't exist and only he and the other players were on the field. That sort of coolness and concentration fascinated Stephanie.

She studied Neil's face, the smooth skin stretched tautly over his cheekbones, the fierce black eyes, the handsomely modeled mouth set in determined lines. Stephanie lowered the binoculars and realized that her stomach was dancing in excitement. She was stirred merely by the sight of his tall form, his masculinity emphasized by the broad-shouldered, low-waisted style of the football uniform. She wished he wasn't flying immediately back to camp tonight, though she told herself it was probably better that he was. Neil had promised not to rush, but her willful emotions weren't complying. They were sweeping her along at a breakneck pace.

The players ended their warmups and streamed off the field. Neil played the first quarter, and she watched anxiously, hands clenched together as they had always been when Ty played. She hoped that Neil would play well and the Pumas would win, but most of all she hoped that he wouldn't get hurt. Any player getting hit made her wince, but it was different with someone she cared about. After Neil left the field, Stephanie lost all interest, but she kept her eyes fixed on the game instead of scrolling on her phone like she would've done if she'd been sitting with the player's wives.

Shortly before half-time Maria Hernández escorted Stephanie and the Ingram brothers downstairs to the broad tunnel by which the players entered the field. A camera man walked backward in front of them. Trust Howard to film the whole thing so that their media department could put together videos and toss them out on all their social media feeds.

When they emerged from the semi-dark tunnel, the stadium lights were dazzling, and Stephanie blinked as her eyes adjusted. To her surprise the team was standing along the fifty-yard line. As Maria had warned her, there was a gaggle of media people a few yards away from the players benches—if specially made cooling seating with misting attachments and retractable wheels could really be called benches.

Maria stepped away as they reached the fifty, and Russell and Winslow escorted Stephanie to the raised dais in the center of the field. There Karen Randall, the head of the Wives' Association, Coach Davis, and Neil waited for her, along with Kimberley, the head of Branding, the Wide Receivers coach and a few other people she didn't know.

Davis nodded at Stephanie, and Neil offered a quiet hello. His dark eyes burned into hers, and Stephanie was intensely aware of him and his happiness at seeing her; it was almost as if he had kissed her. She looked at him for a long moment, then tore her gaze away. She noticed Karen Randall giving her obvious side-eye, and Stephanie knew the Wives' Association would soon be gossiping about her and Neil. Which meant the team would, too. Stephanie glanced up at Neil, so foreign and large in his padded uniform, and discovered that his eyes were still on her. The gossip probably wouldn't bother him at all. Neil simply walked right through speculation and criticism as if they didn't exist.

Russell Ingram made a dull but mercifully brief statement about Ty and the money the Wives Association had raised. He was followed by representatives of the charity and the NFL. Karen handed the check to the hospital administrator. Coach Davis told a funny story about Ty at the Super Bowl and then read from the plaque before handing it to Stephanie. She smiled and nodded her thanks, more moved than she had thought she would be. Tears welled in her eyes.

She was surprised to see Neil step up to the microphone next. Maria hadn't mentioned this part in the run-through. Neil spoke of Ty's talent and exuberant personality and their friendship. "Different as we were, we immediately got each other. On the field we just meshed. Ty always seemed to sense when I was forced out of the pocket and needed him to double back for a pass. I'm not sure I'll ever play with someone again that I have that kind of connection with. Ty was a great player, one of the best I've seen. But all of us lost more than a good player. We lost a loyal friend and a man who made our lives better just by passing through them." There was a crack in Neil's voice as he got to the end of his speech. "There'll never be anyone else like Kenneth Tyler, and for that reason the Phoenix Pumas are retiring his number. Eighty-six will play only in our memories."

Neil turned to Stephanie, who stood rooted to the spot, staring at him. Her entire chest was an ache, and tears spilled out of her eyes. Neil held out a white jersey emblazoned with a huge orange number 86. Stephanie took Ty's jersey with trembling hands, noting the glitter of tears in Neil's own eyes. On one side of the stadium, a banner fell away to show Ty's name and the number 86 attached beneath the tier of luxury boxes. The jumbotron played a video of Ty's best catches, ending with him standing in the end zone after the Super Bowl, arms lifted as confetti rained down all around him. The stadium thundered with applause and cheers. A sob escaped Stephanie's lips as she clutched the jersey to her chest.

Neil put a comforting arm around her shoulders, and she burst into tears, turning her face into his chest. "I'm sorry."

"You didn't tell me you were going to do this!" Her words were barely audible in the noise from the stands.

"I know. I should have. I just thought it would be more special if it was a surprise. Are you angry?"

"No." She stepped back, wiping away her tears and offering up a shaky smile. "You're right. It's very special." Stephanie squared her shoulders and turned to wave to the crowd, pivoting slowly to take in all the sections. However much she hated publicity, she knew Ty loved his fans, and she wanted to acknowledge that affection.

One by one, everyone on the dais came by to shake her hand, then left the platform. Neil grasped Stephanie's arm to help her down the steps. She needed it, because her vision was blurred and her knees shaky.

"Howard agreed to keep the reporters away until after the game, give you some time to recover," Neil told her as they walked to the sideline.

Stephanie glanced up, amusement in her eyes. "I wonder whose idea that was."

Neil grinned, then turned serious. "I'd like to see you after the game."

"I thought you were flying back immediately."

"We are. But maybe you could drive me to the airport?"

"Of course." Her smile broadened. At least she was going to get to spend a little time with Neil alone. "I'll wait for you—I'm sure Howard will have enough press there to keep me occupied."

Maria Hernández was waiting beyond the sidelines, and Neil gave her arm a little squeeze, then turned to trot after the other players. Maria, always prepared, handed Stephanie a little package of tissues to wipe away the remainder of her tears. "You okay?"

"Yes, I'm fine. It was just so touching. Thank you."

The Ingrams were waiting for her, and they walked back to the elevators and the elegant suite above. There Howard was waiting for her, beaming, and handed her a drink.

"Thanks." She took a sip, and her eyes widened. "Woo. That's strong. Careful or I won't be able to do any interviews."

"Nah... you'll be fine." He waved away the idea. "You did great today, kid."

"I want to thank you for putting off the reporters until after the game," Stephanie told him.

"Moran convinced me it'd be better. I already got the money shot, anyway. It'll be all over ESPN tonight." There was a little twinkle in his eyes as he said it, and Stephanie had to laugh. He patted her arm. "You know Ty would have loved it."

"Yes, he would." Maybe Howard wasn't so bad.

Stephanie paid little attention to the second half as she sat at the back of the room, sipping the strong drink. She folded and refolded Ty's jersey, remembering him: His unbelievable catches, his laughter, his humor, his crooked smile. They were right—there was no one else like him. She had loved him so very much. But despite her surprised tears this afternoon, there was only a sweet soft feeling for him inside her now. The primal pain, once so hard to bear, was gone. Her love was a memory, gentle and sweet, but it didn't have the weight it once did. The realization was bittersweet.

Stephanie was jolted from her thoughts by the end of the game. Everyone around her began to rise and move about, getting a last drink while they waited for the crowds to leave the parking lots. Stephanie put aside her empty glass and made the rounds, saying her polite goodbyes.

Howard was waiting for her and led her down to the press area. The question-and-answer session wasn't as bad as she had thought it would be, and before long, Neil and a few other players came out to talk to the media, and she was able to escape from the podium to the large room down the hall where the families and friends of the players waited for them.

The room was noisy with talk and laughter, the atmosphere buoyant. Winning the game always improved the mood, even when it was a meaningless exhibition game like today, but it seemed to Stephanie that the ceremony at halftime had released people's emotions, leaving everyone ready to celebrate. The mood grew even more exuberant when the rookies came in, filled with excitement from playing on an NFL field for the first time.

Several of the wives and players came over to talk to her, including Asa Jackson. He had always been one of her favorite players, despite the friendly rivalry he'd had with Ty since they were both wide receivers. When she'd first met Asa she was surprised they played the same position because of his build. Asa was shorter and more compact; wiry. But after talking to him for a while, Stephanie could see it.

Their backgrounds were different—Ty was a rich White guy from Florida whose family considered four hours on the golf course a tough day and Asa was a Black man from a hardworking middle class family in Long Beach—but their personalities were similar. They had the same drive, the flash, the insane willingness to leap for a ball, arms stretched upward, knowing that they were about to get blasted in the ribs. Asa reached out to envelop Stephanie in a bear hug. "Lady, I gotta tell you," he said, "That man was a runner. Dude was almost as fast as me. And I'll tell you the truth, he could catch them better. He is missed."

"Thank you, Asa." Stephanie smiled at him. "I like the new dreads."

"Thanks." He ran a hand over the two-inch-long strands. "I didn't keep up with shaving my head when Ty got sick, and eventually it was long enough to twist. I wanted a change."

"I get that; I thought about chopping mine off after the funeral, but Ty would've probably haunted me if I had."

Asa laughed. "He did love your hair. Called you Red even when you weren't around."

"That was even how he put my number in his phone." Stephanie shook her head. "When we were first dating, I asked him if he had a Blond and a Brunette in there, too."

"Not after he met you. It was good seeing you, Steph." Asa gave her another, shorter hug and took off for the group waving him down across the room.

Neil walked in and scanned the area. When he saw Stephanie, he grinned, his eyes lighting up, and he strode quickly toward her. He was halted a few times to meet one of the rookies' wife or parents, but finally he reached Stephanie. He pulled her into his arms and hugged her tightly to him. "God, I've missed you."

He released her, planting a quick firm kiss on her lips before he straightened and smiled down into her face. Stephanie's return smile was shaky. She hadn't expected Neil to be so open, so unreserved. She felt as if every eye in the place—those of fans and players—was on them. Nervously she took a step backward. "I missed you too. In fact, I felt guilty because the only reason I wanted to come to the ceremony today was to see you."

Something flashed in his dark eyes. "You want to head to the airport now? That way we could at least talk a little."

"Sure. My car's in the B lot."

"Someone's fancy," he joked, curling an arm around her shoulders and starting for the door. Stephanie was awkward and silent, certain the other players were watching them. What did they think about Ty's widow walking off with his best friend? She was used to seeing these men only in connection with Ty. Being in front of them now with Neil made her feel as if she were betraying her husband. Neil, aware of her stiffness, gave her shoulders a little shake. "Hey loosen up, Stringer. What's the matter?"

"I… I feel so strange being with you with the other guys around." Stephanie answered as the door swung shut behind them. "I mean, they think of me as Ty's wife."

He frowned, and she could feel his body tense. "What does it matter?"

"It's strange, that's all. I don't know how to act."

"You'll get used to it," he assured her.

"I'm not so sure." Stephanie sighed. "Things just aren't easy."

"What fun would life be without challenges?" Neil's voice was light, but she could see the muscle in his jaw tighten.

They reached the car and opened the doors. Stale heat rushed out, and Stephanie slid in carefully to turn on the engine and let the air conditioner run. The steering wheel was too hot to touch, and they sat in the front seat for a few minutes, letting the inside of the car cool. There was an uncomfortable silence between them, which continued as they drove to the airport. Stephanie wasn't sure what to say to end the awkwardness. They always talked easily on the phone, but now there seemed to be a wall between them.

Neil seemed irritated by the fact that she was uncomfortable about revealing their relationship to the other players. But surely he must have expected that. They had said they would take it slow. Now that she thought about it, she was beginning to feel a little annoyed herself. By the time they reached the airport, the air between them was heavy and charged.

Stephanie turned the car into the airport drive and took the exit to the area for chartered flight. She couldn't let him get on the plane without talking about this... whatever it was. She parked in the small lot at the edge of the tarmac and turned to him. "I felt weird this afternoon after the ceremony. The whole second half of the game I sat and thought about Ty—everything I could remember about him. But my memories don't feel…it's as if they are pastels instead of full color. And it was as if Ty'd become—"

"Damn it, Stephanie!" Neil exploded. He wasn't yelling, but his face was thunderous and dark, his black eyes flashing, and his words cut through the air like a knife. "Don't you think about anything else? Is this what it's going to be like—a nonstop rehashing of your life with Ty?"

Stephanie whipped around and got out of the car, surprise, hurt and anger warring inside her. Tears formed, obscuring her vision, but she blinked them away. She turned to face Neil, who had also exited the car, slamming the door behind him. "What the hell is wrong with you?" she yelled. "Either you want to take it slow or you don't. Saying one thing and doing the opposite is crap. I'm not trying to think of Ty, but—"

"But you just can't help it?" Neil's eyes were burning. Lightning fast, he rounded the front of the car and took her by the shoulders, looking intently into her eyes. His body was so close to hers, she could feel his heat. She put her palms on his chest as if to push him away, but she didn't. In fact, she wanted to pull him closer; to feel the fire inside him on her skin. The taut muscle of his chest beneath his shirt sent a shiver of desire through her.

"All I can think about is you, and all you can think about is Ty. Do you intend to love him forever?"

When she didn't answer immediately, he made an impatient noise and his mouth came down on hers. Neil's lips were fiery and demanding, prying hers open to his seeking tongue. The kiss was as passionate as their first, but there was a hard taint to this one that hadn't been there before. It was as if Neil wanted to make sure she never thought of any other man than him ever again. And some perverse part of her wanted that, too. To lose herself in a tidal wave of craving and forget all the complications.

Neil moved in even closer, his body pressing her back against the car. He ground his mouth against hers, sucking her bottom lip into his mouth and lightly teasing at it with his teeth. It sent a jolt straight through Stephanie to her very core. She wanted to lean back on the hood of her car and wrap her legs around him. She wanted him right now. It was all she could do to keep her hands from reaching for his belt buckle. But they were in public. The rest of the team would be here soon. And they were fighting. How could she want to scream at him and tear his clothes off at the same time? It was crazy.

"Stephanie," he groaned as his lips left hers and trailed across her face and neck. One hand came down to cup her breast, moving over her skin through the material. He raised his head. His eyes were fierce pinpoints of desire that held her transfixed. "I want you, and I'm alive. Why won't you let me in?"

Stephanie gazed up at him, pinned by the incredible force of his will.

Neil bent his head to kiss her again, his mouth dominating hers, teeth and tongue and lips demanding surrender. Stephanie was almost faint from the intensity of his kiss. One iron arm was around her, leaving his other hand free to roam her body. His fingers moved firmly, slowly over her, following the contours of her breasts, waist and hips. He traversed the smooth linen covering her thighs and slid up under her skirt, his roughened fingertips rasping over her smooth legs. “I’ll make you forget him,” he grated out, and as treacherous as the words were, her body was even more treacherous. Stephanie wanted to feel exactly how he'd make her forget. Wanted to know what it was to be fully possessed by Neil's passion. His lips left her mouth to prowl over her throat, nipping and teasing at the soft skin.

He left the teasing exploration of her thighs and a small cry escaped her lips at the unfulfilled ache that blossomed between her legs. Neil returned to the soft curve of her breast and she leaned into his hand, urging him on. As he kissed her throat, he brushed the tip of his forefinger over her nipple until it tightened and pushed against the cloth of her dress. With a groan he buried his face in her neck, and his arms went around her like tight steel bands. “You’re killing me. Tell me you don’t love him still.”

Stephanie swallowed, unable to speak. Coherent thought had fled as soon as Neil took her senses hostage. Emotionally she had been pulled in all directions today, and the clash of anger and passion left her trembling with aroused desire, yet stunned and resentful. “Neil, I—I can’t—” she began shakily, hardly knowing what she was saying.

Neil made a disgusted sound deep in his throat, and the skin around his mouth tightened. He released her from his grip and stepped back. “Damn it, how long do you expect me to be a benchwarmer for a ghost?” He jerked away and loped toward the hangar.

Stephanie watched him, her heart pounding violently. What was the matter with Neil? When they retired Ty’s number, she had seen tears in his eyes, too, yet just now he had acted as if he hated Ty. Stephanie hadn’t realized that Neil was capable of such volatile behavior.

Not that she was any better. She was furious at what he had said and the way he had demanded she disavow her husband as if he was some insignificant ex-boyfriend. Neil had no right to ask her to do that! Yet she couldn’t suppress a thrill of excitement at the intensity of his kisses. She had never seen Neil lose control of himself like that. It must have taken a powerful emotion to break through his icy reserve. A delicious shiver darted through her.

Suddenly, irrationally, she was very anxious for Neil to come back from camp.

Chapter Nine

Neil had been itchy the entire flight back to California, pacing the aisle and flexing his hands until Coach Davis had finally warned him he better sit down before he made the flight crew nervous. Hours later, at the Marriott Residence Inn where the players were staying, Neil still couldn't stop stewing. Even a hard workout—or as much of one as he could get in the hotel gym—hadn't stopped the tense energy that was flowing through his veins and bunching up his muscles.

So when Gramps texted that he'd made gumbo in his little kitchenette and other players were coming by to supplement their vending machine dinners, Neil went down the hall to join them. His black mood was unlikely to ruin any of the other guys' good times, and maybe he'd get out of his own head for a bit.

"Hey! Neil!" Gramps Kowalski was sitting cross-legged on the floor in front of the TV where someone had hooked up a Nintendo Switch. Pete Cherneski and Jalyn Williams were smashed together on the small loveseat behind him. It was a modern, low-slung design that had the large men sitting hunched over with their knees up to their chests. It looked more like they were sitting on children's furniture than anything built for them. Asa Jackson was on the floor on the opposite side of the TV from Gramps.

"I see all the lifers are here playing video games while the rookies are hitting the bars."

"Yeah, they'll be regretting it tomorrow when we're running drills in the heat." Asa smirked. "There's a reason we've survived this long."

"Damn it, Bowser!" Jalyn Williams shouted, whipping his controller around as, onscreen, Mario tried to avoid a banana peel on the racetrack in front of him. "What the hell?"

"That's for charging me two hundred dollars to unclog a sink, you Machiavellian little plumber!" Cherneski laughed manically until Jalyn elbowed him in the ribs.

"Coming in hot!" Gramps, playing his usual Princess Peach, threw a red shell and it zeroed in on Asa's Toad who was obviously in the lead.

"Are you kidding me, Kowalski? Again?"

"I've got that good karma—the universe is rewarding me with Mario Kart luck." Gramps grinned.

"If only they'd reward you with such luck in real life." Neil sat down on the arm of the loveseat next to Cherneski, forcing him even closer to Jalyn, who tried to shove Cherneski back to his side of the loveseat. The oversized middle linebacker didn't budge a centimeter.

"I've been riding my motorcycle for a decade and never been in a wreck." Gramps rubbed a hand over his close buzzed salt-and-pepper head. "And in twenty years of playing football, I've never had a concussion. I think my real-life luck is fine."

"Maybe it's just your love life then." Asa laughed. Onscreen, he zipped his character of Toad around from behind Peach to take the lead again.

"There's nothing wrong with my love life. I defy you to find any other guy named Gramps who has as many ladies calling him every weekend as I do."

"All of you peons bow before the king of Mario Kart!" Asa raised his fists in triumph as he crossed the finish line. Then he dropped his controller and turned to Kowalski. "I'm not saying the ladies don't like you, Gramps."

"He's saying all the ladies you like are certifiable." Neil finished.

"Yeah, you gotta admit you got a thing for the crazies." Pete Cherneski shot Gramps a look, then held out his controller to Neil. "I'm gonna go grab a beer; you want next?"

"Sure." Neil slid down to take Cherneski's seat as he got up.

"You guys look hilarious sitting like that." Pete told him.

"Yes. Because you looked so small and dainty here before me." Neil chose Waluigi onscreen and the character made a "WAAA!" sound as he was selected. "Grab me a bowl of gumbo while you're in there!"

"What do I look like, your girlfriend?"

"Had to try." Neil shrugged.

"Speaking of girlfriends…" Asa gave Neil a pointed look as everyone's players lined up for the start of the race.

"What is that supposed to mean?"

"He means what the hell is going on between you and Stephanie?" Jalyn clarified. "My wife keeps bugging me about it, too, ever since Steph came by last week. Wants to know when you two are finally going to bone."

"I'm sure that's exactly how Mel put it." Neil snorted. "So Stephanie talked to Mel?"

"Yeah. Supposedly to catch up with her, but Mel said she kept asking about you and Jill and some other woman, I think—to be honest I was only half listening. Mel got a new tennis skirt, the kids were at summer camp and I got a little distracted."

"I think Stephanie got the idea that there was some other woman when I was with Jill," Neil said. "But I'm not sure if it's even worth clearing up at this point. I think it might already be over."

"This feels like a beer and gumbo conversation." Gramps, as Peach, raced by onscreen, pulling into the lead. "I'll just kick everyone's ass real quick here, and then we can go grab some."

"Always with the advice," Asa shook his head as he pulled into second, crossing the finish line milliseconds after Gramps.

"Oh, no," Jalyn groaned. "Dr. Kowalski is now in session."

"Hey, I've got to do something with my Philosophy degree," Gramps protested.

"Lord knows you'll never get a job with it. Unless you know of someone hiring Philosophers." Jalyn laughed, his Mario pulling into fourth after Neil.

Gramps and Neil handed their controllers off to new players, and they sat down at the tiny kitchen table with a couple of bowls of gumbo and beers.

"Honestly, I don't know what's going on with Stephanie," Neil confided after they'd eaten some of the spicy stew. "I like her, she likes me, but it's not easy."

"Of course not." Gramps cut his clear, ice-blue eyes over to Neil. "Especially today with that ceremony. You two both loved Ty."

"Yeah. But he's gone. And constantly thinking about it, talking about it—it just feeds the guilt." The frustration and anger and whatever had been balled up in his stomach ever since Neil got out of Stephanie's car started to unwind a bit.

"Not talking about it won't change anything," Kowalski pointed out. "Ignoring something doesn't get rid of it."

"Yeah, well, I can't ignore the fact that she still loves Ty. We got into it earlier because she won't say she's over him."

"You tried to get her to say that? Moran, you're an idiot." Gramps dropped his spoon in his bowl. "You come from a big family like me. Did your parents run out of love for the youngest?"

"Are you kidding? Hannah was the only one that didn't give my parents ulcers. She was their good girl—the baby."

"Exactly," Kowalski said. "So why can't Stephanie feel whatever she does for you and still love her dead husband? We all loved Ty. Ty was great. Her feelings for Ty are not gonna change just because you hook up. Doesn't mean she doesn't care about you."

"So I was completely out of line to even ask?"

"Yup." Gramps shrugged and took a gulp of his beer. "Sounds to me like you're pushing her to try and do something that you yourself can't do."

"What's that?"

"Stop caring about Ty. Stop missing Ty. Can you do that? You have your siblings, other friends, maybe even some you knew better than Ty. Does that take away all the years he was your best friend?"

"Of course not. You can't erase a friendship."

"So how realistic is what you're asking of Stephanie?"

"You know—you should have majored in Psychology." Neil pointed at Gramps with his beer. "You're good."

"That was my minor." Gramps laughed.

"So flowers?" Neil asked.

"Yeah, but I want something nice. I mean, I really helped you out. Red roses. And none of the baby's breath filler." Gramps winked. "But your money would probably be better spent getting some for Stephanie."

"Hilarious." Neil paused a second. "Ty told me she loves calla lilies. Should I send those or is that cheating?"

"I don't think she's gonna get you for insider trading."

When Neil returned to his room, he ordered an arrangement of calla lilies and white tulips to be delivered to Stephanie the next morning with the message, "I'm so sorry, Stringer. Please forgive me."

All the next day Neil couldn't stop checking his phone to see if he had received a text from Stephanie, but each time he had no new messages. What if he'd really blown it? Gramps was right. Looking back, he could see the whole thing clearer and clearer. He had felt this nasty, cold sensation in his stomach all during the ceremony. Felt like he'd stolen something from a good man that couldn't defend himself every time he'd locked eyes with Stephanie on that dais.

Neil had been pissed at himself and at the situation, and after the game he'd pushed Stephanie. He kissed her in front of her husband's former team members. He'd known that would make her uncomfortable, but he did it anyway. Like he was trying to prove to himself that it was worth all the guilt because Stephanie wanted him bad enough that she'd kiss him back. Then with each comment Stephanie had made about Ty afterward, it had been like lemon-juice in a paper cut. And he'd been stupid enough to keep pushing her. What did he want her to say—'I like you better than Ty?' Like they were in fourth grade?

The day dragged by, though Neil suspected it wasn't as bad for him and the others that had been playing Mario Kart as it was for the rookies that'd been up drinking all last night. But still, it seemed interminable with the knot of nerves in his stomach. He'd been so distracted in practice this morning that his timing was off. He'd overthrown Asa so many times that the wide receiver was giving Neil the stink eye, and C.J. had intercepted him. Twice. The trash-talking safety would never let him live that down.

Worse, none of Neil's screw-ups had been enough to banish his thoughts about Stephanie. Why hadn't she contacted him after getting the flowers? Was she that furious? Was that too trite a gesture? Too impersonal? Stephanie was not like other women. Clearly, he was going to have to call her and do some major groveling this afternoon after his session with the trainers.

Usually the hot tub and long massage were relaxing, but this afternoon, Neil was too twitchy. It didn't help that the trainer kept talking about the tension in his shoulders and how he needed to relax. There was no way he was going to be able to do that until he got out of here and talked to Stephanie.

Back in his room, he called Stephanie. Listening to her phone ring on and on, he could almost hear milliseconds tick by.

When she finally picked up, he blew out the air he'd been holding in. "I'm so glad you answered." Before she could respond, he raced on, "I thought you might not give me the chance to try and explain myself."

"No!" Stephanie let out that warm familiar laugh, and Neil's shoulders relaxed some. "I was out in my office all day doing Zoom interviews and transcribing my notes afterwards. I didn't take my phone with me in the hopes that I wouldn't procrastinate. I just got back to the main house and saw your flowers—I was about to call and thank you. They're gorgeous!"

"I'm glad you like them." And how inadequate was that to express the relief flooding through him? "Um, listen, Stephanie, I… the ceremony yesterday. It got me thinking about Ty, too, and, I don't know, I guess I was feeling bad or guilty or something, and it just made me all jittery after the game and I was looking for a way to feel better." Neil balled up his left hand and rubbed the knuckles over his jean-clad-thigh so roughly that they felt carpet burnt. He had to explain it Stephanie, had to make it right, but the more he said, the more ashamed he felt. He wanted to just hang up and forget about her. But he knew from experience that that was impossible for him to do. So he pressed on, "And then when I couldn't force things to go the way I wanted them to—I guess… I, well, I turned all that anger I felt at myself back on you and that wasn't okay. I don't know—I'm not explaining it right. But the bottom line is that I know I messed it up. Things are complicated because of Ty and I can't change that no matter how much easier it'd make things. And neither can you. I know that. I don't expect you to pretend like you don't love Ty. That's not fair. And I'm really sorry for even asking you to."

For a tense moment Stephanie didn't say anything. Neil's stomach was trying to turn itself inside out. "Did I lose you?" He had meant to say it casually, commenting on the crappy connection his cell phone had in his hotel room, but it came out more raw and revealing than he intended.

"No." Stephanie sounded stilted herself. "I just... To be honest, I'm sort of stunned. You're much better at apologizing than most guys. It took Ty forever to have a clue what he was feeling, and even then his apologies were pretty half-assed." She sighed. "Sorry. I keep doing that."

"You don't need to police what you say. He was your husband; you love him. I'm going to work on being less jealous. I know I can't compete with his memory."

"You aren't competing with Ty."

"I can't. I know that. But I wish we could start out fresh, without all the past creeping into every moment."

"That's not possible," Stephanie said quietly.

"I know." Neil took a slow breath in. He could feel the hit coming.

"But I think we could try not to let the past mess us up. I'm a very complicated woman, definitely capable of feeling several things all at once." Stephanie laughed.

The tightness in his chest eased. "Yeah. Gramps said something like that last night."

"So that's where all this wisdom came from—you had the sage advice guy from the team helping you out."

"Hey!" Neil put on a mock-insulted tone. "I came up with at least half of my revelations and apologies all on my own."

"I'm sure you did." There was a smile in Stephanie's voice. "I'm just messing with you."

"Do you think maybe when a man is baring his soul in the most uncomfortable way, it might not be a great time to mess with him?"

"I don't know. That sounds kind of like the ideal time to mess with someone."

"You're evil, you know that?" Neil settled down on the uncomfortable hotel room bed and leaned back.

"I do."

"So how did the Zoom interviews go today?" Neil asked.

"Really well. I kept getting so lost in the stories that I would forget to take notes and then have to scramble to get it all down."

"Who did you talk to?"

"My first call was with Detective Fuller. He was the guy who arrested the actual kidnapper. Apparently he never thought Julio Rodriguez did it. There were all kinds of holes in the maid's story."

"And the maid was the one that was dating the real kidnapper, right?"

"Yeah. Detective Fuller was very careful in what he said—you could tell he didn't want to cast a bad light on the original investigation, but he clearly thought it was mishandled from the beginning."

"Probably worried about opening up the department to more lawsuits. Rodriguez's daughter sued, didn't she?"

"She didn't end up filing the suit on the department, even though it was obvious there was some racial bias. Because the maid gave them a false statement, the cops were only guilty of taking someone at their word and having tunnel vision. The criminal case against the maid only amounted to time served by the time her trial was over, so Rodriguez's daughter sued her even though the maid didn't have any money." Stephanie was so into her story that Neil could practically see the way her expressive eyes would light up. Ty had complained that at times Stephanie could go on and on about her work so he couldn't get a word in, but Neil could listen to her talk excitedly for hours. "It was just a way to bring light to the fact that the maid had knowingly accused the wrong man when her boyfriend was behind the kidnapping. The Rodriguezes never got any money from it."

"So have you gotten a chance to talk to Julio yet?" Neil asked.

"No. I seriously doubt I'm going to. He's understandably very suspicious of the media after what he went through. But Fuller thought I was straight forward with him and so he gave Rodriguez's daughter my number. He told me she's always looking for ways to get word out about what happened to her father."

"Trying to keep it from happening to someone else?" Neil guessed.

"I'd imagine that's part of it. But when I spoke with her later this afternoon, she said that the stories on her dad's release and the second trial were not nearly as big as the original story, and a lot of people still think Julio did it. She's hoping a book about the entire thing might exonerate her father in the eyes of the public in a way that him getting out of jail didn't."

"Man. That sucks. Even after all he's been through, he still can't catch a break."

"Yeah. But hopefully not for long. This story feels big. Bigger than anything else I've ever written. It could actually change things for Rodriguez and his family. And I never would've written about it if it weren't for you."

"Well, I can probably think of a few ways you can thank me." Neil grinned.

"I can just see you raising your eyebrow in that cocky way you do." Stephanie said.

"I have no idea what you're talking about." Neil tried to relax his eyebrow back down.

"Sure..."

The teasing tone in her voice curled through him, starting a heat deep inside him that had nothing to do with her words. But before he could respond, there was a rap on his door and a voice said, "Meeting's in five."

"Damn." Neil grimaced. "I've got to go. Deondre's at the door; there's a position meeting."

"Oh. Okay." He smiled at the disappointment in her tone. She didn't want to hang up any more than he did. Muffling the phone, he called, "Hang on a sec." Neil turned back to Stephanie. "Listen… I could call you later?" His voice made the statement into a question.

"I'd like that."

"Yeah. Me, too." He wanted to say more, but he held back the words. No pressure. "Bye, Stringer."

* * *

Much as Stephanie enjoyed Neil's daily phone calls, it wasn't enough. She dreamed about him at night and fantasized about him during all her waking hours when she wasn't working. And even sometimes when she was supposed to be working. The next Sunday she watched the Pumas' game on television. It was pretty boring, but when Neil came onto the field, Stephanie sat forward in her chair, mentally cursing both the helmet for hiding too much of Neil's face and the TV crew for not zooming in on a closeup of him. He played only two quarters, but Stephanie stayed glued to the screen, hoping that the cameras would catch him standing on the sidelines.

Stephanie told herself that she was behaving like a teen, getting excited just at catching a glimpse of Neil, but rational thoughts had little effect on her emotions. She was so keyed-up afterward that it took forever for her to fall asleep. When she finally did, she was rudely awakened by the ring of her cell phone on the bedside table. She fumbled around with it trying to accept the call through the bleariness of her half-dreaming mind.

"Hey, it's Neil." His voice was low, almost a whisper.

"What time is it?" Stephanie rubbed her eyes and struggled to a sitting position.

"I don't know exactly. Late. Everyone's in bed."

"Three o'clock!" Stephanie looked at the time on her phone and then put it back to her ear. "Is something wrong?"

"No. I just wanted to talk to you. I couldn't sleep so I thought I'd make sure you couldn't either." There was a wicked grin in Neil's voice.

"Gee, thanks so much." Stephanie grumbled. But she couldn't wipe the smile off her face.

"I really am sorry to wake you up. I just had to hear your voice. I knew I wouldn't sleep until I did."

Stephanie melted inside at his words. "Good. I watched you on TV tonight."

"Not exactly the Pumas' finest performance, was it?"

"The exhibition games are always full of rookies and mistakes. It was nice seeing you though." She felt almost shy. "Do you feel bad about it?"

"Frustrated. I hate exhibition games. I can't stand hanging around on the sidelines watching everyone else screw up."

"You want to be out there screwing up, too?" Stephanie teased lightly.

"Yeah, I guess so." He chuckled. "You have a great way of putting things into perspective so I don't take myself so seriously." Neil paused. "I wish I could see you tonight."

"I want to be with you too," Stephanie confessed.

"Really?" He sounded inordinately pleased. "Are you coming to the game next Sunday?"

"Do you want me to?"

"I'd like to see you. It'd be nice to know you're in the stands."

Stephanie warmed inside. "Then I'll be there."

"Good. I'll call the office tomorrow and have a seat held for you at the ticket office."

"No, I'd rather buy one. I don't want to sit with the wives and families."

"Why not? They're better seats."

"I know. But I'd rather not sit there. It—I'd feel uncomfortable."

The silence on the other end of the line was deafening. Stephanie could almost sense Neil's tightening. They were wading into the same territory of their fight. Finally he blew out a breath and said, "Okay, if that'll make you feel better."

Stephanie hurried to explain, "It's just that Karen Randall called me last week to 'chat.' We were never friends and it was pretty clear that she just wanted to find out about my private business. You know how that group can be—like a huge, drama filled family riddled with feuds and gossip."

"And you've never liked being a public topic of conversation." Neil finished.

"Exactly."

"I get it. Will you wait for me after the game?"

"Yes." A slow smile spread across Stephanie's face.

"I usually go home after the game and get in the hot tub. Otherwise my muscles hurt like hell the next day. Would you want to come with me? I can take you back to your house later."

The idea of Neil and her half-naked, wet, surrounded by steam—she'd never get back to sleep after they got off the phone. It was also pretty cute how he was carefully skirting the subject of sex, and trying to reassure her that it was fine if she wasn't ready yet. "That sounds good."

"Don't forget to bring your bathing suit if you'd like to get in, too. Or do forget it. I certainly won't complain." The smile in Neil's voice gave Stephanie a shiver.

"I'll keep that in mind," she said in an equally flirty tone.

"I'll let you go now. Again, sorry I woke you up. But I couldn't stand not to talk to you after we got back from the game. I think about you all the time." His low-toned words were heavy with sensual connotations.

"Neil…" She was breathless with a sudden surge of desire.

"If I told you what I'm thinking right now, this would quickly become an obscene phone call. I better hang up or I'll have even more trouble going to sleep than I did before I called. See you Sunday?"

"Yes."

He was silent for a moment, then said hurriedly, "Goodbye, Stephanie."

Stephanie murmured a goodbye and set her phone back on the bedside table. She slid down in her bed and looked up at the ceiling. Yep, it'd be ages before she went back to sleep. She smiled.

* * *

Stephanie's body was practically humming with anticipation as she waited for Neil after the game. She sat on a low concrete wall a good distance away from the cluster of autograph seekers waiting outside the players' entrance. Neil emerged sooner than she had expected and was immediately engulfed by the pack of fans. He looked over their heads, scanning the area until his gaze fell on Stephanie, and he grinned, his eyes lighting up.

God, he was gorgeous. Stephanie unconsciously rose to her feet, as if pulled by the sight of him. She watched Neil as he smiled and nodded, signing autographs with something less than his usual patience as he worked his way through the fans. Finally he extricated himself from the knot of people and strode over to her, his long legs eating up the ground between them.

Stephanie's pulse picked up, anticipation making her stomach flutter. And then he was there, his arms wrapping around her. Stephanie clung to him, her insides in a tumult even as she luxuriated in the scent and heat and feel of him.

"I've been waiting for this all day," he murmured, nuzzling into her neck. "I'd like to take you here right in front of everyone."

"That might be a trifle awkward with all your fans there." Stephanie tried to keep her voice light despite the sparkling sensations his lips and words were sending through her.

"Trifle?" Neil laughed softly, ruffling her hair. "Always showing off that broad vocabulary."

"Can't let people forget I'm a writer," she replied. "Let's go somewhere a bit more private so we don't scandalize this crowd."

"I don't know. Might make me a folk hero." Neil glanced back, then grabbed her hand and pulled her into the shelter of one of the gigantic concrete pillars supporting the stadium. When they were hidden from sight, his arms went around her, lifting her up and into him. His mouth captured hers, seeking, twisting, as his fingers sank into her hips and ground her suggestively against his body. His skin scorched her wherever it touched, and his mouth was a cave of heat. He broke the seal of their mouths to rain kisses over her face and neck, slowing to nibbling caresses over her bare shoulders. His tongue traced moist patterns along the hard line of her collarbone, then paused to explore the vulnerable hollow of her throat.

Stephanie's head fell back as she arched her neck to receive his lips. She was on fire, electrified, helpless. She clung to his shirt as if to anchor herself to reality. Neil sucked in a deep breath and leaned back against the pillar, eyes closed. Stephanie felt the rapid pounding of his heart through his shirt and saw the sheen of moisture on his face and neck. His chest rose and fell quickly, gradually steadying. He braced his legs slightly forward and wide apart, holding her body between his thighs. He swallowed. "I can think of several very lewd acts I would like to commit with you right now."

"Here?" Stephanie responded breathlessly.

He grinned. "I think we better get home first."

They left the shelter of the huge pillar and started toward Stephanie's car. Neil clasped her hand loosely, his fingers slipping between hers in a way that Stephanie thought was the sexiest thing since the last time he touched her. He walked carefully apart from her, but the heat of his palm told her of his desire.

"How'd you like the game?" Neil asked.

"It was fine... well, except for seeing you get sacked."

"Yeah, that hurt," Neil said, but he was laughing. It had obviously bothered her more than it had him.

"And I wasn't a huge fan of the guy with the Puma logo painted on his beer belly who kept hitting on me."

That made Neil laugh even louder. "I think I'd rather get sacked."

When they reached her car, Stephanie held out the keys to Neil in a questioning gesture. "Would you like to drive?"

"No, you do it. I want to look at you."

Stephanie blushed. "You'll make me nervous."

"Good." Neil grinned at her wickedly.

She started the car and turned it toward the freeway. Neil lounged in the bucket seat beside her, his tall, hard body incongruous in the small car. He watched her just as he'd said he would, but rather than making her nervous, his gaze filled her with a liquid heat. Stephanie felt a flush rising up her throat and cheeks and she sought desperately for trivial conversation. "You played very well today."

He shrugged. "We won. But I've had better days." Carelessly he analyzed the game, breaking some of the overwhelming sexual tension hanging in the air. They talked easily all the way out to his house, but Stephanie suspected that only a fraction of his attention was on their words. She wondered what he was thinking. She'd never imagined such a sensual nature lay beneath his cool exterior.

When she reached the turnoff to his house she slowed down and watched intently for all the treacherous potholes and bumps which infested the road. "Every time I drive up here I bet I take a year off the life of my car."

"Not taking it to the shop while the check engine light is on probably doesn't help either." Neil grinned and gave a quick nod at her dash that, as usual, was lit up like a Christmas tree. If a Christmas tree was made entirely out of maintenance warnings.

"If I lose a hubcap, I swear I'm never coming back again."

"I may have to resurface the drive, then."

They drove through the rough desert terrain of cacti and boulders, climbing the barren mountain until the modern buildings of Phoenix lay scattered below them. Stephanie stopped in front of Neil's house and stepped out, taking in the scene before her. "I always forget how beautiful it is up here," she breathed.

"You should be here during a thunderstorm. You can see the lightning all over the valley and on the mountains beyond. It's like a gigantic fireworks display."

Stephanie turned away from the view and started toward Neil's house. It was a one-story structure that sprawled across the face of the mountain. Made Pueblo style, with rough timbers thrusting out of the roof, it was a neutral adobe and blended in with the landscape around it, assisted by the many large windows. The entire side that faced the valley was plate-glass. Stephanie knew that the view at sunset must be breathtaking. Hidden by a high wooden fence, the pool and spa lay to one side of the house.

Stephanie liked Neil's house. Though obviously expensive, it shared none of the ostentation Ty's home had had. It was sparsely furnished with roughhewn furniture that didn't draw your attention. The decoration in this room was its view, and nothing detracted from it. There were few rooms in the house, but all were large and airy, bringing the spacious outdoors inside.

"I have to hit the whirlpool," Neil said. "Did you bring a suit?"

"Yes."

"That's too bad. I was hoping to convince you that you'd just have to skinny dip. I was even willing to forego my own suit if it'd make you more comfortable." He winked at her.

"Maybe I should've lied then," Stephanie said saucily before ducking into the bathroom to change. She pulled on the one-piece black suit with the plunging neckline and high cut legs. It was more modest than some of her bikinis but, strangely, also sexier. She gazed at her image in the mirror and wondered if it was too much.

Not that it really mattered. Neil didn't seem to need her to do anything special to excite him. Everything seemed to be happening faster than she'd planned, but the tingling throughout her body told her she wasn't going to put on the brakes. There were no thoughts of Ty in her—or of anything except the effervescence in her chest and the heavy ache in her abdomen. She wanted Neil. She wanted to feel his hands and mouth on her, to see his firm naked body and hot black eyes, heavy-lidded with passion. Stephanie blushed and turned away from the mirror. She opened the door and walked out to meet Neil.

He was already in the hot tub. As he heard the sliding glass door open behind him, he turned and slowly climbed out. He stood on the deck, still as a statue. Stephanie watched him as steam rose from his recently submerged skin. It gave him an other-worldly appearance that was both frightening and intriguing. Stephanie shifted under his gaze. With the clinging of his already wet trunks, the effect of her swimsuit on him was obvious. Neil came closer, his eyes devouring her.

Slowly, his eyes never leaving hers, he raised his wet hands to encircle her neck, then he smoothed his hands down and across the bare expanse of her shoulders and chest, leaving a warm trail behind. Almost reverently his fingers moved down her back, rounding over her hips, and slid back up to her waist, digging into her flesh in the most deliciously sharp way. Stephanie had never felt such urgency, such need. The very strength of his desire was ratcheting hers higher.

She felt awash in her own sensuality, yet curiously safe and secure because it was Neil. He would never hurt her, she knew. Neil closed his eyes, his breath rasping in his throat, and he rested his forehead against hers.

"I don't… want to rush you." His voice was husky. "But I want you here with me tonight." He gathered her hair in one large hand and lifted it from her neck, twining it around his hand and forearm. "Is there any chance I can persuade you to stay?"

Stephanie tilted her head back to look at him. "Why don't you try?"

Chapter Ten

Neil's eyes widened slightly at the invitation in Stephanie's expression. He bent and grazed his mouth against hers once, twice, then his lips hovered just above hers as the tip of his tongue traced the shape of her mouth. His fingertips moved down her body, following their earlier path. They touched her as softly as moth wings, inviting without demanding. Teasing, arousing. Slowly, Neil reminded himself. Stephanie's intimation that she might sleep with him made him pound with desire. He wanted to sweep her up in his arms and carry her straight to his bed. He yearned to see her, touch her, bury himself deep inside her with all the force and hunger of years of waiting.

But he had to hold back. Wait for her to welcome him. To beg for him. Just the thought of her whimpering his name, arching her back, aching for him made him want to lift her off her feet and press her against the wall of his house, shoving her bathing suit aside as she wrapped her long legs around him... But he forced his mind away from his swirling fantasies. Instead, he took her hands in his. Stephanie glanced up at him in faint surprise. He smiled and turned away, leading her to the sunken pool of bubbling, frothing water.

Neil sat down in front of a pulsating jet of water. Stephanie sat across from him like she always had. That had been their normal configuration—she and Ty on one side, and Neil and his girl across from them. Neil noticed but banished the thought from his mind. That was the past. All he could possibly have with Stephanie was the future. He was not going to spoil it by thinking about what came before.

Neil stretched out his legs, ankles crossed, feet on the seat beside Stephanie. Steam rose around them in the evening air, which was cool in the desert after the sun went down. He leaned back his head and closed his eyes, concentrating on the soothing action of the water on his muscles. He wouldn't think about tomorrow and the soreness. That was the way he always got through the pain, whatever form it took. He would cut it from his mind, relegate it to another time and place. Unacknowledged, the pain never seemed as great as it was.

It was his special talent, this ability to section things off and lock them away in his brain, and it had enabled him to play hurt or scared or unhappy without letting it affect his game. In college he'd once played almost three quarters after his left arm was injured, refusing to acknowledge the pain until after the game. Afterwards, when the team doctor x-rayed it, he discovered that Neil's forearm was actually fractured. It had made a good story for his college coach to tell to prove Neil's toughness.

That talent had also gotten him through many an aching night watching Stephanie with Ty.

Stephanie seemed to be equally relaxed by the heated water, but after a while she got out, saying it was getting too hot for her. She sat down on the edge of the tub and dangled her feet in the water as she let the desert air fan her wet body. Neil studied her, his dark eyes narrow slits. Stephanie's suit clung even more tightly to her body now that it was soaked, and the cool air on her skin had caused her nipples to pucker. As he stared, they tightened even more.

Neil stood up and crossed the hot tub. He knelt on the seat and touched his lips to one of her nipples. Stephanie shivered and sank her fingers into his dampened hair as he pulled the nipple into his mouth, material and all. His tongue worked magic on her, stroking and lashing the bud until she was gasping with pleasure. His teeth nibbled and rolled the nipple. Stephanie groaned his name, and Neil pulled away to begin on the other breast. By the time he finished with it she was moving restlessly on her perch.

He looked up at her, his eyes dark pools, his usually impassive face slack and stamped with hunger. He reached up and pulled her into the water with him. Standing in the center of the water, he wrapped his arms around her and held her high so that her face was level with his. He kissed her hungrily, moving his lips against hers, taking her mouth like a treasure—precious, but indisputably his. Stephanie's tongue met his, welcoming him until his breath blew hot and demanding on her cheek.

Stephanie wrapped her dangling legs around Neil's waist. Their position sent a strong shudder through Neil, and his kisses turned wild and hot. He had wanted her for so long, had fought and denied his hunger so many times, and now she was offering herself to him. Everything he'd dreamed of was in his hands, and the idea sent flames of desire shooting through him, fogging his mind. He couldn't get enough of her. His hands were everywhere and his mouth seized hers, fiery and demanding.

Stephanie's fingers worked through his hair, kneading his scalp, and he tightened his arms around her, pressing her even more intimately against him. His hands slid down to cup her ass, circling and caressing, slipping along her wet thighs. He dug his fingers into her hips, grinding his body into hers. A groan escaped him and he pulled away from their kiss, burying his face in her neck and shoulder.

"Stephanie…" His breath came in short, hard gasps and his muscles quivered with barely restrained tension. "I'm too… far ahead of you." He nuzzled her tender flesh, his lips moist and velvety soft upon her. "I'm already about to explode."

Reluctantly he loosened his arms and set her down on the floor of the tub. She looked up at him. "Go ahead." She gazed straight into his eyes, challenging him, and just that expression alone was almost enough to take him apart. "I want you to."

"Not yet. I want it to be as good for you as it is for me." His black eyes glowed. "Better, even."

"Trust me, I'm ready."

He grinned, his white teeth slashing through the dark. "Oh, no, you're not nearly ready. That was just a warmup. You need more time and attention."

Stephanie turned away and sat down in the water, huddling her legs up against her chest. "Did Ty tell you that?" she asked resentfully. "I know men talk about their hookups—but I never thought it continued when they became their wives. Did he tell you everything about me?"

"No," Neil responded firmly, sitting down beside her. "Ty never said a word to me about your sex life." It was a small lie; there had been a couple of times when Ty was drunk and had remarked on Stephanie's skills in pleasing him. But it hadn't happened often. Neil hadn't encouraged it because it ripped him apart with jealousy. "It's something I guessed about you. I've known you for a while, remember?"

"Not that way." She let her legs slide back down, though she still wouldn't look at him. "Well, I'm not that far behind you, I don't think. There's no need to wait… to deny ourselves…"

Neil chuckled. "Believe me, I won't be denying either of us. I intend to enjoy every second. I simply need to take a breather, that's all." Leaning in close, he whispered in her ear. "There's nothing wrong with going slow. It's not a race." He rose and started up the steps. "I'm going to take a dip in the pool to cool off. Want to come? It feels good after the hot tub. I promise." He extended one hand to her.

"Okay." She took his hand and climbed out of the tub. Neil flicked a switch on the wall of the house, and lights sprang on beneath the water. Neil dove into the swimming pool and swam toward the opposite end. Stephanie followed more slowly, easing down the ladder. The water sparkled, deliciously cool after the heat of the whirlpool. Stephanie pushed herself away from the side in a smooth, slow glide and stroked her way across the pool. She swam in a leisurely manner, often pausing to rest beside the rim and idly swish her legs through the water.

Neil, on the other hand, zipped up and down the length of the pool like a swimmer in training for the Olympics. When at last he stopped in the deep end of the pool, one hand grasping the rim, Stephanie swam over to him. "You aren't even breathing hard!" she exclaimed accusingly.

He shrugged and grinned, wiping the drops of water from his face. "I was just working off some excess energy. I swim about three miles every morning."

"Jocks!" Stephanie shook her head.

He touched the tip of her nose with his forefinger. "But for some reason you're attracted to us."

"Apparently," Stephanie agreed, assuming a puzzled look. "I'll never understand why."

"Oh, no?" He moved closer, his eyebrow with the scar running through it arching in a leer. "Maybe you like the staying power."

"Don't be crude."

"Can't help it. I'm a jock, remember?" His large hand cradled her cheek, one finger tracing the lines of her face. "You're so beautiful. All during camp I'd lie awake at night and think about you." The timbre of his voice lowered. Stephanie's gaze dropped to his mouth. "I want you, Stephanie."

His forefinger grazed her lower lip, and her mouth opened to allow his finger access, then closed over it, trapping his finger in a velvet clamp. Neil's chest began to rise and fall rapidly. Stephanie ran the tip of her moist tongue along the side of his finger, her lips sucking at it ever so lightly. Neil hissed in a sharp breath from between clenched teeth. Stephanie smiled and opened her mouth wider, worrying over his finger with her teeth as her tongue made swirling designs on his flesh.

Neil murmured hoarsely and closed his eyes, gripping the rim of the pool so tightly that his knuckles whitened. Finally Stephanie released his finger, but she took his hand in hers and with slow, aching deliberation brought each of his other fingers to her mouth to give them the same treatment. When she finished, Neil's arm lashed out to pull her tightly against him and his legs wrapped around her like steel cords. He shoved them away from the edge and with one powerful arm stroked down the pool. Stephanie lay pressed intimately against him, as every atom of Neil's body throbbed with desire.

When he reached the shallow end of the pool Neil stood and swung her into his arms like she weighed nothing, then climbed the steps and strode across the cement to the hot tub. Gently he set Stephanie on her feet. He hooked his thumbs into the straps of her swimsuit and pulled it down, rolling it over the swelling white flesh of her breasts. He stopped when she was naked to the waist and gazed at her breasts, memorizing them. He cupped the full mounds, his fingers dark against Stephanie's pale skin as he took their weight in his hands. She let out a small noise of pleasure, and desire thundered through his veins. He pushed the soft globes together, lifting them, and bent to circle the pink-brown centers with his tongue. Stephanie moved restlessly and he lifted her, his arms beneath her hips so he could more easily take her nipples in his mouth, sucking first on one and then the other. When he set her back down, he supported her for a moment. He wasn't sure her legs would hold her, the way she looked.

Neil peeled her bathing suit down past her hips, smoothing it over her slender thighs. It fell to her ankles and she stepped out of the wet suit. Heat flooded Neil and his tongue crept out to moisten his lips. He looked at her like a starved man at a feast that had suddenly been set before him.

At last he stripped off his swimming trunks. Stephanie watched him the entire time. Even though she flushed at the sight of his naked body and glanced away, her eyes came right back, drawn as if to a magnet. Neil spent hours working out and he knew that every muscle was sculpted to be as powerful as possible. He felt no embarrassment. He loved Stephanie's eyes on him, reveled in the desire that washed across her face as she looked at him.

He stepped into the whirling hot tub and Stephanie followed. Neil reached back behind them. The top step to Neil's hot-tub was a storage step that lifted open like a trunk. It held towels and various supplies and a small box that he'd never once removed in Stephanie's presence. There was no denying the power of the spa, and he kept a stash of condoms here for that very reason. He hoped that Stephanie didn't think too hard about how many times and with what other women he'd removed this box. They both had pasts, but right now he wanted to ignore all that. He took a condom out and lay it on the rim of the tub in easy reach for when Stephanie was ready.

He repositioned himself before the pounding jet of water, but this time he pulled Stephanie onto his lap, facing him. She drew in her breath as she straddled his legs with her own. Neil kissed her over and over, his strong fingers played over her breasts, rolling the nipples between his thumb and forefinger, squeezing lightly.

His fingers roamed her body masterfully. His mouth explored her ears and throat and shoulders, teasing with his tongue. Stephanie moaned and moved restlessly. She rose on her knees, her mouth seeking its mate, and his hand slipped between her legs. Stephanie drew in a sharp breath, and Neil chuckled deep in his throat. He cupped her in the palm of his hand and his fingers teased at the satiny folds until Stephanie writhed against his hand, seeking release.

She pulled her mouth away to whisper raggedly, "Please, Neil, I want you. I want… to feel you inside me."

He groaned and buried his face in her hair, his hands clenching behind her back. He had imagined her saying those very words a million times, but it didn't come close to comparing to the real thing. "No, not quite yet."

"Neil!"

"Shhh. I'll know when you're ready." He wrapped an arm around her lower back and stood, turning both of them and setting her down on the bench. Then he put one big hand on either side of her small waist and flipped her around so she was kneeling in front of the rushing jet and he was positioned behind her. He snaked his hand around to the front of her body, teasing her nipples as he pressed against her body, aching for his own release, but determined to concentrate on hers.

His other hand moved to her soft inner recesses and he eased a finger inside. Stephanie twisted and moaned as his finger and his thumb simultaneously pressed and stroked. He maneuvered her a little closer to the wall of the hot tub, so that the jet of water was gushing over his hand and her flesh. Stephanie whimpered. She moved her hips roughly against his hand, seeking, begging. He could hear her desperation as she gasped out his name.

Finally, when she was at the jagged edge of control, he stood clear of the water and handed her the condom. She tore it open with an eagerness that would have almost made him laugh if it wasn't so sexy. She rolled it down and Neil let out a groan as he watched Stephanie's graceful fingers play across him. Sinking on to the bench seat he eased her back so that she was once again astride him, this time deftly positioning them so that he began to slide into her. A little sob of pleasure escaped Stephanie's lips as she eased down slowly until their bodies were touching at every point they could.

All the fantasies Neil had ever had about Stephanie combined couldn't have begun to equal the way it felt to be inside of her. To watch her nipples harden as the hair on his chest rasped over them. To hear her moans grow louder and louder as he slipped his hand between their joined bodies to find the slick delicate flesh there. His thumb made tight, fast circles as her cries became more desperate with every movement. Her sharp sounds of ecstasy urged Neil on, and he increased the pressure, taking her to the outer reaches of passion.

The water slapped stingingly against his back as Stephanie moved faster and faster, compelled by a deep and primal need. Neil's fingers dug into her hips as he thrust into Stephanie with every suppressed feeling he'd ever had for her. With all the passion he'd been forced to hide for years. For so long he'd wanted to make Stephanie his, and now she finally was. He could see the hunger stamped on her face. Neil's own desire was reflected back in her stormy grey eyes that darkened as she got closer and closer.

"Neil," his name was a groan ripped from her body as Stephanie began to tense around him. Readying. Almost there. Neil could feel her shaking at the precipice, which hurtled him closer to his own edge. Perspiration dotted his forehead, and his breathing was shallow. His grip on his fierce control was almost exhausted. "You feel amazing," Neil's voice was low, guttural.

Stephanie began to move even harder and faster. Neil thrust with abandon, an untamed, instinctive drive for fulfillment. "I'm almost there." He could barely get the words out, consumed by the sensation of Stephanie digging her fingernails into his back, clinging to him, quivering with the force of her need. She cried out as the knot of longing within her exploded, washing outward. Neil lost all awareness as he followed, his body hit by a tidal wave of pleasure. He gave a primitive shudder as he found his own release.

They melted together, limp and exhausted. But the temperature of the water, unnoticed in their excitement, was almost unbearable now to their sensitized nerves. Reluctantly they parted and climbed out. Neil pulled two large, fluffy towels from the storage step and wrapped one of them around Stephanie. She leaned against him, dazed and glowing, content to let him take control. He dried off haphazardly and lifted Stephanie into his arms again. He caught the handle of the sliding door with his elbow and pushed it open, then stepped inside. Stephanie reached back and closed it after them. He smiled and kissed her lightly on the forehead before he walked down the hall, cradling her against his chest. It seemed to him that he carried his entire world in his arms. When he reached his room they tumbled into his bed, happily intertwined, and slid into a deep sleep.

* * *

Stephanie was awakened the next morning by light kisses being feathered over her face. Her eyelids fluttered open, and she focused on Neil's tanned face, inches away from her, relaxed and smiling. "Hello, Stringer." He straightened, picking up her hand and turning it over to kiss the palm. "Sorry to wake you, but I didn't want you to think I'd stolen away in the night."

"If you never came back, I'd just have to console myself with your multi-millionaire-dollar home." Stephanie teased.

"Unfortunately for you, and your bank account, I'll be back."

"What time is it? Where are you going?"

"Practice. It's eight, and it takes me thirty minutes to get to the field." He rose and slipped his cellphone into his jeans pocket, preparing to leave.

"Practice? On Monday? I thought that was your day off, like salons and barbershops."

"Not anymore. Though the Pumas are identical to hair dressers in almost every other way." Neil grinned. "They decided we got too stiff taking Monday off, so now we have a light practice and take Tuesday off. Will you be here when I get back?"

"How else will I establish my squatter's rights?" Stephanie sat up and rubbed her face sleepily. "But really I should probably go home and work."

"Then I'll drop by your house after I get done. We can go out to dinner." He leaned over her, one sinewy brown arm on either side of her. Softly, almost nervously, he asked, "Are you okay? I mean, do you have any regrets?"

Maddeningly, Stephanie felt herself blushing. "No," she breathed. She put her hands on his arms and slid them upward, loving the crisp feel of his hair under her hands. "I've never felt anything like that before. It was never like that with Ty." Why had she blurted that out? This was probably one of the worst times to remind Neil of her relationship with Ty. Stephanie turned her gaze away, chewing on her lower lip.

Suddenly Neil sat down on the bed, his arms going under her, and he nestled his head against her breasts. Rubbing his cheek against her smooth skin, he murmured, "I don't want to go away even for a few hours."

"Coach Davis would fine you. What is it now? A thousand bucks?"

"More than that." He paused. "It'd be worth it."

Her breath caught. "Then… then you enjoyed it, too?"

He chuckled and sat up. "My God, yes. Couldn't you tell?"

"I wasn't sure. You—you did so much for me, and I hardly did anything for you."

"Everything I did to you excited me just as much as it did you. Touching you is so unbelievable—I can't even describe how much pleasure you gave me."

"Really?" Stephanie gazed searchingly into his eyes.

"Really." He bent to kiss her deeply. When he pulled away at last Stephanie was shaken, and Neil's breath was decidedly uneven. "Should I skip practice?"

Reluctantly Stephanie shook her head. "No. I don't want you to get stiff." Her blue-grey eyes sparkled mischievously. "That might cramp our…uh…leisure activities."

Neil laughed. "I certainly wouldn't want to do that."

He gave her a quick, firm kiss and stood up. "See you this evening." He started toward the door but turned back to Stephanie, looking a little hesitant. "I, um... next weekend is the first season opener. I wondered if you were going to come to see it."

"Yes."

"And you'll use my ticket?"

Stephanie dreaded sitting with the wives. The only one she was really friends with was Mel Williams. She'd be uncomfortable under all the speculative gazes. Especially Karen Randall; she was such a gossip. But it was obviously important to Neil that she sit there. It represented something to him, she guessed, a declaration of their relationship. He had given her so much recently that it seemed selfish of her to not give him this. And maybe she could accidentally spill an entire cup of soda in one of Karen Randall's expensive purses to improve the experience. "Yes, I'll use your ticket."

"And there's that thing afterwards—will you go to that with me?"

"What thing?"

"You know, the opening party."

"Oh." The management threw a big party after the first regular season home game. It was the social event of the year for the players and their wives, the one occasion when coaches, players, clerks, management and even the owners mingled freely. The rest of the time everyone pretty much stayed within their own sphere. "I'd forgotten about that. I… yes, of course I'll come." Personally, huge parties weren't her thing. Ty had always wanted her there with him, but then he'd dragged her from group to group being charming, networking and talking about new sports cars or hot stock tips or something else equally uninteresting to Stephanie. She'd never really understood why Ty insisted she be there since she never had anything to say on any of those topics, but it was obvious this party mattered to Neil, too, based on the look in his eyes.

He grinned broadly and came back to her for another long kiss. He pulled back reluctantly. "I have to go. Goodbye."

"Bye."

He turned and left. Stephanie listened to the sound of his footsteps on the wood flooring.

She linked her hands behind her head and contemplated the ceiling, her lips curving into a smile. She had never experienced anything like last night. Much as she had loved Ty, he had never lavished the kind of time and attention on her as Neil had. She closed her eyes, remembering the surging, turbulent need that had eclipsed everything else. Neil had brought out a kind of abandon in her that was totally out of the norm. Ty had never had such an intense effect on her and he had never been more worried about her pleasure than his own. No wonder Neil always had plenty of available women wanting another date.

Stephanie felt a stab of guilt. It seemed disloyal to Ty to enjoy herself so much with another man. She had loved him so much. So why hadn't sex with the man she loved been as good as it was last night with Neil, whom she didn't love? It didn't seem right. Stephanie went into the bathroom and stopped dead at the sight of her reflection. Her hair looked like a bird's nest after swimming in chlorine and then sleeping with it wet. How did Neil even keep a straight face while they were talking? She looked positively electrified.

Stephanie started the water in the shower. There was a showerhead high on one wall, obviously meant for the 6' 5" Neil. The one in Ty's house had been the same way, and it was annoying. But here, on the opposite wall was a much lower one, obviously meant for a woman. Convenient for a bachelor, Stephanie thought grimly and turned on the spray. It was instantly warm and she stepped under it, letting the sound of rushing water drive out thoughts of other women sharing Neil's shower.

Thirty minutes later, dressed in last night's clothes, Stephanie let herself out the front door. She was hungry, and it seemed strange to go through Neil's kitchen without him there. She jumped in her car and headed for Phoenix. She should work today, but she was too giddy after last night to get anything constructive done. As usual, there was nothing to eat at her place, so Stephanie decided to stop for a chocolate croissant and coffee and then go shopping. She wanted to buy a dress that would make Neil's jaw drop open when he picked her up for dinner tonight.

After she located the perfect backless dress, Stephanie stopped at a small eatery near the Biltmore Fashion Park where she'd been shopping. She'd only had one croissant and she was getting hungry again. As she ate her pasta salad, she saw a familiar, tall woman approaching. It was Jill Byerly. The last thing she wanted to do today was run into one of Neil's exes. But it was obvious the woman had spotted her.

"Jill!" Stephanie pasted a pleasant smile on her face.

Jill strode over to her table with that model's walk that Stephanie had envied. "Imagine seeing you shopping here." Jill gestured with her exorbitantly expensive sunglasses toward Stephanie's small bag.

"I needed a dress." Stephanie could feel her smile getting tighter already. "Would you like to join me?"

"No, thank you. I'm on my way to a modeling job, actually. Not that I could eat that many carbs even if I wasn't." Jill gave Stephanie and her food a judgmental glance.

"Right." Stephanie had always been puzzled by the other woman's dislike for her. She'd never felt that she'd done anything to offend her, and Stephanie certainly couldn't see any reason for the downright hostility in Jill's eyes now.

Jill's tone was hard and bitter as she went on, "Karen Randall called me a couple of days ago. She told me you and Neil are a thing now."

Stephanie's stomach sank. It hadn't occurred to her that Jill might know about her and Neil. No doubt she was still interested in Neil and was jealous of their relationship. "Well, I… it isn't anything serious."

Jill made an inelegant snort. “Maybe not to you. Actually, I’m surprised Neil waited long enough for Ty’s corpse to get cold.”

“Excuse me?” Stephanie gasped. “What the hell are you talking about?”

Jill shot her a scornful look. “Oh, come on, don’t tell me you still don’t know.”

“Know what?”

“That Neil is in love with you. He’s been in love with you ever since you met.”

Chapter Eleven

Stephanie stared at Jill for a moment, then exclaimed, "Neil's not in love with me—we just started dating!"

Jill's pretty lips thinned into a vicious line. "No? Ask anybody. Everyone who saw Neil with you knew. The only ones too dumb to figure it out were you and Ty. Neil always wanted you, but he was too noble to try to steal you from his best friend. I never had a chance with him!" Her nostrils flared with anger. "No matter what I did or how good I looked, I couldn't ever compete because I wasn't you."

Stephanie couldn't pull her thoughts together enough to say anything. It was crazy. How could Neil have been in love with her for years and years and she'd never even picked up a clue? That was certainly not something she would put on her resume as an investigative reporter. Maybe Jill was only lashing out in hurt because Neil had rejected her. That must be it. Stephanie groped for something to say. "Neil and I were good friends, but there was never anything going on between us. Not until a few weeks ago. Maybe you saw our close friendship, and in your mind you turned it into something it wasn't."

Jill laughed humorlessly. "No. You've been blind." She turned to leave, flinging a parting shot over her shoulder. "I hope Neil's happy now that he's gotten what he always wanted." Her tone indicated the exact opposite of her words.

Stephanie watched the woman walk away, then looked back down at her food. Her appetite had vanished. She piled the containers together on the tray and swept them into the trash. Shakily she gathered her package and purse and left. As she went to her car, she ran over Jill's assertions in her mind. Neil and Ty were best friends; she and Neil had gotten along well themselves; and the three of them had been together a lot. Perhaps that had started rumors. Pete Cherneski had jokingly called them 'the thruple,' but surely their teammates hadn't actually thought there was anything to the nickname.

If Neil had felt anything more for her, he would have told her at some point. Or would he? Stephanie had to admit that it would fit Neil's personality to love her without letting on. He was too loyal to hurt Ty and too kind to saddle her with the knowledge of his unrequited feelings. He was also the only person she knew who had the iron will it would take to love someone they saw all the time without ever expressing it.

Now that she thought about it, Stephanie remembered a few occasions when she had caught Neil watching her with a dark, pained expression. There had been the time he had danced with her because Ty was taking shots with the guys and her favorite song had come on in the bar. Then suddenly Neil had pulled away as if he were angry and stalked out of the room. His tirade the other day after the game about her still loving Ty—it had felt like an argument between a couple that came up over and over, even though it had been brand new to her. Had he been having that argument for years in his head? He'd said something on that day when she'd made him lunch after her meeting with Howard Perry. Stephanie tried to remember Neil's exact words, but she couldn't—still, she'd come away from that conversation thinking he'd been involved with or in love with a married woman. Was the person that Stephanie was trying to dig up info on at Mel Williams's house actually…her?

And, of course, there had been that time Ty had slapped her. The growing tumor in Ty's brain had started to affect his personality early on, though they hadn't known the cause at the time. Ty had turned moody, lashing out at friends for no reason or storming off the field in a rage. Stephanie didn't know what had precipitated his fury that particular evening, but he had begun striding around the room, complaining about football fans. Stephanie, irritated by all of his recent moodiness, had answered sharply, and he had turned his anger on her. She wasn't one to back down from an argument, and soon they were in the middle of a full-fledged screaming match. In an outburst of fury, Ty had slapped her. She had fallen back into the wall, and for a moment they'd stared at each other in blank surprise.

Ty had groaned and sank down heavily on the couch, digging his fingers into his scalp. Stephanie had immediately run outside to her car and driven all the way to Neil's mountainside home in a furious haze without thinking of where she was going. Her first instinct had been to seek safety, and she'd gone to Neil's on autopilot.

When Neil had seen her tear-streaked face, already swelling and bruised, his expression had turned to shock. He had pulled her inside, pouring out questions, and Jill had appeared in the front hallway behind him, her eyes wide with astonishment. When Stephanie told him what had happened, Neil's face had twisted, his dark eyes blazing with an unholy fire.

"I'll kill that asshole," he'd grated, and pushed past her, striding toward his car.

Stephanie had run after him, Jill not far behind her. The two women had grasped his arms, one on each side, and managed to slow him down long enough for the red rage to clear. Then he had gone back inside and gently applied an ice pack to Stephanie's swollen cheek while they discussed what was wrong with Ty. It was then that they decided Ty had to visit a doctor.

Had that moment when Neil charged out into the night, intent on getting revenge, been an indication of his feelings for her? Had sudden stress ripped away a mask that he usually carefully cultivated? This morning she had been happy in her new relationship, but this changed everything. If Neil had been in love with her all this time, last night meant something vastly different to him than it did to her. How did they go back to casually dating now that she knew that his own feelings ran so much deeper than hers? She was poised on the edge of something, but Neil was already far down the path.

Stephanie wasted most of the afternoon in pointless worrying and had barely gotten dressed by the time Neil came over after practice. She'd decided not to wear the new dress after all and went casual in jeans and a tank top. The doorbell sounded, and she noticed that her palms were sweaty on her door handle. She would have to talk to him right away or she'd never be able to eat around the nervous knot in her stomach.

Neil lounged against the wall of her small front porch, arms folded across his chest and one booted foot hooked casually over the other. His eyes were snapping with life. Stephanie's nerves set up a strange tingling. Her voice was almost shy. "Hi."

He grinned and unfolded himself, covering the ground between them in one huge step. He seized her upper arms in his steel grasp and pulled her up into a long, breathless kiss. Stephanie's heart tripped into a fluttering beat, and by the time he released her, she was almost dizzy.

He followed her into the house. Stephanie's heartbeat steadied, and her breathing returned to normal. She searched for something innocuous to say. Now that he was here, she didn't know how to broach the subject. "How was practice?"

He groaned comically. "Painful? Like it always is the day after a game." His eyes twinkled. "I didn't pay proper attention to soaking my muscles in the hot tub last night."

A blush rose on Stephanie's cheeks and warmth spread in her abdomen. Neil sat down on the couch and tugged at her hand, indicating that she should sit down beside him. Stephanie pulled back. "I better get started fixing dinner."

His eyebrows went up. "It's only five. I may be moving like a senior citizen right now, but I don't need to eat dinner before six pm." When she didn't smile at his joke, a little frown flashed between his eyes. "Besides, I wanted to take you out some place nice."

"Oh, no, I'd rather cook tonight." She cleared her throat. "How about a drink?"

"I'm good. Just sit down and talk to me." Again he pulled her hand, and she sat down, fitting all too easily against his side. "How was your day? Did you do more interviews or are you on to writing at this point?"

"I didn't do much of anything. I couldn't settle down to work. And don't grin at me like that."

"Sorry." He pulled the suggestive smile from his face, but his eyes twinkled more than ever.

"You're impossible."

"So what did you do instead of working?"

"I shopped at Biltmore Park." The introduction to her subject was suddenly there, staring her in the face. Stephanie chewed on her lower lip.

She had to know. She would have to ask him and the sooner the better, no matter how much she hated it. "I ran into Jill Byerly there."

"Oh?" He stiffened almost imperceptibly. If Stephanie hadn't been pressed against his side she wouldn't have noticed it. "How is she?"

"Bitter, I think."

Neil sighed. "Jill knew where she stood from the start. I didn't want to hurt her."

"She told me she never stood a chance with you. Is that true?"

"More or less. I knew from the beginning that I wouldn't fall in love with her."

"Why?"

Neil shot Stephanie a wary glance. "What does it matter? It was over a long time ago. My relationship with Jill has nothing to do with us."

"That's not what Jill said."

His face was still, almost resigned. "What did Jill say?"

"That you've been in love with me ever since we met. Is that true?"

"You make it sound as if it were a crime."

"Of course not. But it's important."

He regarded her for a moment. "All right. Yes. I fell in love with you years ago. If Ty hadn't been my best friend, I'd have done my best to break you up. There. Does that satisfy you?"

Stephanie shook her head. "I never knew. I really didn't have any idea."

"I didn't want you to. It wouldn't have been fair to you or Ty. It wouldn't have helped matters." Neil took one of her hands in his. "But that doesn't affect what you and I have now."

"Doesn't it?" she asked distractedly, pulling her hand from his and rising to her feet. "I feel as if I've known you all this time under false pretenses."

"You think I'm a liar? I can't be trusted?"

"No, of course not. I mean, not exactly."

"What good would it have done to tell you? We couldn't have been friends any longer. It would have been too awkward. And Ty would have hated me." Neil stood up, too. "He was the closest person to me in the world besides my brother Charles, and he never would've spoken to me again. And that's the best-case scenario—you know Ty probably would've gotten drunk and wanted to fight me and then what? I beat him up? I let him beat me up? You know it wasn't in either one of us to back down. It would have ruined everything. And I'd have had nothing. Not knowing didn't hurt you and Ty."

"But you must have been hurt!"

"I have only myself to blame. If I chose it, what's wrong with that?"

"I feel guilty, now, like I hurt you and took advantage of your feelings for me. When I think of all the times I leaned on you during Ty's illness—sometimes literally. And I must have come between you and Ty."

"You did not come between me and Ty. If anything, he was between you and me. You'd have been mine a long time ago if it hadn't been for him. You didn't hurt me. We weren't unfaithful to Ty. Where's the harm?"

"I don't know. Maybe there was none. But it makes me feel uneasy." She looked at Neil, frowning. "I'm so sorry."

"Don't pity me," he cut her off sharply. "I don't need or want that, especially not from you. I chose to love you, and I chose to conceal it in order to remain friends with you and Ty. There's nothing you could have done and no reason for you to feel bad. I made my decision. I lived with it. End of story."

"I'm not pitying you. But I feel hurt for your hurt. Sympathy isn't bad, Neil."

"Neither is loving you. I don't think there was ever any wrong in it."

Stephanie sighed. "I'm sure there wasn't. But don't you see how it puts us in an awkward situation now?"

"No, how?"

"Now I know. Now if you get hurt, it will be my fault. I don't want to cause you pain. I like you far too much."

"Believe me, you aren't causing me any pain by sleeping with me. Just the opposite, I'd say."

"Maybe right now. But it doesn't seem fair to you. There's a..." She made a vague gesture, searching for the right word. "An inequity."

"An inequity?" His brows rose. "This isn't some article about civil rights. And who said love is ever fair? I feel how I feel. You feel how you feel. That's the way it always is in relationships. You think everyone that falls in love does it at the same speed? That's life. There are no guarantees. And I'm not asking you for one."

"Yeah, but someday a physical relationship won't seem like enough anymore. You'll want love."

Neil was silent for a moment, studying her. In a low voice he asked, "What makes you think I won't get what I want? Do you plan to never fall in love again? Was Ty your one and only?"

She blinked. "No. I imagine I'll fall in love again someday. At least, I hope so. But…"

"But it won't be with me?"

Stephanie blushed. "No, I didn't mean that. It—of course I might fall in love with you. But the point is, I don't know. What if I don't? Then you'll get hurt."

"Stringer…" He turned away, then walked back toward her, his hands jammed in the rear pockets of his jeans. "You know what makes me a successful quarterback?"

Stephanie stared, confused by his sudden change of topic. "What in the world are you talking about?"

"I'm talking about my personality. I have pretty average talent for pro football. Ty was a natural. I'm not. What I am is determined. I can concentrate on my goal and not be distracted. And I'm patient. I'm willing to work for things. I don't try to win in one glorious play. That's why I know I'll get you someday." He gave her a cocky little smile.

"Oh, really?" That smirk shouldn't melt her right down to her toes, but it did. Stephanie crossed her arms, one eyebrow lifting in playful challenge.

"Yeah, really." He withdrew one hand from his pocket to tilt up her chin. "I won't push. I won't pressure you into committing. I'm willing to wait, but I won't ever forget what I'm after. I love you, and I'll do everything I can to make you love me." He paused. "There's another thing I do well. I roll with the punches. I've learned how to deal with defeat. It's not something I enjoy, but I'm able to go after something with all my heart and at the same time accept the fact that I may not get it."

"And that applies to me as well?"

He smiled. "Does that bother you?"

"Comparing me to a football game? No, why should it?" she replied tartly.

His smile broadened into a chuckle, and he took her hands in his. "You are the most important thing in my life. But you don't need to protect me. I'm not a child. My eyes are wide open. And last night was the happiest I've been in years. I want some more happiness. I want to give some to you as well. It's that simple."

Stephanie frowned. "I don't think things are ever as simple as you make them sound."

"You'd be surprised how unnecessarily complex I make them sometimes. After Ty died, I felt horribly guilty for loving you, as if my love had somehow killed him. I thought about all the times when I had wished he was out of the picture so I could make you mine, and I hated myself because it felt like those wishes had come true. It was awful. That's one reason I stayed away after I'd finished helping you with the funeral." Neil sighed. "Finally I saw that I was ruining my future like it was penance for Ty's death. But nothing we do or don't do will bring him back. Letting the past control us, make us miserable, is pointless. Ty wouldn't want us to do that. He lived every moment to the fullest. Let's forget about the past and the future. Let's just be here, together, in the present."

His thumbs began to draw slow, steady circles on the backs of her hands, a caressing invitation, a beckoning to return from the chasm of her thoughts. It was a small gesture, not overpoweringly sexy, yet it stirred her desire. She wanted Neil. Last night he had made her feel as no other man ever had. Her memories of it were enough to start a low, throbbing heat in her.

She looked up at Neil and a smile crept across her face. She thought of the joy he'd taken in her pleasure last night, even after years of pent-up passions. Stephanie wanted to please him. To give him all the fire he'd wanted from her for so long. "Why are we standing here talking?" she asked in an injured tone. "I'd think you'd have me in the bedroom by now."

"An accomplished player like me?" His grin was wide and relieved. "Maybe my reputation exceeds my ability."

"I don't think so." Stephanie turned her hands so that their palms fit together. "Come on. I have a surprise for you."

"What?" He followed as she dropped one of his hands and tugged at the other, guiding him from the room.

"How about a massage? I thought you might like one after working out and discovering all those stiff muscles."

"Sounds perfect."

They reached her bedroom and Stephanie motioned him toward her bed. "Then take off your clothes and lie down."

"All my clothes?"

Stephanie chuckled. "A massage usually works better that way."

Neil joined in her laughter. "Sorry. I'm just naturally shy," he quipped and began unbuttoning his shirt.

"I was there last night, remember? You're not even a little bit shy about your body. Not that you have any reason to be." She gave him a flirty smile before ducking into the bathroom to search for the oil she'd always used for Ty's rubdowns. It had been so long since she used it; it was bound to be in the back of the cabinet—if she'd even brought it with her when she moved. She breathed a small sigh of relief when she found the bottle.

Neil had already pulled aside the comforter and was lying face down across her bed when she returned. Stephanie slipped off everything but her underwear and pulled off her ring, laying it on her dresser. She settled down beside Neil, clad only in her flesh-colored lace panties and bra. She plunged her fingers into his thick black hair and began to work. Neil made a contented noise and his well-muscled body relaxed all over. Stephanie smiled and continued moving down from his head to his neck. Then she poured a bit of oil into her palm and let it warm as her eyes moved down the length of his body. A bruise the size of a softball marred his back just below the left shoulder blade. Stephanie drew in her breath sharply. "Neil! What happened?"

"What?" His head came up and he glanced around. "What are you talking about?"

"This bruise." Stephanie reached out tentatively to touch the edge of it.

"Oh, that." Neil shrugged. "I don't know. I got it during practice or the game."

How could she have forgotten? Ty had always been cut and bruised after playing. Her eyes skimmed over Neil's back, looking more attentively this time. She touched a small scar low on his back. "What's this?"

"I got cut by a cleat in high school."

Stephanie closed her eyes, remembering the tape around Ty's ribs after he had cracked them. It had hurt him to breathe, and laughing had been pure agony. She thought of the scars that had etched his fair skin, the knob on his collarbone where he had broken it and it had reknit poorly. She opened her eyes and found the scar on Neil's elbow where they'd done the surgery. She looked at the bruises dotting his hips and legs. She knew that if he rolled over she'd find them all over his front too. The little finger of his passing hand was permanently bent at an unnatural angle above the knuckle because it had been broken so many times.

"Why do you guys do it?" she breathed, fear and sickness clutching at her stomach. What was she getting herself into? Life with another man who did his best to get bruised and torn and battered every Sunday?

"Goes with the territory."

"I wonder if the territory's worth it," Stephanie retorted sharply.

"Sometimes I wonder that myself." He cocked his head to grin up at her. "Maybe I'm a masochist."

"That thought has crossed my mind."

"But aren't things better when you have to struggle to get them?"

"Struggle I can understand. Mutilating yourself, I can't."

"It's just a ploy to get your sympathy. Hey, what happened to that massage?" He went on teasingly, "Were you overcome by the sight of my magnificent body?"

She rolled her eyes and smiled. "Just letting the oil warm up." She rubbed the oil between her palms and set to work on his back, carefully avoiding that painful-looking bruise. She would have to get accustomed to this rough world again.

Her fingers dug in deeply, working out the knots in Neil's corded muscles. She moved down his back, then did each arm in turn, supporting it as she kneaded the warmed oil into his skin. Neil sighed blissfully, and groaned now and then as she soothed a particularly sore spot. "Can I arrange for this after every game?"

"We might be able to work something out. Do you like it?"

"Yes. Except you're turning me on so much that I don't know if I want to wait for you to get out all the kinks before I return the favor."

"Really, Neil," she said with mock sternness. "I have not been giving you a sexy rubdown."

"No? Could have fooled me."

"I guess I'll have to show you the difference, then." Stephanie's hands slithered over his oiled back and dug into his buttocks, eliciting a muffled groan from Neil. She stroked, kneaded and lifted, letting her thumbs drift down between his legs, teasing at the sensitive, hair-roughened flesh. Neil moved his legs restlessly, his fingers digging into the sheets. Stephanie's fingers moved over his thighs, still rubbing the tense muscles, but also teasing with her fingertips.

Tantalizing and inflaming Neil's senses was equally arousing for her. Every melting of a taut line in his face added to the liquid fire in her abdomen. Stephanie worked her way down his legs, bending over to kiss the tender skin behind his knees. Neil jerked involuntarily and murmured her name.

"Stephanie! What are you trying to do to me?" Neil rolled over on his back.

"Looks like I've already done it," Stephanie remarked, glancing significantly at his body's unmistakable message. "Didn't you like it?"

"Like isn't the word for it."

"Then lie still. I haven't finished yet." She kissed her way up his legs as she slid sinuously up his body, her flesh skimming over his. Neil's breath rasped in his throat, his chest rising and falling unevenly. Finally he grasped her shoulders and pulled her up to the level of his face. Fierce black eyes blazed into hers as he raised his head to kiss her, blotting out everything else. Stephanie clung to him, their mouths greedy on each other, tongues mingling, teeth hard and sharp beneath the velvet cover of lips. Neil wrapped his legs around hers as he turned over, pinning her beneath him, and ended their kiss.

He rose to his knees to look down at her, his legs like iron trapping hers. The sprinkling of hair on his thighs rasped teasingly against her skin. His hands went to cover her breasts, his widespread fingers rough against the lace of her bra. He watched her with heavy-lidded hunger as her nipples hardened underneath his thumbs. Stephanie's breath came faster. She felt each whorl and line of his thumbs as if they were raking across her nipples with no fabric between them, sending shivers of violent pleasure through her. He smiled in supreme satisfaction as Stephanie arched her back and moaned with longing.

"I need you now," she told him thickly.

He closed his eyes. "Not fair," he rose from the bed. "I told you, first I have to return the favor."

"Huh?" Her mind was dazed with pleasure.

"I'm going to give you a massage. Turn over."

Stephanie groaned but did as he told her, anticipation blossoming in her abdomen. He unhooked her bra and slid it from under her, then insinuated his fingers beneath the lacy panties and tugged them down her legs. He dropped the gossamer garments onto the floor and his hands returned to her body. His touch was light as a feather, exploring her everywhere, not massaging so much as teasing and arousing. He traveled up and down her back and legs, coming close to, grazing but never quite touching the hot, throbbing locus of her senses, even though she moved her legs apart, inviting his hand.

He began to kiss down her neck, making wet, intricate patterns on her back and the sensitive sides of her breasts. Stephanie writhed under his mouth, aching, longing for the satisfaction only he could bring. She had never felt anything like the fire running rampant through her body when Neil touched her. The ache between her legs was enormous and uncontrollable. She was aware of nothing except Neil's hands and mouth. He was driving her crazy with his slow exploration of her entire body. In another moment she was certain that she would start whimpering for him, begging.

Finally his hand slid between her legs, and the long-awaited contact was electric. Callused flesh touched moist smoothness. Heat melded to heat, and pressure answered ache. Stephanie squeezed her legs together, capturing his fingers, urging him to finish his delightful torment. She twisted, moving her hips to match the rhythm of his fingers. His hand left her too soon and she turned over on her back, her eyes liquid with passion.

Neil positioned himself between her legs and grabbed a condom he had obviously stowed on her bedside table while she was searching the bathroom cabinets. Stephanie eagerly helped him roll it on and he groaned. Sliding his hands beneath her hips Neil paused for a moment, not entering her yet.

"Neil, please. I need to feel you inside of me. Please."

With a low groan, he slowly pushed into her welcoming warmth. Stephanie moved in counterpoint, luxuriating in the fullness of his deep thrust. She closed her eyes at the exquisite pleasure of his possession. She felt as if she could go on this way forever, yet the budding need deep within wanted more… and speed… and now.

Neil was breathing shakily as he buried his face in her breasts. Stephanie knew his desire was taking over, urging him on. Stephanie wrapped her legs tightly around his back. Every nerve in her body seemed to have gathered into a fist in her abdomen, and with each movement the fist drew tighter and tighter until Stephanie was sobbing for release. Suddenly Neil cried out and his face contorted as he shuddered under the onslaught.

The force of it swept Stephanie along to her own climax. Sparks showered through her body, setting off a wild, tingling fire all over her. She buried her face in Neil's shoulder to muffle the sounds which were torn from her.

They lay together afterward, not daring to speak, hardly daring to breathe. Finally Neil rolled from on top of her and disposed of the condom quickly, coming back to pull her against him, her back to his front. One of his arms looped around her waist, and the other pillowed her head. Stephanie could feel the faint brush of his breath against her hair. Neither spoke. The nestling of their bodies held the moment close in a way that was beyond words.

Chapter Twelve

Stephanie had known it for only two nights, but the lack of Neil's body warmth awakened her. Sunlight pierced the cracks of the miniblinds, bathing the room with a glow indicating that it was late morning. Stephanie blinked and pushed back her tangled hair with one hand. Where was Neil?

She spotted movement in the mirror of the tiny bathroom adjoining the bedroom, and she turned in that direction. Neil stood at the sink, clad only in his boxer-briefs, his lower face lathered in purple foam. He tilted back his head so he could shave under his throat, wincing as the razor pulled. "Damn!"

Stephanie giggled, and he turned to shoot her a dirty look. "What is it that women have against sharp razors? A guy could kill himself with this thing."

Stephanie sat up in bed, propping a pillow behind her. "It's meant for shaving legs, not faces. It's perfectly adequate for that." He grimaced and continued to shave. Stephanie smiled. "The purple shaving cream looks nice with your hair."

Neil made a mock growl. "It smells to high heaven."

"It's 'delicately scented with lavender—to turn your shave into a relaxing spa experience,'" Stephanie quoted with a touch of humor.

"It's certainly the most relaxing throat-slitting experience I've ever had." A grin quirked his mouth. "I'm guessing that the same faultless logic is what led them to add purple dye to the lather?"

"Your guess is as good as mine. I get it because it's cheap." Stephanie leaned her head against the headboard of the bed and watched him shave. There was something comfortingly familiar about the ritual. She was suddenly aware of how much she had missed a male presence in her home. The grief of the past year and a half had made this a barren, lonely landscape, but Stephanie hadn't really realized it until now. Having someone here—tears stung her eyes—no, having Neil here in her home made everything brighter.

She left her bed and went into the bathroom to wrap her arms around his waist from behind and reached up on her tiptoes to kiss the outthrust of his shoulder blade. Neil smiled at her in the mirror and reached behind him with his free arm to press her against him. She kissed him again, then left him reluctantly. She stepped into the shower and turned on the faucet. Moments later she heard the shower door open again, and she turned to see Neil joining her. Playfully he squeezed some of her soap out into his hands and lathered her body, his play rapidly becoming a sensual game. She returned the favor, and soon he jumped out, running across the room still half covered in soap and getting water all over her floor so he could get a condom. She pretended to be mad at him for probably warping her wood floors but she quickly welcomed him back, her legs gripping his waist as he pushed her into the cold tile with each deep thrust, the shower spraying over them warmly.

Later they dried each other off, and Neil pulled on his clothes. "I can tell I'm going to have to bring a few things over here," he joked, "or I'll have to live in one set of clothes and have a perpetually bloodied face." He stopped abruptly and shot her a slightly wary glance.

Stephanie realized that he was waiting for her permission to fulfill his humorously worded request. She smiled, her heart swelling with joy. As important as it was to her not to rush things, she couldn't deny how much she wanted Neil to be around more. "Of course. I wouldn't want you to bleed to death."

He grinned and winked, then strolled out of the room, whistling under his breath. Stephanie slipped on some clothes, her favorite necklace and earrings and reached for her wedding ring on top of the dresser, where she had put it the previous night before giving Neil his massage. Her hand paused in midair. She studied the ring for a moment. Then her fingers curled around the cool metal, enclosing the ring in her palm. She slid open a tiny drawer of her jewelry box and placed her wedding ring inside it. Closing the drawer, she walked to the kitchen to join Neil.

* * *

The game the following Sunday wasn't as awkward as Stephanie thought it would be, and after sitting with Mel Williams for a few hours, she remembered how much fun she could have at them. And while Stephanie hadn't ended up pouring any beverages in Karen Randall's purse, she made sure a few errant cheesy popcorn kernels found their way into the woman's fancy white handbag.

The wives all trailed out of the stadium together, Mel chattering excitedly to Stephanie about how this was the one night a year that she got to dress up in an evening gown and forget that she had three boys at home probably all badgering their babysitter to let them stay up late.

Stephanie drove straight home to get ready for the party. When Neil arrived precisely on the dot of 7:30, she was only half-dressed. She was digging in her closet for the other strappy high heel that went with her outfit as she heard him stroll down the hall and into her bedroom.

"I know, I know," she said without turning around. "I'm late, but I'm not as far behind as I look. I only have to put on my dress and—aha!" She found the shoe and turned around, holding it up triumphantly.

Neil smiled, his dark eyes heated as they swept down her body, clad only in a lacy, plunge-necked bodysuit. "You look perfect just like that."

Stephanie flushed, the heat of desire spreading through her body. Hand on her cocked hip, she said, "You think this is what they meant by black-tie optional?"

"Probably not, but it would make things interesting. Of course, then I'd have to fight my teammates off with a chair."

"Some of your teammates are pretty big; you think a chair is going to do it?"

"You're right. I'm going home to get my tranquilizer darts." Neil turned like he was about to leave, but Stephanie reached out for his hand.

"I won't have you tranq-ing your competition." She gave his wrist a playful squeeze. "It's very unsportsmanlike."

He easily pulled out of her grasp and spread his hands on her hips. "Well, I intend to have you all to myself tonight, no matter what it takes."

"Hmm," Stephanie said thoughtfully. "In that case, maybe I should wear a dress."

"I'm good with that... as long as I have a private showing." Neil bent to kiss her, but Stephanie turned her face away.

"No way. I already did my make-up. You are not messing up my lipstick."

He grinned. "Well, then… I'll just have to limit myself to non-make-up areas." He kissed the crook of her neck, the velvet touch of his lips on her bare skin sending shivers through her.

"You're not playing fair," she murmured as he kissed his way up her neck, but she tilted her head to expose more of her throat to his seduction.

He let out a soft laugh, his breath on her flesh sparking even more tingles in her. "I don't play fair. I play to win."

She all but melted as his hands joined in the assault on her senses. But finally she pulled herself together enough to break away. "Stop that. I have to get dressed for a very important date. With a special guy."

"Yeah?" He stepped back, leaning his shoulder against the wall. "How special?"

Stephanie gave him a seductive smile. "I'll show you how special when we get back." She moved away to pull on a robe.

Neil groaned. "Now you're the one not playing fair."

"Go," Stephanie said with mock sternness and pointed to the bedroom door.

"Okay. I give in." He went to the door, but turned in the doorway to look at her. "You're beautiful. You know that?"

Stephanie flushed, smiling as she watched him walk away. Turning, she picked up the dress lying on her bed and pulled it on. It was an ankle-length white crepe sheath, very simple in design. In the back it was slit up to the knees to allow for easy walking. The strapless neckline dipped down in a narrow vee between her breasts. It was a beautiful dress, very understated but elegant, especially with the French-twist hairstyle she'd chosen. However, it definitely needed some jewelry to set it off. Stephanie dug through her necklaces and pulled out a chunky gold necklace.

She slipped on her high heels and went out to join Neil, holding up the necklace. "What do you think about this with the dress?"

He rose to his feet, a stunned expression on his face, and ran his eyes over her figure. "Gorgeous. Not the necklace. You."

"Thank you."

"But I think this will look better." He held out a flat, hinged box. "Lucky you chose tonight to wear that."

Surprised, Stephanie took the box and opened it. Inside, nestled in cream velvet, was the delicate rose-gold jewelry set she had admired in Sedona when the two of them had taken a daytrip there. "Neil, it's beautiful!" She set the jewelry in her hand aside and reverently lifted out the necklace to put it on. It nestled perfectly against the hollow of her throat. Stephanie fitted the bracelet around her wrist and slipped the unique bar and chain, threader-style earrings through her ear piercings. One look in the mirror assured her that the jewelry looked even more beautiful with this dress. She couldn't have asked for more perfect accessories.

"Neil, I… they're stunning. I wanted them that day we went to the shop, but I didn't know you'd—I mean… I probably should say, 'You shouldn't have,' but I'm so happy you did." She turned to him, her expression bright and sparkling. "I promise I'll keep them always."

"That look in your eyes is all the promise I need."

* * *

The party was held, as always, at the Biltmore, the prototype of the Phoenix resorts. The large room had a portable bar in each corner, a stage set up for a band, a dance floor, large round tables for eating and long tables loaded with appetizers. The Ingrams stood by the door to meet the players and their wives personally, a nice touch made possible by the fact that Coach Davis and his wife were beside them greeting everyone by name first, thus clueing in the owners.

Neil and Stephanie walked through the room, stopping to chat with Jalyn and Mel Williams by the appetizers. Neil kept his arm possessively around Stephanie's waist, filled with pride that he finally got to introduce her to people as being with him. Just the thought warmed him.

Neil kept the conversation going with Jalyn and Mel until he saw Pete Cherneski sit down to eat. Neil immediately headed to the table and pulled out a chair for Stephanie. She'd told Neil in the past that she thought Pete was bizarre, and while Neil had explained that Pete was a typical linebacker, weird but big-hearted, Neil had noticed that she still hadn't exactly made it a priority to get to know him. Luckily, Gramps and Asa were sitting at the table, too, so Stephanie wouldn't feel pressured to talk with Cherneski if she didn't want to.

Clearly, she was smart enough to see the ploy behind their seating arrangement, though, because the first thing she did was zero in on Pete.

"You are so sweet to have brought over enough appetizers for everyone." She nodded at the array of dishes across the table where he sat. "I just got these mushroom puffs for myself."

Pete looked around him at the plates of wontons, crab cakes, cocktail shrimp, spinach and artichoke tarts, and hummus and pita slices. "I also got these for myself."

Stephanie gave him a big smile and then leaned in to whisper to Neil, "Is this one of his strange jokes I don't get?"

Neil did his best to keep a straight face. "Maybe he's just hungry."

Stephanie straightened back up and tried again. "So I guess you didn't get a chance to grab dinner after the game. Me neither. I'm starving."

"And all you got to eat is mushroom puffs?" He looked at her like she was the one that was weird. "I had a large pizza before I came. But this food is free. I always have room for free food."

"I didn't want to eat the Ingrams out of house and home," Stephanie joked.

"What are you? 5'8" and 120?" Pete asked and Stephanie was so taken aback that she dropped out of her polite face for a second and looked supremely annoyed. "I doubt you could eat them out of house and home if you tried."

Asa covered his mouth with a napkin to muffle a sudden coughing fit. Stephanie opened her mouth and closed it again. Three times. Neil clamped down on the laugh threatening to explode out of him. She looked like the cutest guppy ever.

"He's got you there." Gramps pointed at Stephanie with his beer bottle.

"And you know the Ingrams are rich, right?" Pete continued to stare at Stephanie like she was possibly a little bit dim. "Like, they own half of Phoenix and they're pretty good with their money. They can afford to feed you. I mean, if they can feed a football team, am I right?" he asked the table.

"My little cousin Mike is the worst amateur day trader ever, and he could probably cover your groceries for a year," Asa confirmed, his eyes dancing.

"Okay." Stephanie held up her hands and narrowed her eyes. "I take exception to this whole exchange. My appetite is perfectly in line with someone that is not incredibly active, right, Neil?"

"'Not incredibly active?' Didn't you throw out a pedometer that Ty gave you because it never registered more than three thousand steps a day?"

"It was obviously broken."

"Obviously." Neil nodded, his shoulders shaking.

Stephanie let out a slow breath through her nose and turned to Gramps.

"So are you glad to be back from camp or do you miss California?" Stephanie asked, popping a mushroom puff in her mouth. Neil groaned inwardly, wishing he'd warned her beforehand.

"Training camp is kind of hard for me. More the time of year than anything." Gramps spoke as vaguely as Neil had ever heard him on the subject. Of course, Neil wouldn't want to get into it at a party either.

"Why's that? Not a summer heat guy?"

"My dad died when I was in training camp at college." Gramps never lied, even little white ones for social niceties sake. Neil figured his attempt to skirt the situation at the start was about as close as he got to it.

"Oh, I'm so sorry. I had no idea." Stephanie reached out like she wanted to comfort Gramps, but then just dropped her hands in her lap, her forehead wrinkled with concern.

"Hey, don't worry about it." Gramps smiled at her reassuringly. "Our relationship was complicated, but we weren't close. And there's no reason you would have known. Plus, my life took a not-all-bad detour after that."

"That was a poor segue if you wanted to change the subject." Neil shook his head. "There is nothing Stephanie likes to talk about more than how you got where you are in life. She may start taking notes for your biography."

"It'd probably be a bestseller." Stephanie shot Neil an exaggerated glare before turning back to Gramps. "So what was the detour?"

"There were some tangles with the law, and I got suspended from my college team for a while because of that. But it was also when I got most of my tattoos and bought my motorcycle—which I have no regrets about," Kowalski said firmly. "During some court-ordered therapy, I discovered stoicism, which fascinated me. Eventually I changed my major to philosophy and got a minor in psychology."

"And now you get to be the unpaid life coach to an entire football team." Neil laughed.

"Yeah, well, I said it made my life better; I didn't say it made me any money." Gramps shrugged.

"So did you bring a girlfriend tonight?" Stephanie asked Gramps, determinedly taking another stab at conversation.

"Please, God, say no." Neil looked up as if pleading with a higher power.

"I'm not dating anyone right now." Gramps punched Neil in the bicep. "But don't believe anything these guys say about my exes."

"Oh, no, you should definitely believe it." Asa pantomimed a looping circle around his ear.

"I'm going to go get a refill. When I get back, you will have moved on to another subject." Gramps gave Neil and Asa each a long look.

"So should I be jealous that you're trying to find out Gramps' status?" Neil asked Stephanie when he'd walked away.

"I was just thinking about how cute he is. That slight Louisiana drawl, the piercing blue eyes, the strong jaw, and that shaved head you just want to rub."

"Okay… so I was kidding, but now I'm getting a little bit worried. I'm not going to have to get into a fist-fight with the nicest guy on the team, am I?" Neil raised his eyebrows.

"Obviously I wasn't asking for me," Stephanie retorted. "But I was thinking when he was talking about how much he's worked on himself over the years—maybe he'd be good for Claire. They're both in their thirties and she'd love to meet a guy that isn't incredibly boring or married."

"Yeah..." Neil tilted his head. "I'm not sure Claire is really Gramps' type. He's usually into girls that play roller derby and have purple hair and lots of tattoos."

"Maybe his relationships would last longer with a non-crazy girl."

"Oh, that's not the crazy part." Asa jumped in. "Moran's just giving you Gramps' type. The drug habits, insane jealousy and getting into bar brawls is the part that makes them crazy."

"Yeah, there was that one girl that spelled out her name in Kowalski's clothes on the front lawn, doused them in gasoline and lit them on fire," Pete added after he polished off his last wonton. "Must have been a year before the AVA bald-spot in his grass faded."

"I always said he was lucky it wasn't Elizabeth or he would've had to wear his uniform to go shopping for an entirely new wardrobe." Neil clinked bottles with Asa and Pete.

"What did he do, cheat on her?" Stephanie asked.

"We had an away game the same weekend as her favorite band was playing here in Phoenix."

"Seriously?"

"Like I said. Crazy." Asa nodded.

"See?" Stephanie pointed at Asa. "Even more reason he should give Claire a chance. Shhhh...he's coming back." She turned her warning finger on Neil. "And I'm not giving up on this."

"Oh, trust me. I know."

"I swear, if y'all are still talking about my girlfriends, I'm going to let the whole defensive line blitz y'all next game." Gramps slid back into his seat.

"Nope. Definitely not." Neil shook his head.

"We took you very seriously, man." Asa added. "We're just uh...about to watch Pete do a magic trick, right?"

Pete sat up at attention, patting down his suit pockets. "Oh, yeah. I have some cards here somewhere and, uh, Stephanie wanted to help me practice the, um, Triumph card trick."

Stephanie looked at Pete blankly.

"Y'all are terrible liars." Gramps rolled his eyes. "Speaking of, I'm starting a weekly poker game and you are all invited."

Pete tapped his cards out onto the table, and Neil leaned into Stephanie. "Don't laugh if he messes it up," Neil whispered. "Cherneski takes his burgeoning magic skills very seriously... But he will definitely mess it up."

"Maybe he wouldn't if he had more supportive friends," she countered. Neil smiled at her; it was adorable the way she came to every players' defense, no matter how jumbo-sized and impervious to insults they were.

"Okay, pick a card, any card." Pete held the fanned-out deck in front of Stephanie so she could see the cards. Neil moved in closer, waiting for her to choose one.

"Get out of here." She pushed Neil back playfully. "Pete asked me." Once she was satisfied no one could see the card she selected, she tapped her finger on it.

"Wonderful choice! Not that I know which one you chose. Obviously I have no idea, as this is a pack of brand new unmarked cards," Pete assured them. "I'll just do the one-handed shuffle, here, that I've been working on, and mix your card back in." Pete applied pressure on the deck of cards he held in one hand. "Super quick and easy," he editorialized, but the way he squinted his eyes and stuck the tip of his tongue out the side of his mouth in concentration contradicted his words.

When Pete pulled back with his index finger while pivoting the back half of the deck around with his thumb, Stephanie leaned away instinctively and Neil casually placed a finger on his lips to smother a laugh. Pete carefully maneuvered one edge of the split deck into the other side using a subtle little see-saw motion until, suddenly, the cards flew up into the air with the force of a shaken bottle of champagne and rained down over everyone at their table and the next one over.

"Crap!" Pete exclaimed. "I really thought I had it that time." He dropped down on his hands and knees, scurrying under the table. Everyone at the table stared at each other, unsure what to do as they listened to Pete obviously flipping over cards beneath them. He gave several grunts of frustration and bumped his back into the table, making all the glasses sway precariously.

“Having a little trouble there, Cherneski?” Gramps leaned over to peer at his friend, whose back half was now sticking out from beneath the table cloth. Pete’s butt swaying back and forth as he searched made Neil thinking of his childhood dog Rambo digging a hole.

“Can I giggle yet?” Stephanie stage whispered to Neil; she looked almost purple from holding it in. Neil nodded to her, his shoulders already shaking in silent sobs of laughter. There was nothing silent about Asa’s laughter, and he kept raising his beer to his lips but not drinking it—probably to avoid choking.

At the tables all around them, people had turned to look at them. Muffled—and not-so-muffled—laughs broke out. One of the players stood up, craning his neck to see. “What the—oh, it’s Cherneski.”

He dropped back into his seat to the laughter of his table-mates.

“Is this your card?” Pete’s head unexpectedly popped up from under the table between Neil and Stephanie’s seats. His face was awash in anticipation and he held up the queen of hearts.

“No.” Stephanie could barely get the word out with a straight face. “I’m sorry.”

“Damn it!” Pete disappeared back under the table again, and Stephanie started laughing so hard tears came out the corners of her eyes.

“Man, while you’re under there, you might wanna see if you can find where you misplaced your dignity.” Asa howled.

“Screw you, Asa, this trick is amazing.”

“That’s one word for it,” Stephanie gasped, wiping at her eyes.

Finally, after collecting all the cards from the floor, Pete stood back up and started pawing through the cards still on their table.

At that moment, a regal looking older woman—Neil suspected she was probably a relative of the Ingram’s—stood up and cleared her throat loudly. “Excuse me.”

She held aloft her dessert dish, where a card stood, one corner embedded in the whipped cream like the cherry on top of a sundae.

A roar of laughter erupted from the guests watching, which by this point had grown to half the room.

“Aha! Thank you, Madame!” Pete gave her a formal bow and took the dessert from her hands. Whirling around, he presented the plate to

Stephanie with a flourish, like a waiter offering a fine bottle of wine. "Is this your card?"

"Yes!" Stephanie did her best delighted and amazed expression, but Neil wasn't buying it.

"That is some trick, man—let me get you a drink." Gramps stood, patted Pete on the back and they turned to the bar. "You'll have to show my little nephew—he loves magic."

"It's all in the wrist." Cherneski said with pride as they walked away, and the rest of the room settled back into conversation.

"Was that actually your card?" Neil leaned into Stephanie conspiratorially.

"No!" She burst out laughing again. "But I didn't want to take the chance he'd try it all over again. He could've put that fancy woman's eye out. Do you think he could tell I was lying?" She chewed on her bottom lip in the way Neil had always found so sexy.

"I think your secret is safe." He nodded his head at Pete who was talking excitedly to the bartender and waving his arms wildly in a pantomime of the trick.

"This has been really fun so far." Stephanie wrapped her hands around Neil's arm and rested her cheek on his shoulder. Her face was bright, her eyes glowing.

"You say that like you're surprised." Neil grinned.

"I don't know. I guess I kind of am. Usually these parties seem so extravagant and flashy and filled with people bragging and trying to impress each other. But it's been fun just goofing off and relaxing over here with your friends."

"Ty was always the life of the party, but it did get hard to keep up with him sometimes. I can drink most people under the table, but even I couldn't hang in a drinking contest with Ty." Neil laughed, remembering how rowdy they used to get when he tried.

"You could hang better than I could! Three drinks and I was done."

"And he was just getting started." Neil finished. "He was damn entertaining, though."

"Yeah… of course, I'm not sure anything has ever made me laugh as hard as Pete crawling around on all fours."

"See! I told you that you just had to give him a chance."

"And you were right. He's definitely not someone I would've made friends with on my own, but I think he is growing on me."

"He does that. Like an invasive species."

"But in a good way." Stephanie added.

The band started at nine, and from then on Stephanie used all of her many charms to keep Neil on the dance floor as much as she could. Neil made a token protest about his lack of dance skills, but in fact he didn't mind. He enjoyed the time with Stephanie in his arms, their bodies brushing against each other. His thoughts went automatically to other times they had been even closer, and he couldn't help but remember the way her soft skin felt against his when there was no clothing between them. Neil gathered her tighter in his arms with each dance, letting his head rest on the top of her hair as they transitioned into a slow song.

Once, when they returned to the table, Pete asked Stephanie to dance, and Neil watched her walk away with the burly linebacker. A faint smile hovered on his lips. Cherneski had two left feet on the dance floor—although it never stopped him from getting out there—but Stephanie was floatingly graceful. Neil enjoyed watching her like this, unobserved. He was able to drink in the tender line of her throat, the glossy spice of her hair, the exquisite angles and curves of her body. Lord, she was beautiful.

Neil couldn't remember ever being this happy. It was as if everything he'd always wanted had been suddenly dropped at his feet. Stephanie was as lovely, as warm, as passionate as he'd always dreamed—and more. Once Neil had believed that he loved her as much as it was possible to love anyone, but now he knew he'd been wrong. Every moment he was with her he fell more deeply in love. There were aspects to her personality that he had never guessed—secret desires, fears and hopes. And everything he found out about her made him love her all the more.

There was only one imperfection in all his bliss: Stephanie didn't love him. She enjoyed his company and their very healthy sex life; she cared for him a lot. But she didn't love him in the all-consuming way that he loved her. Neil tapped his fingers on the table. He wasn't used to not winning. Whatever he wanted, he went after and usually got. It would be the same here. It had to be.

Chapter Thirteen

They left long before the party ended, more anxious to be alone than to enjoy the good food, drinks and conversation. As Neil drove home, Stephanie snuggled against him, resting her head on his arm, one hand spread across his thigh.

Suddenly, the wheel jerked under Neil's hand and a loud sound like a firecracker exploding came from below the passenger side of his car. Much as he loved the Stingray, the power steering was less than ideal—even without a flat tire, which he now most definitely had.

"Did a tire just blow-up?" Stephanie's eyes were wide as Neil checked her side mirror to make sure he could pull off the highway. Thankfully they were on the less frequently traveled road near his house. There wasn't much of a shoulder here, but there was far less traffic. That'd make it slightly less dangerous to change the tire of a dark colored car on a road with no streetlights. Neil rolled slowly until he found a stretch of desert off the road that was bare of any cacti, enabling him to pull further away from the highway.

"Are you calling Triple A?" Stephanie asked.

"Nah. I have my spare and all the tools in the trunk. I'll be done before they could even make it all the way out here."

Neil threw his jacket and tie in the back of the car and rolled up his sleeves.

"You're going to get your white shirt all dirty." Stephanie wiggled her eyebrows suggestively. "You could just take it off."

"Do you have some secret mechanic fetish?"

"Um, what girl doesn't? That's like a nurse or stewardess to guys."

Neil gazed into her eyes as he slowly undid each button. At first Stephanie giggled, but by the time he tossed his shirt on the rest of the pile of clothes she was no longer laughing. "So, are you observing?" He opened his door and pulled the latch to release the trunk.

"Oh, I'm definitely following those abs wherever they go." She trailed him around to the trunk. Neil left both the inside dome light and the headlights on to break up the inky darkness of the desert night. Too bad it wasn't a full moon.

"Do you need help?" Stephanie asked.

"Since the Stingray is so low to the ground and the tire is completely blown, I'm going to have trouble even getting the car high enough to get the jack under it. I'll need to drive the flat up on something, then jack it up on the frame rail in front of the vertical door gap."

"You know that what you just said meant about as much to me as when you describe a specific play the team is working on, right?"

"If you could find me a large rock while I unload my tools that would help me out. Preferably a rock without any sharp edges, and one end higher than the other."

"Luckily we are in a desert with a lot of big rocks." Stephanie wandered further away from Neil. "Though, I'm not sure how many ramp-rocks I'll be able to locate."

Neil got out the tools and laid them out next to the car on the passenger side.

"Here! It looks like a big wedge of cheese." Stephanie stood a few yards away pointing down at her find. "There's no way I can pick it up though."

Neil came over and slid a hand around her tiny waist, pulling her close against his bare chest. Her soft dress brushed his nipples and he could feel every inch of his body responding to her.

"Thank you. You are my good luck charm." He bent his head to hers as she smiled up at him. Neil kissed her curving lips, then released her. Heaving the rock up carefully so as not to tweak his elbow, he positioned it under the flat before getting back in the car to drive up on it.

"What else can I do?" Stephanie asked Neil after he got back out.

"This isn't NASCAR so I don't have the equipment to team-change a tire." He gave her a quick kiss on the forehead, "Much as I appreciate your offer." Neil started the process of jacking up the car to get enough clearance to insert the jack stands under the frame. "It'll take me fifteen minutes, twenty tops. Just relax, play a game on your phone or something, and I'll be done before you know it."

It only took him about ten to get the new tire on, and he was already tightening the first bolt when Stephanie came back over to where he was crouching in front of the spare. "My phone died. I forgot to charge it before the party. And now I'm bored."

Neil shook his head, not looking away from his work. "I'm sorry my manly show of skill isn't enough to entertain you." He laughed. "But I'm almost done here." He started tightening the next bolt.

"Maybe you can help me be less bored." Stephanie, behind him, ran her hands through his hair as he gave the bolt a hard turn.

"That feels good." Neil stopped what he was doing and let his eyes close as he concentrated on her fingers working into his scalp. She massaged further down his neck and then slid her arms around to his front. Leaning forward, she ran her hands over his chest, then rolled one of his nipples between her delicate fingers. He opened his eyes and spun around on his knees so his back was to the spare tire. Stephanie was bent at the waist and her dress gaped open so he could see the sheer lacy thing she'd been wearing earlier when he arrived at her house.

Neil groaned low in his throat and grabbed her by the hips then turned them both back around, pressing Stephanie against the side of his car, right over the wheel well. The tire could wait. He pushed her back so she was sitting on the side of the hood. Neil wrapped his hands around her ankles, spreading her gorgeous legs and positioning himself between them. Her nails bit into his shoulders as he slid one hand under her skirt and pushed the flimsy lace to one side.

"God, you're wet." He shoved her skirt all the way up as he ran a trail of kisses up her thigh.

"Must be that mechanic thing." She was obviously going for a light tone, but her breath caught in her throat as Neil's mouth found his mark. Stephanie braced her hands against the hood of the car and Neil concentrated on the button of pleasure at her center, alternating between lashing his tongue and drawing her into the cavern of his mouth. He added a finger and Stephanie tightened her grip on the car. Neil smiled against her softness. He hoped she left fingernail marks on the Stingray. He didn't care about the paint job. He just wanted her to lose her mind.

Stephanie moaned and grabbed Neil's head as he added another finger. She grasped at his hair, pulling and twisting in a way that sent sparks through him. Neil grew harder, straining against his tuxedo pants, pulsing with need, but he took his time, making Stephanie moan and whimper. She writhed over his mouth, moving her hips in the same rhythm as his tongue. Slowly, Neil built up speed until his tongue and his fingers had brought her right up to the line. She squeezed him with her thighs. "I'm so close, Neil." Just hearing Stephanie say his name like that, so full of passion, pushed Neil into high-gear.

"Not yet." His mouth left her, but he kept his hand moving against her, though slightly slower.

"Neil, I need it. I need you." Stephanie's hands roamed over him desperately, down his bare chest and squeezing him through his pants.

Neil let out a growl. His body was thrumming with anticipation and he stood, pressing himself hard into her, lifting her ass up with one arm and using the other to guide her to wrap her long legs around his waist.

"We going somewhere?" Stephanie laughed.

"I want to see you." Neil walked to the front of the car and sat down on the hood with Stephanie on top of him.

"We're going to crush the jack things."

"They'll be fine. And I don't really care right now. All I want is to be inside of you." He shifted to pull a condom from his pants pocket under Stephanie's leg.

"Did you set this whole thing up?" Stephanie narrowed her eyes playfully.

"I was actually thinking we might sneak off to the bathroom at the party or something." He grinned.

"This, under the stars? Way better." Stephanie pulled his belt open with a ferocity that told him she'd had about as much foreplay as she could take. He knew exactly how she felt.

Neil leaned back on his elbows, watching Stephanie slowly roll the condom down. As she lowered her warm, tight body onto him, he let out an involuntary groan and grabbed her face with both hands. He kissed her hard, his fingers digging into her hair, destroying the updo. She reached back and with a little twist of her hand, her hair came tumbling down around her shoulders.

"God, you are sexy." Neil grated out.

He did his best to keep the rhythm of his hips slow, letting her orgasm build again, filling her with as much anticipation as he felt, but with the cold steel of the car under him, the velvet sky of stars above and Stephanie moving on top of him, it was almost impossible to keep a coherent thought in his head. He kissed her again, capturing her bottom lip with his teeth and sucking it into his mouth. He breathed in her breath. There was nothing in the world but Stephanie.

She was the most beautiful thing he had ever seen. Neil watched her eyes flutter closed, saw the hint of moisture on her bottom lip shining in the beam of the headlights. He was on her lips. Neil savored the feeling of being inside her and he knew that she was inside him, too. Under his skin. A part of the marrow in his bones. He wanted her there, entwined with his very matter. He wanted to be even closer to her; to capture some small part of her so that it could never leave him. Stephanie rocked her hips faster and Neil let his hands wander. He pushed the skirt of her dress even higher, finding the small spot between her legs again, spurring her on. He wanted to leave his imprint on her, too.

"Oh, Neil." Her head tilted back, her graceful neck paler than normal in the headlights, her red highlights sparking like embers. She was fire and light and warmth and everything Neil had ever wanted and so much more than he could've dreamed.

Stephanie's nipples strained against the cloth still covering them. With one hand still working to bring her ever higher, Neil let his other one slip beneath the neckline of her dress and the lace of her bodysuit. The feel of her supple breasts and pointing nipples almost sent him over the edge, but he held on, coaxing her. Her nipple got harder as he squeezed it and he brought her to him, yanking the top of her dress down so he could draw her breast into his mouth.

"Oh, my God." Stephanie's voice was loud, splitting the night air.

Neil studied her as his tongue played across her nipple: her head was thrown back, eyes closed, lips parted sensually. A warm breeze caressed his skin. They were outside where anyone could come upon them… Stephanie was now almost totally naked, but she didn't care… She was grinding her hips into him with abandon as he teased her nipple with his teeth. Neil wanted it to go on forever, but he could feel her tightening around him and her movements sped up even more.

Neil was quickly losing all semblance of control, gripping her dress where it was bunched up around her waist and bucking his hips as he thrust hard into her. Stephanie cried out with pleasure as a fierce groan was torn from Neil's throat. Then the waves rolled through her body, pulling him with her and over the brink. Stephanie collapsed on his chest, panting hard and murmuring soft words he couldn't quite make out.

"That was…" She looked up into his eyes. "I have no words."

"It was certainly my favorite flat tire ever." Neil grinned, wrapping her hair around his hand and pulling her down for a long kiss.

* * *

Stephanie shifted the overflowing file which lay in her lap. It contained print-outs of all the email responses from people involved in the Willoughby kidnapping and subsequent investigations and trials. It also held her transcribed notes from those who had granted interviews. She was going through the file, weeding out the terse and suspicious replies—as well as the obvious lies—from the useful material.

She lifted her eyes from her task and glanced across the room at Neil. He lay on the sofa, feet up on one end and head on the other, looking intently at the iPad propped up on his chest. Studying diagrams of plays, he was utterly absorbed. Stephanie had thought she was good at focusing on something to the exclusion of all else, particularly when she was reading, but Neil made her concentration seem laughable.

She watched him, a smile hovering on her lips. The past two weeks had been close to perfect. Since she and Neil were already good friends, there hadn't been much of the 'discovering annoying habits and personality quirks,' that so often came along with the good parts of the beginnings of a relationship. They knew the subjects they enjoyed talking about with each other, and their senses of humor matched. And whenever they were together, sexual excitement bubbled just beneath the surface. Neil's sheer hunger for Stephanie was more seductive than anything Stephanie had ever known. She'd always thought she was more warmly affectionate than she was sexual. But with Neil she discovered that her warmth was not limited. She had a deeply passionate side which only he'd been able to bring to the surface.

They had spent every night together except for the Friday and Saturday of the previous week, when the team had flown out of town for a game. Stephanie had missed Neil those two days more than she would have thought possible. It was odd. With Ty she had preferred out-of-town games because she didn't have to endure his pregame nerves and bad temper. She frowned and studied Neil more sharply. There wasn't a sign of nerves in his whole limp body. She sat forward with interest. "Hey," she began, "Neil…" She cleared her throat with deliberate loudness when he didn't glance up from the football film he was watching. "Mr. Moran."

Neil looked up questioningly. "What?"

"Are you really not nervous or are you just good at hiding it?"

"Hiding what?" He frowned, puzzled.

"The tension, the fear, the excitement—you know, about the game tomorrow."

"Oh." His brow cleared. "I'm as excited as you can get about an ordinary game after years of playing. Tomorrow morning sometime I'll start pumping adrenaline. No point in wasting it today."

Stephanie chuckled. "You're the only person I've ever met who can turn off your adrenaline because it's pointless."

"Pretty cold-blooded, huh?" Neil grinned and sat up, bracing his elbows on his knees. "It's not that I don't get excited. I do. I love football. But I've learned to channel the tension into something more constructive than jumping with nerves the day before a game." He gestured with his hands as he tried to explain. "When I was in high school, I'd get so high on anticipation that I couldn't sleep the night before. I'd charge through Friday and not remember a thing I learned in class. It was okay in high school, but in college, I couldn't pour out that much energy and still compete on the field. Everybody else was too good. One day, when I was all charged up before a game, one of my friends kept taunting me. It was about something so stupid that now I can't even remember what it was, but because I was all amped, I slammed my fist into a metal locker and broke my little finger. I couldn't play the next day. That's when the coach took me aside and explained I was killing my own game. After that I made it my mission to learn how to relax."

"You mean deep breathing and all that?"

"Yeah. Focusing my mind on something else. The excitement's still there, but I bundle it up and set it aside until it's useful."

Stephanie shook her head. "You're amazing; I could never do that. Are you able to get rid of the fear that way, too?"

"What fear?" Neil looked faintly puzzled and then his expression cleared. "You mean, why am I not pale and sweating and throwing up like Ty?"

"Yeah. He was awful to be around the day before a game. One minute he'd tell me how he had run this cornerback into the ground last time they played each other, then the next minute he'd worry that the other guy had gotten better or that he himself had lost his speed…"

"…or a hundred other things," Neil finished for her. "Sure. That was Ty. He had a real love/hate relationship with football. He was an impressive player, but he was filled with insecurities. I have some of that fear—I suspect anyone who performs does. Actors, singers, athletes. Don't writers? You know—what if I fail? What if they hate it? What if I've been fooling myself all these years and I don't really have any talent?"

"Yeah," Stephanie admitted. "Sometimes when I sit down at the computer to start writing, I'm absolutely frozen with fear, and I think of a hundred other occupations I should have pursued instead."

"I think it's pretty natural." Neil agreed. "I have it, too, but not to the extent Ty did. Maybe because I wasn't as naturally gifted and had to work for it more. I know if I practice enough, if I concentrate, lay the foundation, it'll be there for me to fall back on—the muscle memory, the hours of sweat. I wonder if, when it just comes easily, it makes you question it more. Like it's an act of God, and the first time you screw up, you think that's it, I'm finished, there's nothing I can do to get it back."

"That makes sense." Stephanie nodded. "If you feel like it was handed to you, it might feel like it could also be taken away."

"See, when I screw up, I know that I've done it a hundred times before and I just have to try again and I'll get it right." Neil tilted his head considerimgly. "Plus, Ty could never achieve enough for his father. You know how his old man was."

"To be honest, all I really know is the stuff Ty told me. His dad never talked to me all that much. I got the feeling he didn't think I was very interesting."

"Trust me, it had nothing to do with you. The only thing he considered a suitable hobby was golf, and even that didn't really matter. Football was all that counted, and being the best at it was all that was acceptable. Ty never loved football in the same way I did. He didn't feel the sheer excitement of playing, of pitting yourself against the other team. It wasn't a game for him, but a way of proving himself over and over. He was always afraid he wouldn't measure up."

Stephanie had assumed that Ty's feelings about football were natural, that Neil, too, looked on the game more as an enemy than a friend. She understood now that wasn't true. Neil's eyes lit up when he talked about the game. "You genuinely love football, don't you?"

"Sure." He sounded surprised, as if anything else was impossible. "It's pretty much been my life since I was little. I love playing and planning. Competition. Winning."

"But what about all the injuries?" Stephanie's stomach was a knot of nerves every time the offense was on the field, and she cringed whenever Neil got sacked. "Your arm—the sprained this or the broken that. I've seen you play with cracked ribs."

"Yeah, that was no fun. But injuries are part of the game. You try to avoid them, but they're going to happen. You just have to work through them."

"I don't understand you. Aren't you scared when those guys are coming at you to slam you to the ground? It's dangerous."

"Sure." He shrugged. "But the danger's part of the fun, isn't it?"

Stephanie rolled her eyes, and said with mock disdain, "Men."

Neil laughed. "I know it can't go on forever. I'll have to give up football in a few years. And I'll be able to live without it. But I'll keep playing as long as I can. I don't intend to retire until I have to."

"Then I hope that day's a long, long way off." Stephanie crossed the room to kneel beside the couch and nestle her head against his chest. His arms curled around her. He bent his head to kiss her hair.

"I want Claire to be as happy as I am right now. "

Neil groaned. "Don't tell me you were really serious about getting her and Gramps together."

"Why not? He's a great guy, and he has his life together. But with the motorcycle, the tattoos and his past problems, he's still interesting enough that Claire won't think he's totally dull and predictable. And he could obviously use a more stable girlfriend."

"A: I'm not one hundred percent sold on Claire's stability. And B: what makes you think Gramps wants a more stable girlfriend? Maybe he likes coming to the rescue of girls that can't stay out of trouble."

"There is still plenty he can rescue about Claire. And she won't light his clothes or his lawn on fire if they break up. Please? What would it hurt?"

"I don't know. Maybe nothing. I'm not sure why, but I can't picture Gramps and Claire together. Still, I guess it's a decision for the two of them, not me—and not you either." Neil gave Stephanie a pointed look.

"I won't push, promise! We'll just get them together, all have dinner and see what happens."

"What if 'what happens' is it is a date from hell and we're stuck in it with them?"

"We can lessen the tension then; make it easier on them."

"I'm not worried about making it easier on them—I want it to be easier on me." Neil laughed.

"Please…" Stephanie batted her eyelashes in a comically exaggerated manner.

"It'll have to be casual; I can't see Gramps agreeing to a setup. He's never hurting for dates and that's a lot to ask of a guy who can easily find a woman on his own."

"Yeah. We'll have to make it seem natural, not like a blind date." Stephanie sat up straighter as she clearly started scheming. "I'll invite Claire over to have dinner with the two of us—she's dying to know more about you so I'm sure she'll come. Then, that same day, I'll drop you off at practice in my car and you can bum a ride home with Gramps."

Home. Neil smiled to himself; he liked the way she considered where she lived his home.

"While you're driving you can tell him I'm cooking and ask him to eat with us to thank him for the ride," Stephanie continued. "Couldn't that work?"

"It could. Gramps doesn't live far from your house, so it would seem natural. But are you sure you really want to get into this?"

Stephanie grinned. "Yes, I really do. I've never been a matchmaker, but I feel so happy that I'm almost overflowing. I want to share it with my friend. I want to give Claire a chance at what we've got. Does that make sense?"

Neil's smile was slow and brought warmth to his dark eyes. "Yeah. It makes sense. And it makes me very happy."

Chapter Fourteen

Looking back on it, Stephanie realized that she should have known her arranged meeting between Claire and Gramps had all the ingredients for disaster. But she was too cheerful to consider it. She invited Claire for Wednesday evening, and Claire accepted eagerly, elated at the chance to get to know Neil Moran better. Stephanie drove Neil to the practice field that morning, setting the stage for Gramps to bring him back to her place. She quit work early to tidy up and start dinner, careful not to fix anything elaborate. It was, after all, supposed to be an ordinary dinner with a close friend. When the doorbell rang she realized there was one problem with setting it up that way.

Claire, normally obsessed with fashion and makeup, stood on Stephanie's doorstep completely barefaced, with three star-shaped yellow acne stickers on her forehead. Her platinum blond bob looked like she'd slept on it wet and it had dried smushed flat on one side and wildly bushy on the other. Stephanie had never known Claire not to dress with flair—even if it was just a casual outfit for running to the store. But today she had on an oversized T-shirt and sweatpants—that she usually wore when bleaching her hair, judging by the random splotches of yellowish white on the heather gray fabric—and checkerboard Vans that had almost as many holes in them as they did black and white squares.

Claire walked past Stephanie, not noticing the stunned expression on Stephanie's face. Gramps didn't seem at all judgmental, but once Claire saw how cute he was and figured out what was going on, she was going to be so pissed at Stephanie for not giving her any warning. Stephanie glanced at her phone, wondering if Claire would have time to run home and back if she told her the plan now. Of course, Claire was running late, and the guys would be here any minute. And as soon as Stephanie clued her in to the real setup, Claire might be so furious she wouldn't return. Stephanie chewed on her lip. Whatever. She'd just have to hope that her friend would eventually forgive her. Maybe Gramps would like the little acne stickers; he liked tattoos so it wasn't totally out of the realm of possibility. Was it?

Claire, who had flopped down on the living room couch, let out a groan. "God, what a headache!" she rubbed her temples. "To tell you the truth, I almost cancelled tonight, but my curiosity was stronger than my headache. I decided, what the hell, Neil won't be interested in looking at me with you here, so I'll go as I am. It's been one hell of a day. I took four aspirins this afternoon, and they haven't made a dent. Do you think it's a migraine?"

"I don't know. I've never had one. I could fix you a drink. Or would that make it worse?"

"No clue. Let's find out. Maybe it'll stop the pain—or send me to the hospital where I can get the really good drugs," Claire cracked.

Stephanie returned to her kitchen and mixed two vodka sodas. She came back and sat down across from Claire. Claire took a sip and sighed. "At least it tastes good, even if it doesn't cure my headache. You wouldn't believe the problems I had today." She began to recount the multitude of things that had gone wrong at the theater and at home as she nursed her cocktail. "Mmm, I'm beginning to feel a little better. Maybe another couple of drinks and I'll feel human… or I'll slide off your couch and pass out under your coffee table."

Suddenly Stephanie jumped to her feet. "Oh, no, the casserole! I was supposed to turn off the oven and let it sit for fifteen minutes." She ran to the kitchen and pulled out the dish, burning her fingers where her old oven mitt had gotten thin. She sucked on the burned fingers as she lifted the lid and peered inside. Not burned, but definitely scorched around the edges. Well, if she cut off the outside of the casserole and served it with vegetables and a salad, maybe no one would notice. She grabbed a bag of frozen broccoli out of the freezer and was washing lettuce when she heard the slamming of car doors. Neil was here. She went back out to the living room, arriving just as Neil stepped inside, Gramps behind him…and right behind Gramps was Pete Cherneski.

Stephanie, who had been stepping forward to kiss Neil hello, froze in her tracks. "Hey, Stringer," Neil began a little stiltedly. "I invited Gramps and Pete in for drinks since they gave me a ride home. Hope you don't mind."

"No, of course not," Stephanie managed to get out. "Hello, Gramps, that was sweet of you to drive Neil. And Pete! Come in, everybody, and sit down." She led them into the living room where Claire still sat. Maybe Neil's offer of drinks would work best. There was no way her casserole would feed three football players, especially given the amount of food she'd seen Pete Cherneski put away.

She turned to Claire with a bright smile. "Claire, this is Justin Kowalski. He gave Neil a ride home. And this is Pete Cherneski. They both play on the Pumas with Neil."

Claire looked up and smiled charmingly. "Hello, nice to meet you both."

"Claire's a good friend of mine," Stephanie explained. "She runs a new theater here."

"Movies?" Pete asked, irritating Stephanie by plunking himself down on the couch beside Claire, leaving Gramps to the chair. How had Pete gotten involved in this? Stephanie had started to like him at the party—even if he was either strangely literal or his delivery was so dry that she didn't get half his jokes. And Pete was good-looking in a rough sort of way. But at the moment he was royally messing with her plans.

Claire had already turned to him and was explaining her work when Pete cut her off mid-sentence. "Do you have stars stuck to your forehead?"

"Oh, God." Claire held up her hand, shielding her forehead from his view. "I'd completely forgotten."

"I like it. I have a niece that paints rainbows on my face—and also on anything I happen to leave at my sister's place."

"I wasn't expecting Neil to have friends with him," Claire narrowed her eyes at Stephanie. "And then Steph made me a drink and… you know how that goes. They're actually acne stickers."

"That's cool." Pete broke into a grin. "They help? I get that under my helmet in the heat. Maybe you could text me a link to where you found them."

"Sure." Claire whipped out her phone. "Here, give me your number, and I'll do it now."

Stephanie took a deep breath. Never in a million years would she have guessed this blind date would include Pete Cherneski and Claire exchanging beauty tips. Stephanie turned to Gramps.

"What can I get you to drink?"

"A scotch neat?" Gramps looked at her questioningly.

"I have scotch, so that's no problem."

"I'll take bourbon if you have it, Steph," Pete volunteered. "The cheaper the better. Reminds me of my younger days."

"I used to drink only bottom shelf in college so people wouldn't guess my family had money," Claire offered.

What was going on here? Claire was usually embarrassed about her family's wealth. She certainly hadn't told Stephanie about it until she'd known her for a while—and here she was spilling about it to Pete Cherneski at first sight?

"You couldn't pay me to drink it now, though," Claire went on.

"Not even for old time's sake? Come on, we can pretend we're twenty-one and have no sense." Pete waggled his eyebrows.

"Why not?" Claire giggled. "I'm already half-sloshed drinking on an empty stomach. Stephanie, my dear, two of your not-finest bourbons."

"I don't have any bottom shelf liquor," Stephanie replied "But I can put some vinegar in your drinks if that'll help."

The cheap bourbon duo cracked up laughing.

"That's not a no." Gramps pointed out.

"Neil, can you help me?" Stephanie asked in her sweetest voice.

Stephanie marched into the kitchen and straight across to the farthest corner of the room. She turned. "What is going on?" she whispered indignantly.

"So far it seems like your friend Claire is acting weird—or normal for her, I guess, since she was pretty strange the first time I met her—" Neil teased. "And she's also coming off like a borderline alcoholic. Odd strategy, but maybe it'll make Gramps think she's his type?"

"It's not a strategy! She had no idea about Gramps. Still doesn't—I wasn't coaching her! This is such a disaster. Claire had a headache and was a little loopy before the drink. I probably should have made her a weaker drink. Or a smaller one. Or both." Stephanie chewed on her lip. "But we can get to my screw up later. Currently we're discussing the train-wreck that hitched a ride to your wagon. And by that, I mean Pete."

"Oh, wow, that was mixing at least two metaphors—I'm not even sure, it was so convoluted. You must be really upset." Neil pulled her to him in a hug, laughing into her hair.

"Don't laugh! Pete could eat anyone out of house and home. I'll have to get a second mortgage just to restock my pantry and fridge. Why is he here?"

"I guess I'm not cut out for intrigue." Neil shrugged. "I asked Gramps to drop me off, and Cherneski was standing there. He heard me and said he needed a ride too. What could I say? 'No, you can't come because Stephanie's trying to lure Gramps into a trap?' I figured you'd rather have Gramps with Cherneski along than not at all, so I invited them to come in for a drink."

Stephanie sighed. "You're right. I can't blame you. This is all my fault. I'm afraid Claire is going to be so mad at me. And now I'll never get another chance to set her up. Then I burned the casserole. And my hand. And then—" She looked over at the counter where the package of frozen broccoli sat in a puddle of water. "Oh, crap. Now the vegetables are going to be super mushy."

Neil laughed again and pulled her closer. "Everything is going to be okay. I will make everyone's drinks. Claire doesn't seem to be pissed off at all. The guys won't cry over not having vegetables. Pete likes any food that's free, remember? You can use the melting broccoli to ice your hand so at least it's not a total waste. Go sit down and relax and I'll bring you a drink, too."

"Sans vinegar?" Stephanie threw him a sparkling smile. Neil really was the best.

"For you, definitely. I can add a bit to Pete's though, if it'll make you feel better."

"Maybe a smidge." She laughed and leaned her head against his shoulder. "He probably wouldn't even notice."

"I can guarantee you, he wouldn't."

"I guess that takes all the fun out of it then." Stephanie heaved a mock sigh. "Thanks, Neil. I don't know what I'd do without you."

"Luckily, you don't have to find out." He swatted her on the butt. "Now go relax like I told you to."

"Yes, sir." Stephanie gave him a little salute, but it was ruined by the bag of broccoli clutched in her hand.

Stephanie did her best to shake off any funk and put a smile on her face as she walked back into the living room. "I'm making dinner—would you guys like to stay for some food?"

She didn't add that the quality was not assured. Maybe if she got enough drinks in them no one would even notice.

"Sure," Pete agreed enthusiastically.

With a sinking heart Stephanie watched Gramps shake his head. "Nope, I have to take off. One of my favorite bands is playing at the Blue Shack tonight."

"That old bar is still around?" Claire scrunched up her forehead, wrinkling her star stickers. "I thought it closed while I was off at school."

"Nope. Still there. It's become a friendly neighborhood biker bar these last few years." Gramps took a swig of the scotch Neil handed him.

"I don't know what Gramps would do if they closed. That's his favorite place in Phoenix." Neil said as he handed Stephanie a fresh vodka soda.

"Who is Gramps?" Claire pointed at him. "I thought your name was Justin. And you're my age, right?"

"Yeah. Football nickname." He shrugged.

"He's old for a player." Pete explained.

"So you're like models, over the hill before you're thirty-five?"

"I don't know much about models, but that sounds about right." Gramps nodded.

"What band is playing at the Blue Shack?" Stephanie asked, trying to keep a bit of conversation going between the two. Claire loved performance art as well as theater, and live music was a close third.

"This metal band, Gatecreeper."

"Oh." Stephanie leaned back in her chair. That was definitely not Claire's kind of music.

"Sounds interesting." Claire said, but it came out more like a question. "I don't know much about metal. But I love jazz and swing music."

"Really?" Pete looked entranced. "I did cotillion with my sister when I was a kid, and I was really good at the jitterbug. That's like swing dancing, isn't it?"

"Yes!" Claire giggled. "You'll have to show me later."

Stephanie downed the rest of her drink. Gramps left fifteen minutes later, and Claire excused herself to run to the restroom.

"Wow." Pete was shaking his head as he watched Claire disappear down the hall. "Your friend is super-hot."

"Yes…" Stephanie wasn't entirely sure if Pete was being sarcastic or if he was the type of guy who didn't need makeup and high heels to be able to tell a woman was attractive. "She's extremely pretty."

"And so... unique. You know? She's like an old-school movie star from the thirties. Only without the fancy clothes and caked-on makeup. She's just so cool and authentic."

"She is." Stephanie felt a laugh bubbling up inside her. Everything had gone wrong. And yet somehow, she'd managed to find a guy who was interested in Claire and wasn't even the tiniest bit like her ex-husband. Claire's ex had mainly used her for arm-candy. At least, until he decided he wanted younger arm candy. "I'm glad you're staying for dinner, Pete."

"Me, too." Cherneski grinned.

Belatedly, Stephanie remembered that she had not fixed the salad. By the time it was ready, the casserole was cold as well as burned around the edges. The salad was tasty, at least, although she realized she forgotten tomatoes half-way through eating it.

Claire had gone back into her litany of complaints about the day, but Pete broke in, describing in detail how she could fix her broken garbage disposal without having to wait for her over-priced plumber to have an appointment open. Strangely, Claire seemed to find the idea fascinating. She and Pete continued to knock back drinks and were definitely more than half-drunk when Stephanie got out the prepackaged cheesecake for dessert.

Now that her plumbing problems were apparently solved, Claire had launched into a detailed description of her headache when Pete exclaimed, "All your nerve endings are in your feet, you know."

Claire began to giggle and even Stephanie couldn't help but laugh. Neil didn't seem fazed in the least by Pete's non-sequitur, merely getting a second slice of cheesecake. Obviously, he'd heard Pete's spiel before.

"I'm telling you the truth," Pete protested, and promptly slid off his chair. For a moment Stephanie thought he had passed out, but then she realized that he was under the dining table pulling off Claire's Vans.

"Do all nights with Pete end up with him under a table?" Stephanie stage-whispered to Neil.

"A lot of them," Pete answered from below them. "Now, Claire, this is the trick for next time you have a headache. So pay attention."

Claire sat up straighter and put on what she probably meant to be an alert expression. With as many drinks as she'd had, she looked more like she'd just been pinched.

"Every nerve in our bodies ends somewhere in our feet. You can get rid of headaches, backaches, anything, by massaging your feet. I know. I've studied reflexology." Pete punctuated his words by throwing Claire's no-show socks onto the floor. A few seconds later she came several inches up off her chair and let out a yelp. Pete shifted around, bumping the table, and Neil grabbed the bottle of wine before it spilled all over the cheesecake.

"Nice catch." Stephanie smiled. "I guess you can do more than throw."

"Just looking out for my baby." He winked.

"I would say you're embarrassing me in front of our guests, but I'm not really sure how that would be possible right now."

"Oh, you thought I was calling you my baby?" Neil reached his long arm back to set the wine bottle safely on the kitchen counter. "I was talking about this cheesecake."

Stephanie picked up a crouton from the nearly empty salad bowl and threw it at his head. Even after several drinks his reflexes were good enough that he caught it in his mouth, "Thanks, Stringer."

"I hate you." She scrunched up her face in displeasure.

"No." Neil shook his head confidently. "You really don't."

Stephanie smiled. "Not even a little bit."

"I'm sorry. But I have to see what is going on here." Neil pointed at Claire, whose various sounds and faces were bordering on ecstasy, and he sat down cross-legged on the floor to watch Pete work. Stephanie grabbed her drink and sat beside him on the hard tile, laying her head on his shoulder.

"Well, if nothing else, at least tonight was interesting." She sighed.

"We can always remember the night we all literally drank ourselves under the table," Neil agreed.

"Something to tell the grandkids someday," Stephanie said off-handedly, then suddenly realized the full implication of her words. She glanced over to see if the remark had registered on Neil in the same way, but his face was placid as he watched Pete's performance.

Claire, when she stopped laughing, announced that her head was amazingly better. Stephanie thought to herself that after the number of drinks Claire had consumed, she doubted that Claire could tell if she had a head at all. Claire, now revived, lingered for another hour, and Pete showed no signs of leaving, either.

When Claire rose to go home, Pete stood up too, and turned to Claire. "I was thinking of taking a Lyft home so Neil won't have to go out after he's been drinking. Would you like to ride with me? I live in central Phoenix so I can have them drop you off wherever really easily." He opened up the app on his phone and showed it to her. "And we'll drop you off first so I can make sure you get in safely."

Claire tilted her head, considering the offer. Stephanie agreed that her friend was in no condition to drive home, but she thought she should offer Claire an out, so she told her, "You can also sleep in my office out back if you'd like. You'd have privacy and the couch folds out into a comfy bed."

"Hmmm, I really think I can drive," Claire frowned then looked up into Pete's face and smiled. "But I've never taken a Lyft before. Sounds like a fun way to round out our night of pretending to be twenty-one."

"How have you never taken a Lyft?" Pete asked as he headed toward the door, holding it open for Claire as she hugged Neil and Stephanie goodbye.

"A sad fact from the life of a poor little rich girl." She giggled, then covered her mouth with her hand. "Maybe I am less sober than I thought."

"Perhaps." Stephanie laughed as she closed the door behind them.

They went back to the living room and Neil sank onto the couch, pulling Stephanie into his lap. She leaned against his chest, utterly warm and at home. "I think I'll give up matchmaking."

"It might be a wise idea."

She sighed and snuggled closer. She'd never felt happier in her life. No matter what had happened, everything was all right. Because Neil was there. It came upon her softly; no bolt of lightning or clap of thunder. She didn't feel the least bit nervous. Quite naturally Stephanie nuzzled Neil's neck and murmured, "I love you."

* * *

In the following weeks Neil's time was dominated by football. There weren't only the games, but also practice, workouts, position meetings, and studying tape—it seemed as if half his evenings were spent with Neil bent over his iPad, breaking down opposing teams' defenses. Not to mention all the time he spent in hydrotherapy, ice baths, massage, and electric stimulation to recover from the beating his body took every week. But he spent every other possible minute with Stephanie.

Luckily her work was thriving, too, so she didn't have a ton of time to think about how much she missed Neil when he was doing football stuff. Plus, her brimming emotions for Neil filled her with energy and creativity. And Neil's relationship to her work was different than Ty's had been—he seemed genuinely interested and often asked about it, which was a welcome change.

One evening after practice Neil came in, his face a mask of exquisite calm. "So, Stringer," he casually looped an arm around her shoulders as she sat on the couch reading. "How would you feel about an interview with the Willoughbys?"

Stephanie stared at him, her Kindle dropping from her hands onto the couch. "What? Are you feeling okay? The Willoughbys never give interviews."

He grinned. "I wouldn't be so sure. It seems Bernard Willoughby is a football fan, more specifically a Pumas fan, and even more specifically, a Neil Moran fan."

"You're kidding!"

"Is it that hard to believe?" He wrapped his arm tighter around her and she leaned in to kiss him.

"Of course not." She smiled. "How do you even know this?"

"Russell Ingram knows Bernard Willoughby. The Ingrams sold him the property that he converted into the Fortress. Russell said he'd set up an introduction for me, and I just might be willing to ask Willoughby about an interview with you—if the price is right." Neil arched his eyebrow that was bisected by an old scar.

"You are too cute when you do that. I'm going to utterly fail at these negotiations." Stephanie laughed. "What are your opening terms?"

"Hmmmm… it is a very valuable prize." Neil tapped a finger against his mouth. "How about you cook me dinner every Tuesday and Thursday—topless."

"Dream on." She swatted him with a pillow.

"Oh, I will." He grinned mischievously. "How about sexy Saturdays? You spend the entire day in lingerie."

"That might be a little uncomfortable if I have to run to the grocery store. Also, you're out of town every other Saturday."

"You can always send me photos to remind me of what I'm missing."

"Also not going to happen."

"Fine." He sighed heavily. "You're a much tougher negotiator than you led me to believe." A moment later he perked up. "I've got it."

"What?"

"A kiss every morning even if you're still half-asleep."

"Now that I can do." Stephanie leaned in to give him a preview. "Happily."

"So are you going to the game on Sunday?"

"Of course!" She did her best to keep the smile on her face relaxed.

Stephanie didn't want him to see how much she dreaded going to the games. It was the only thing that had clouded the happiness of these last few weeks. But it wasn't like there was anything that Stephanie could do about it—this was the thing Neil loved: football.

It wasn't about the amount of time it took up—even though that was huge—it was her fear for Neil's safety. Stephanie didn't know how the other wives and girlfriends could stand it. She was like a live wire during every game. Each hit Neil took, she cringed inside, and she would clench her hands so tightly that her nails bit into her flesh until he was up on his feet again. Every game seemed to be harder for her to sit through than the last.

It had been bad enough when she was married to Ty, but it was even worse now. Now she knew what it was like to have the man you loved taken away from you. She understood what it was like to sit in hospitals waiting for the results of surgery. She knew it wasn't the same as it had been with Ty; he had died of something else altogether. But the cause didn't make any difference; the pain would remain the same.

Though she couldn't stand the jangle of nerves when she watched, she wasn't able to ignore the games as she'd done in the past, either. Stephanie wanted to be there for Neil. She knew it was important to him and she couldn't stand not to know what was happening when he played.

Besides, not going to the game wouldn't keep her from seeing the cuts and bruises and him icing his bad elbow when he got home. Hours before the game her stomach would begin to knot, and as the weeks passed the time of her nervousness extended, so that she was now a mess all day Saturday as well as Sunday.

Stephanie hated that she couldn't even talk about it with the person who was closest to her because it would sound like she was nagging Neil. And she was not going to demand that he give up what he loved for her. They would argue, he would refuse and then that would really spoil things. Or he would just give her meaningless reassurances. Neil would retire before too many years; he'd told her that. She just had to wait.

Was she really thinking long term now? That thought made her stomach dance, too, and her mind skittered away from it. She was not going to think about the future. She had learned too well that all she had was the here and now. And here and now she was happy.

But by the time Sunday rolled around, she was a mess again. The morning before the game against the San Diego Sharks, Stephanie did a super-tough yoga session. Well, for someone in her lack-of-shape it was super-tough. Claire probably would have laughed at her panting and sweating all through the video. After that Stephanie went through a relaxation exercise as she drove to the stadium.

The yoga and calming visualization combo was her most recent attempt to get through the games without as much stress. So far, she hadn't seen that it helped. It was November now, and every game was important. But the one today with San Diego was more important than others. The Sharks were the Pumas' biggest rival in their division and were just behind Phoenix in the standings.

Most of the other wives, including Mel, were intent on the game. Stephanie watched closely, too, but all she really cared about was whether the offensive line would hold when Neil stepped into the pocket. In most games, when the blitz got through, Neil was able to escape and complete the pass or throw it away. But today he was sacked twice in the first half.

Late in the third quarter, Neil dropped back and was flattened by a San Diego linebacker. Somehow Asa still managed to come back and catch the fluttering pass. The crowd roared, but Stephanie was unable to speak, unable to move. All she could see was Neil's limp form lying motionless on the field.

Chapter Fifteen

Stephanie stood, frozen, as players turned and started toward Neil and trainers trotted out onto the field. They were followed by the quarterbacks' coach and the team doctor. Then Coach Davis took off his headset and walked out there, too. The crowd that had been roaring was hushed now, all eyes on the motionless figure on the field.

It was her worst nightmare realized. Memories of every player she had seen lying like that raced through her mind as two assistants rushed out with a stretcher and laid it down on the ground beside Neil. Stephanie pressed her hands to her stomach, and Mel Williams wrapped a comforting arm around her. Neil was so still. They knelt on either side of him, immobilizing his neck and lifting him over to the stretcher. The injury cart trundled onto the field as the trainers began to strap Neil down on the stretcher, locking his head and neck in place.

She had to go to him. Stephanie pushed past the wives in the row beside her and started toward the stairs, her thoughts a jumble. She raced up the cement steps and along the hall to the stairs leading down to the tunnel and locker room. As she reached the tunnel, the electric cart crossed her path, heading to the outside door, and she caught a glimpse of Neil's face. His eyes were closed, his normally olive skin sallow. Her heart squeezed in her chest and she couldn't speak. The cart passed her and drove on to the outside doors. She could see an ambulance waiting outside, doors open.

Stephanie's knees were suddenly like water, and she braced herself against the wall, telling herself to breathe. An ambulance at the door didn't mean Neil was going to die.

"Ms. Tyler!" She turned to see a man jogging toward her. Stephanie ran to meet him. She knew the man; he was one of the trainers, though her mind was too numb to recall his name. He reached out and took her arm, saying in a calming voice, "It's all right. Don't worry. He's conscious again, and he moved his feet and arms. We're thinking it's only a concussion."

Only a concussion. How warped were they that being knocked out was considered good news? "Where are they taking him?"

"St. Anthony's."

Stephanie paled. That was where Ty had been.

He hastened to assure her, "It's all right. That's where we always take them. It's a good hospital."

"I know." Stephanie wished her heart believed her words.

"They won't let us in the ambulance," he went on. "Come on, I'll drive you to the hospital. You shouldn't be behind the wheel right now."

Stephanie nodded. She wanted desperately to be with Neil, but demanding that she be let on the ambulance would only slow them down. She let him lead her away. "Thank you, Hal." Right. That was his name.

They followed the ambulance, which hadn't turned on its lights and sirens. That was a good sign, right? Memories of Ty lying in his hospital bed, face drawn and pale, kept running through her head, mingling with her glimpse of Neil on the stretcher.

Hal didn't try to talk, thank God. He pulled in behind the ambulance at the emergency entrance, telling Stephanie he'd park and join them. She jumped out. They had transferred Neil to a gurney, and she glimpsed it rolling in through the wide doors. She hurried after it, ignoring the front desk. Fortunately, they were occupied and didn't glance over at her.

She strode along purposefully, glancing into the open cubicles. She found Neil in the third one. He was sitting up on the examination table, his long legs, still in uniform, dangling over the side. They'd removed his jersey and shoulder pads. A doctor was shining a light in Neil's eyes.

Stephanie stepped into the room and Neil saw her. A sickly grin spread across his face. His usually sharp black eyes were dull and cloudy. "Hey, Stringer. What are you doing here? Where's Ty?"

"Ty?" she repeated in shock, her eyes widening.

"Pretty pass, wasn't it?" he went on, not noticing her stunned expression. "Nobody but my man could catch it, huh?"

The doctor motioned to the nurse beside him, and she hustled Stephanie out of the room. "I'm afraid you'll have to leave, ma'am. Mr. Moran is being examined."

Stephanie let the woman drag her along. She wanted to talk to her. "What's the matter with him? He's talking about Ty as if he were alive. Ty was a teammate that died a year and a half ago."

"Mr. Moran is a little confused right now. It's very common for a concussed patient to exhibit some disorientation," the nurse told her in a soothing voice as she placed Stephanie in a chair. "If you'll wait here, the doctor will let you know Mr. Moran's condition as soon as possible. Are you his wife?"

"No, he's not married. I'm his—" She paused. "Girlfriend" was something she'd been in high school. When life was simple. There was no easy label for what she was to Neil. "We're very close. We've been friends for years."

The nurse smiled and returned to the exam room, pulling the curtains closed. Stephanie stared out the window at the end of the room. Why was Neil talking about Ty as if he'd just thrown a pass to him? Why had his mind chosen that moment to return to? Stephanie glanced down at her hand. It was trembling on the arm of her chair.

She didn't know how long she'd been there—it seemed an eternity—before Hal came up to her. She started to rise, but he motioned her back down. "I went in there, but they kicked me out."

"Yeah, me too. Hal... Neil asked me if Ty was here," she told him, frowning.

He sat down across from her. "I wouldn't think anything about it if I was you. He hasn't lost his mind. I've seen it before. They get hit, and they don't remember what happened right before. Sometimes they wake up thinking they're somewhere else. In some other time. Neil seems to think it's after the Minnesota game three years ago when he threw that unbelievable pass to Ty. Neil had a concussion then too. He'll straighten it out. Neil's tough, the least fragile quarterback I've ever seen."

Hal's words reassured her slightly, but Stephanie couldn't shake the fear. She didn't want Neil to be tough. She wanted him to be safe. Neil had sounded too much like Ty when he was dying. There had been times when

Ty thought Neil was his father or that a nurse was Stephanie. And nothing had been as sharp as the pain of Ty's looking straight at her and not recognizing her. Of course, she knew Neil's confusion was a result of being knocked out. It wasn't caused by a tumor. It didn't mean he was going to die. But... what if there was blood seeping in his brain and they just didn't realize it? Or a blood clot that burst later on?

What if Neil died? What if she lost him? She didn't know what she would do, how she would live. Stephanie realized that she would be much less able to deal with Neil's death than Ty's. She loved Neil so much—more than she had Ty, she realized with shock. Ty had been a very special person, a free spirit. She had always had the vague feeling that he was merely visiting her life. But Neil was a part of her. He was entwined in her life, threaded into the fabric of her very soul. That was why she had been more scared that he would get injured in a game. If Neil were hurt, she hurt also. And if she lost him, she would lose a huge chunk of herself.

Stephanie jumped up, her heart pounding, and began to pace. But when the white-coated doctor emerged from the examining room and walked over to Hal, she scurried back. "…a concussion," he was saying as she came up. "He seems to have the usual symptoms—dizziness, confusion, some loss of memory. I don't think there's anything seriously wrong, but I'd like to keep him under observation for another day or two."

"Thank you, doctor." Stephanie relaxed somewhat.

"Of course, he shouldn't return to football for a while," the doctor went on. "We need to watch for migraines, sensitivity to light, headaches, and so on."

"Yeah, we have a concussion protocol," Hal assured him. "He'll have to pass all the stages and an independent physician's examination before he can get back out on the field." Hal looked worried. Stephanie suspected his frown was more about Neil being unable to play a few games than about how Neil felt. Hal seemed to be an okay guy, but money was what drove management, and that meant winning games.

"May I see him now?" Stephanie asked.

"Yes. They're taking him to the fourth floor. Ask one of the nurses at the desk for his room number."

When she tiptoed into Neil's room a few minutes later, he was lying in bed with his eyes closed. His face was still pale, but when he opened his eyes the dullness was gone. He smiled weakly. "Hi, Steph. Good thing it was just my head that got hit, huh? Otherwise it might have done some damage."

Stephanie frowned and took one of his hands in both of hers. "You don't have to pretend with me."

"I don't? Good. Then I'll admit my head hurts like hell." He paused. "When I first woke up I didn't know where I was. I thought it was that Minnesota game."

"I know."

"I'm sorry if I acted weird." His current tone was still strange to Stephanie. He seemed unpolished, almost childlike. And for some reason it scared her. Maybe because he was always the one in control. He took care of her. She wasn't sure what her role was in this new situation. Or if she was even capable of doing it. She tried her best to look reassuring.

"It's okay," Stephanie told him.

"It was the strangest thing. For just a few minutes there, Ty was alive again in my head. I hope I didn't upset you."

Stephanie forced a bright smile onto her face. "No," she lied. "I just thought—well, there goes Neil again. Doesn't know what's going on."

"Don't make me laugh. My head is killing me."

"I'm sure it is."

"How'd the game end up?"

"Seriously?" Stephanie made an exasperated noise. "You were right—your skull's too thick to damage. Did you think I hung around in the stands while you were being taken out unconscious on a stretcher?"

"I thought you might have checked after you got to the hospital."

"I wasn't in the waiting room watching it on my phone, either." She shook her head. "I was worried then, too."

"I shouldn't be glad you were worried, but I am." Neil smiled, and she returned it tremulously, barely fighting back the tears. It was difficult to act calm and cheerful when inside she was a wreck, but she forced herself to handle it, staying another hour before Asa and Gramps showed up. She gave them both hugs, relieved that they'd come to visit and she could slip away without feeling guilty.

Stephanie was drained, as if she had been working hard for days. She trailed slowly back to the waiting room and plopped down on a chair. She should call for a Lyft since her car was still at the stadium. Or one of the guys would probably be fine with dropping her off. Should she go to the stadium or just go to her house? Working out the logistics of getting home suddenly seemed like a monumental task that she wasn't sure she was up to.

Fortunately, Hal came walking in and said he would take her home and arrange for her car to be driven back to the house. He was as quiet on the drive home as he had been going to the hospital, which Stephanie was also thankful for. She didn't think she could face making chit-chat.

Fully clothed, Stephanie crawled into bed. She was exhausted and though she thought she'd go to sleep immediately even if it was still early in the evening, she found that she couldn't. Adrenaline still coursed through her. She got up and went to her kitchen where she'd left her laptop. She spent the rest of the evening at her kitchen table reading about concussions, brain injuries and neurodegenerative conditions like CTE. Finally, she turned off the computer, her mind swimming with the onslaught of knowledge. Crossing her arms on the table, she laid her head on them. She felt unutterably weary and sad.

I can't do this. Day in, day out. I can't do it.

Neil loved football and had no intention of retiring until he was too old to play anymore. He was in great physical shape. Even though he was thirty, he might stay in football another five years, maybe even more. Tom Brady was still playing at forty. Every year Neil would be out there risking his neck, the entire regular season plus four exhibition games and however-many playoffs, and she would be watching, consumed by fear, praying that he'd make it through one more game. Whenever he was tackled, she'd feel the crash and agonize. More than that, she'd experience once more the heart-stopping terror that this time he wouldn't get up. That this time when she reached the hospital he wouldn't be sitting up, smiling at her. Or that this time, he might not remember who she was. She couldn't stand it. She just couldn't.

Stephanie finally pulled herself up and went to bed, but the same thoughts kept running over and over in her head, interrupted now and then by the heartbreaking thought of what the alternative was to this vision of her future. If she couldn't take it, she would be out of Neil's life. She couldn't bear that thought either. She broke down and cried, sobbing out her fear and anguish.

Stephanie woke up early the next morning and knew she had made her decision. She couldn't continue this. She'd lost one love; she couldn't stand to lose another. Hard as it would be to break up with Neil, it would be far worse later—she fell in love with him more every day. She couldn't do it now, while he was still in the hospital recuperating. She would have to wait until he was better. At least that would give her a few more precious days with him.

A glance in the mirror told her that she looked as dead as she felt inside. Her eyes were puffy and red from her long bout of tears, and her skin was ashen. She showered and dressed, braiding her hair in a single thick rope. Makeup helped her eyes and skin, and a cup of coffee raised her energy level, but her stomach rejected the very idea of food.

When she arrived at the hospital, she met Neil as he was emerging from his room. He was dressed and, other than being pale, he looked much like his normal self. "Stephanie. Hey." He curled his arm around her and kissed her lightly. "You almost missed me. I'm leaving."

"The hospital? You're leaving the hospital? Are you crazy?"

"Can you lower the volume? I feel like I've got about five hangovers this morning."

Hal stepped out of Neil's room behind him, and Stephanie turned on him. "Are you responsible for this?"

The man stared, stopped in his tracks by the cold fury glittering in Stephanie's usually warm blue-gray eyes. "Wha—" he began to stutter.

Neil came to his rescue. "Don't blame him, Steph. He just happened to be here when I checked out. Otherwise I'd have gone home in a Lyft."

"The doctor wanted to keep you here for another day," Stephanie argued, suddenly furious at Neil's lackadaisical attitude toward his injury. "You could have bleeding or your brain might swell."

Neil shook his head, then winced at the pain. "The doctor said this morning that there wasn't any sign of that. I'm fine. I promise."

"Did he say it was all right for you to leave?"

"He said I didn't have to stay."

Stephanie snorted. "More likely he said he couldn't keep you from killing yourself if you were bound and determined to do it." She released a long sigh. "All right. I give up. You'll do exactly what you want, no matter the risk. Come on, I'll drive you home."

Neil turned to Hal with a smile. "Sorry. I just got a better offer."

"Can't say I blame you," Hal returned jokingly, but he kept a wary eye on Stephanie and gave her a wide berth as he left. He called over his shoulder, "See you in a couple of days."

"A couple of days?" Stephanie whirled to face Neil. "You're going back to football in a couple of days?"

"I don't know. I have to follow the concussion protocol."

Stephanie rolled her eyes. "Oh, right, the precious protocol. I read about the NFL protocol last night. In colleges, you have to wait a week after you've had your last symptom before you can even go back to mild exercise. Yours? It's basically, well, as soon as you say your symptoms are gone, you go back to exercise, and if you still feel okay, then you step it up to aerobic exercise, and so on for, like, 5 stages, and then you're back out on the field. Somebody like you—you can suck it up and say you feel fine, and you can be back by the next game."

"Well, it's more than that," he replied, his voice irritatingly reasonable. "You have to be examined by the team doctor and an independent doctor, and they both have to give their okay."

Stephanie let out an exasperated noise. "Don't. Just don't." She turned and stalked off to the elevator. She could hardly believe Neil's careless attitude, but it certainly justified the decision she'd made last night. Here she was in a mess of turmoil over his safety, and Neil didn't even seem to care. He certainly wasn't thinking about how it affected her—how worried she was about him. He'd go back to playing despite the doctor, despite her, despite everything.

Neil followed her and slid one arm around her shoulders, bending down to whisper in her ear, "I'm all right, Stringer. Really. This happened to me before, and I know what I can and can't do. I'm not an idiot. I promise I won't hurt myself."

"It's pointless to argue." Stephanie looked up at him. His face was so familiar, so dear to her. How could she follow through with her decision? How could she not? Neil caught her to him, wrapping both arms around her. "Don't look at me like that. There's nothing to be concerned about."

That's what Ty had always said too. Shoulder and ankle taped, yellow and purple bruises on his back, a shot of painkiller. He always went out on the field no matter how hurt he was. Neil would do the same. He wouldn't admit he was too hurt to play until it was too late. Stephanie pulled away, turning her head so he couldn't see the sparkle of tears in her eyes. The elevator door opened and she stepped inside.

She drove Neil to his house, where one of the coaching assistants had left his car after the game. It was a long drive, and the silence Stephanie maintained was filled with tension. Neil probably wanted to talk about it, to settle her concerns. Fix the problem and move ahead; that was Neil.

But she didn't want to get into it now. Neil had a terrible headache, and he needed to lie down in a dark room and rest—she'd read up on that, too. He certainly didn't need to have an argument. And it would be cold to tell him about her decision while he was trying to recover.

If she was honest with herself, Stephanie didn't want to tell him yet. Neil might be fine with giving up a day of observation at the hospital, but she wasn't fine with giving up this last little bit of time with him. She'd made up her mind to tell him after he recovered, and the idea of doing it any earlier than she'd planned gave her a horrible sinking feeling.

Stephanie drove carefully up the bumpy driveway, being mindful of Neil's concussion—even if he wasn't going to be. They went inside, Stephanie carrying all the paraphernalia the hospital had dumped on them.

She insisted that he lie down despite his protests, but Neil took her hand and pulled her over to the couch.

"Come on, sit down and talk to me."

She sat beside him, his arm around her shoulders, and Stephanie felt tears pricking at her eyelids. This was one of the last times they would sit like this; she felt like a condemned prisoner, ticking off the hours she had left, dreading the moment even as she soaked in the last bits of pleasure.

Neil stroked his hand up and down her arm. "I know you're unhappy about me going back, but I promise it'll be okay. I've done it lots of other times."

"I know. That's the problem. You'll do it again and again. You'll slap a bandage on it or put an IV of plasma platelet replacement in your arm. You'll wrap tape around your ribs or your ankle. And you'll go back in."

"Steph..."

"What? It's true. Isn't it?" Stephanie jumped up, too agitated to sit still. "Injuries are something to hide so you don't lose playing time. Or trophies that show how tough you are—broken bones or illness can't bring you down like a mere mortal. The only bad injury is the final one, right?"

"It's not like that."

"It is!" Her insides were icy with fear. This wasn't the way to do this, the way she'd planned. But somehow she couldn't keep the words from pouring out. "It's idiotic. Risking breaking your neck, and for what? To win a stupid game. As if that's the most important thing in life. No, the only thing in life. Wives, children—we're just supporting characters, things to be loved when you have time off from your first love: Football. The game. WINNING." She whipped around and stalked away, furious with herself for losing control of her anger, furious with Neil for pushing her to talk about it when all she'd wanted to do was stay in denial a little longer. Stay with him a little longer.

"Stephanie..." Neil said in a soothing voice, standing up and coming over to her. "Come on, you're blowing this all out of proportion."

"Don't patronize me," Stephanie snapped. "Don't act like what you do is normal."

He rubbed his forehead, his face pinched. She knew he was in pain, and guilt flooded her. She shouldn't have gone into this. But now it was too late to turn back. She couldn't undo what had already been said. Tears filled her eyes and began to pour down her cheeks. "Neil, I can't do this anymore."

He stiffened. "Do what?"

"Stay with you."

"You're leaving me?" His face was suddenly expressionless, his eyes cold. "Because I got knocked out?"

"No, not that. I'm leaving because I love you, but I can't be with you."

"What? How can you say those two things in the same breath?"

"It's true. I can't live like this. I can't love another football player. I refuse to be a widow again."

"Stephanie, that's ridiculous."

"Football players don't die?"

"Of course they do, but not from playing football." Neil said with exasperation.

"Last night while I was researching your injury—"

"You did research? Like I'm some sort of story you want to find the right angle on?"

"Of course not. This is coming out all wrong—I wasn't casually researching; I was worried about you! So scared I couldn't sleep and I wanted to reassure myself; find proof that I was overreacting. But I'm not. I read about a boy in Tempe who passed out in football practice, and by the time they got him to the hospital he was dead. He'd had a heart attack."

"I remember that. It was a fluke," Neil argued. "It's not the norm. He had a heart condition that nobody knew about. By the time you get to where I am, you know if you have a heart condition. It's entirely different."

"You can't tell me that there haven't been pro players who have been paralyzed. And what about CTE?"

"Okay, yes, things like that have happened. And CTE is something to worry about. That's why they're making changes, especially with young players. Helmets with more cushion, less contact in practice. But it comes from repeated blows to the head—the kind of thing that linemen and running backs or linebackers get. I'm the safest guy on the field. They don't hit me in practice; there are big penalties for roughing the passer."

"Don't pretend you don't get injured. I've seen you play. You'll be out there playing when you're hurt, trying to get your head bashed in again or your elbow re-broken or your shoulder dislocated. I can't take the anxiety. Don't you understand? I love you too much! I hurt when you're hurt. Every week it gets worse. Please, try to understand the agony of sitting in the stands watching someone you love getting thrown to the ground, of seeing him lie there motionless or writhing in pain. I realized Sunday that I love you more than I ever did Ty, and I can't bear the pain."

Neil's eyes blazed. "Damn it! How can you sit there and claim you love me more than you loved Ty and yet tell me you're going to walk? It makes no sense. Won't it hurt when you leave me?"

"Yes, of course." She couldn't meet his eyes. "But the pain will go away in time. I won't feel it forever."

"No? Then it must be easier for you, Stephanie, because I'll feel it every day for the rest of my life. You're lying, you know, even to yourself. You aren't dropping me because you're scared I'll get hurt on the field. I'm healthy and resilient. I have fewer injuries than most quarterbacks my age. And how many more years will I play? Maybe three. My football career is almost over. You won't be facing it 'for the rest of your life.' You're not leaving because I'm a football player. Ty didn't die because he was a football player. He died from a brain tumor. He could have been an accountant or a lawyer or anything else, and he would have died just the same way."

"How do you know? They don't know for sure that repeated trauma might not play a role. They didn't know anything about its connection to dementia until recently."

"You're talking crazy." Neil's eyes were hard and full of frozen fire. "I'll tell you why you're leaving. You're still too bound up with Ty. You feel guilty because you love me instead of mourning for your dead husband. So you're going to punish us both for our disloyalty by running away."

"That's not true!" Stephanie protested.

He turned away from her, jerking his head toward the front door. "Go on, then. Go back to your safe, solitary life."

"No, I'm not going to just leave you here by yourself. I'll stay until you're better. I want to make sure you're okay."

Neil whipped around, his eyes glittering and his face taut. His voice wasn't loud, but it was cold and clipped with barely contained fury. "I don't want your pity. I'm fine; if I need help, I can a call a friend."

Tears rolled down Stephanie's face; she felt ripped apart. "I am your friend, Neil. I'll always be there for you as a friend. Just like you were there for me."

He let out a bitter laugh. "No. I never would have done this to you. And we're not friends anymore. I don't know if we ever really were."

His words hit her like a physical blow. "Please, Neil, don't say that. Don't make this any harder than it already is."

She reached out to touch his arm, but he stepped away.

"No. I must not make it harder on you, must I?" he asked caustically. "Not fragile little Stephanie, who can't bear life as it is. The good and the bad. God, what an idiot I've been all these years—wasting my heart on someone who isn't strong enough to be in love, no matter the sacrifices. Well, I'm not going to spend the rest of my life chasing after you, begging for your attention. I'm done, Stephanie."

He turned away, but paused at the edge of the room and said in an emotionless voice, "I'll pack up whatever things you have here and have them sent to you." Then he strode down the hall to his bedroom and closed the door softly behind him.

Stephanie stared after him. She felt as if she might shatter if she moved. Neil was gone. Out of her life forever. That was what she'd wanted, wasn't it? No, not what she wanted. What had to happen for her own mental well-being. She'd made the right decision, the only choice she could make.

Now she just had to learn to live with it.

Chapter Sixteen

Stephanie had expected pain and loneliness after her breakup with Neil, but she had never imagined that it would be as bad as this. There wasn't the shock there had been with Ty or the agony of witnessing his suffering, but the sheer sorrow was greater. The knowledge that she had chosen this course made it even harder to bear. She told herself that it was for the best, that the worst of the pain would soon pass.

It didn't help.

She missed Neil physically, emotionally, mentally—every way possible. She missed his warm presence in her bed at night, the knowledgeable touch of his fingers on her body, the exquisite pleasure of his lips. Sometimes she woke up sweating and throbbing with passion after a dream about him. At those times she ached so much that she would reach for her phone, but she always managed to put it down before hitting his number.

It wasn't only the sex she missed. It was depressing to face each day without Neil's presence at her breakfast table, barefoot and shirtless, his hair disheveled. She pictured in her mind the way he drank his coffee and yawned until his jaw popped, the way he'd reach out to pull her into his lap as she passed by.

It would have been easier to take if breaking up with Neil had actually stopped her worrying, but every Sunday Stephanie had to consciously stop herself from turning on the TV or checking ESPN. Still, even though she didn't watch, her anxiety meter switched on every Sunday afternoon. She tried to tell herself that, too, would change in time.

But right now, the memories made her silent house unbearable. Stephanie found herself storing up thoughts about her book to relate to Neil at the end of the day, and it was always a shock to her system when she remembered that he wouldn't be there to hear them. It seemed as if her life was now utterly empty. The love built on their friendship meant their lives were intertwined—how had she ever believed she could simply cut Neil out? It was ridiculous. Could worrying about his safety for the next few years really be worse than this agony?

There wasn't a day that passed that she didn't think about calling Neil, going to him, telling him she had been wrong. But then she thought of how cold, hard and angry he had been when she broke up with him. He'd sounded as if he hated her. There was no reason to think that had changed. Neil was the kind of guy who did what he said he was going to. He'd packed up a box of her things and had someone bring it over to her, just like he'd said he would. He was actively working on getting over her. And he would succeed.

She couldn't go back. He wouldn't want her. God, she'd really screwed everything up. It was like someone had handed her a beautiful present: the best relationship of her life. But instead of cherishing it and thanking her lucky stars every single day, she'd taken that present and punted it off a bridge.

The only thing that kept her going was her work and she was grateful for it. There was a former character actor, now living in New York, who had known Gabrielle Willoughby's actress mother, Angela Drake. Stephanie wasn't sure he'd really been that close to her during her daughter's kidnapping, but Stephanie had to investigate all the leads she still had. It wasn't like she was going to get that interview with Willoughby that Neil had been planning to set up for her.

Before their break-up Stephanie hadn't wanted to go to New York because she hadn't wanted to leave Neil. But now there was nothing stopping her, so she booked an inexpensive Airbnb and spent Thanksgiving week in New York. She had hoped the holiday might seem less lonely if she was away from home. But she felt just as bad, if not worse. It had been all she could do not to call Neil.

Strangely, here in New York, she was unable to resist turning on the game. Before it began, there was an interview with Neil. Stephanie watched him hungrily, her eyes taking in every detail. He was his usual assured self. There were no signs of grief.

Not that she wanted him to be unhappy. That was the last thing she wanted. If there were any way she could have ended it without hurting him, she would have. But she couldn't stop the sharp thought that he, unlike her, had been able to move on. Could he have loved her that much if now he could look so calm?

Neil's playing was erratic—brilliant one moment, awful the next. His unswerving concentration was usually his greatest asset, but it was obviously failing him. After a controversial call he actually got into a screaming match with a referee. That wasn't at all like Neil. Stephanie clenched her hands.

Had she done this? She'd never dreamed that she might damage his game. That was the one area of Neil's life that nothing had ever seemed to affect. She was torn with guilt, but she shook herself. This was crazy. She didn't have that kind of power. It was pure ego to think she did. The whole team was having a bad day. They'd be fine next week. It was just one loss.

But while the rest of the team was fine the next week, Neil wasn't. And Stephanie, now back at home, couldn't pull herself away from the TV even as it hurt her to watch Neil pacing on the sidelines, dark eyes shooting sparks. The game cut to a commercial and there Neil was again, shaving and wearing nothing but a white towel around his waist as he extolled the merits of the razor he used. Stephanie wanted to throw the remote into her flatscreen. But instead she just leaned forward and studied him. His broad tanned chest; his muscled arms; his sinewy hands. Neil's black eyes twinkled and that irresistible dimple on one side of his mouth popped in as he smiled.

Stephanie clicked off the TV and leaned her head back on the couch, staring up into the nothingness of her white ceiling. She wanted to scream in frustration, but she had to pull herself together. Her entire life was waiting for her. Her entire empty life. She began to cry.

Emotionally exhausted, she must have fallen asleep because she was awakened by her phone ringing next to her on the couch. She'd been avoiding Claire's calls since the break-up. No doubt it was her trying again. Stephanie had already said a groggy hello before she realized that it wasn't Claire's number that had flashed on her phone. It was Neil's.

There was a dead silence on the other end. Had he been able to hear the aftermath of a crying bout in her voice? For a moment Stephanie couldn't breathe. She swallowed and forced out his name. "Neil?"

"Yeah. Uh, sorry. It rang so many times I thought it was your voicemail picking up."

"Nope. Just me." She hoped her voice wasn't trembling the way her hands were.

"I called because I, well, uh—I have that dinner invitation from Bernard Willoughby. I talked to him before the game. He's willing to meet you and hear about your book. Then he'll decide whether he'll let you question him and Gabrielle further."

It was the best news she could have gotten, but Stephanie's heart sank. For a brief moment, joy had flared to life in her, but this was obviously the only reason Neil had called her—not to say he'd missed her. Not that she had any right to even hope for that; not with the way she'd ended things.

"That'd be great," she forced herself to say, striving to sound as neutral as he did. "When?"

"Friday evening. Is that too little notice?"

"No. It'll be fine."

"He expects me to come along." Neil paused. "Like I told you, he has a thing about football. I think the main reason he agreed to consider you was because you're Ty's widow. He had a lot of respect for Ty's ability. Anyway, he wants me there, too. I couldn't get out of it."

"That's…uh…all right with me." She had trouble speaking past the tears that were gathering again. He couldn't even stand the thought of being around her for one night. He either really hated her now—or, almost worse than that, he'd found he'd never really cared about her as much as he'd thought he did.

"Good. I'll see you Friday," he said shortly. "I'll come by about five-thirty. We're expected at his compound at eight."

"I'll be ready."

"Goodbye, Stephanie."

"Goodbye," her voice came out as barely a whisper, but he'd already hung up the phone.

* * *

Stephanie answered her front door on Friday looking even more beautiful than she had on the day she'd broken up with Neil. The last time he'd seen her. Except in his mind. She resided there every second of every day. Neil had been furious with her at first. At times even hated her. But he'd never for a moment stopped thinking of her.

Stephanie's smile looked forced as she said hello.

"Hey, St—Stephanie." He caught himself before he called her Stringer. "Ready to go?"

"Yes. Just let me grab my purse."

"I'll wait out here." He turned away and gazed out across the grass of her yard. Whoever was cutting it now was trimming it too short. It was going to burn up in the Arizona sun. He hoped it was just some inexperienced yard guy—maybe from another, cooler climate—and not a new boyfriend. Red hot anger swept through Neil at the thought. He didn't know how he still had any left.

He had taken his anger onto the field with him, and most of the time it had hurt his game. It gave him drive and energy, but his accuracy and concentration were gone. He threw his passes so hard that the receivers couldn't hold on to them. He'd never been so erratic in his career.

But he tried to hold on to the anger anyway. When the anger left him, he was in agony. It drained him of his willpower, and he would replay over and over again that early conversation with Stephanie after she found out he was in love with her. She had warned him that they shouldn't get involved. His casual reply that he could handle it rang in his ears. What an idiot he had been. This was far worse than his early unrequited love had been. He'd never imagined the sharpness of this pain, how much he'd miss her, how his body would ache for hers even more now that he knew every inch of her.

Yet through all of the rage and pain, there was the lingering hope that she would regret her decision. But after three weeks went by without hearing from her, even he had to admit she wasn't going to come back. So when Willoughby gave him the opportunity to see her again, he'd been so excited and nervous that he'd gone momentarily speechless when she answered her phone. He wanted to see her again—had to see her—but now he wondered if it was a mistake. Stephanie seemed utterly disinterested in him.

She closed the front door behind her, and Neil escorted her to his car, opening the door for her but being careful not to touch her. “Thank you for getting me the invitation,” she said in a stilted voice as he slid into the driver’s seat and turned the key.

“You’re welcome. It was no trouble.” Neil couldn’t help but think that it didn’t look like she’d spent any sleepless nights going over their breakup. She was cold, and he felt so stiff and awkward that he could think of nothing to say. All he wanted to do was grab her and kiss her. He kept his breathing even and focused on the road ahead, but it took all of his willpower and left him feeling remote and out of place. They could have been strangers sitting here in the car together.

After a few grim minutes of silence, Neil put on some music. But every time a song came on about a breakup, he skipped quickly to the next track. He was embarrassed; it was immature. But he couldn’t stand to listen to someone sing about being torn up inside when he felt like he was currently bleeding out from an invisible wound.

Stephanie didn’t seem to notice, though. She leaned her head back against the seat and closed her eyes. She often fell asleep while riding in a car, but he couldn’t understand how she could do that right now. He was so wound up that it would probably be hours before he’d fall asleep after he got home tonight. No doubt he’d spend half the night wandering around, pacing the floor or lying rigid in bed, trying not to think about Stephanie.

Neil’s bitter thoughts continued all through the drive south. Just north of Tucson he had to keep an eye out for the small private drive he was going to take the rest of the way. It didn’t even come up on Google maps for privacy reasons. Neil slowed the car, his eyes flickering over the cacti and rocks of the landscape.

“What are you looking for?” Stephanie’s words broke the long silence.

“A private road. Mr. Willoughby said the turnoff was right after a pair of large red boulders.”

Neil had to turn around twice, but finally he saw the faint indications of tire tracks. Neil drove slowly, constantly looking for evidence that they were still on the right path.

“You’d be stuck out here for days if it rained,” Stephanie commented.

“Hopefully it doesn’t rain tonight or we’ll have to dig my car out.”

"Surely, he has a paved driveway." She frowned.

"We won't be parking there, though." Neil hadn't told Stephanie all the arrangements he'd had to agree to before securing their invitation. Partly because he didn't want her to know how hard he'd actually worked to wrangle it, partly because of some fear she might not agree, and once they were on their way, he'd been muted by his out-of-control emotions.

"What does that mean?"

"We have to park by the guard's station at the first fence. One of Willoughby's drivers slash bodyguards will come out to meet us in their SUV. We have to leave all phones and recording devices in the car, and they'll pat us down and use a metal detector to make sure we aren't smuggling in anything. Also, you can't bring a weapon. But I figured that wouldn't be a problem for you."

"You mean I can't be packing heat? I'm so disappointed." Stephanie's warm smile, her witty comments ripped through Neil like a cold knife even as he chuckled.

"I know it'll be hard for you." He slowed even further as they neared the gate, and he pulled even with an SUV that was already waiting for them.

The black tinted window slid down and Neil used the old-fashioned handle in the Stingray to roll down his own window. The man wore an expression that was somehow both entirely blank and also intimidating. "Park where you are, empty your pockets of any cell phones, cameras or recording devices and leave them when you exit your car."

"Sure." Neil nodded and rolled his window back up.

"He's vaguely terrifying." Stephanie said as she emptied her purse of everything the guard might object to.

The man was waiting beside his vehicle, feet shoulder width apart, arms hanging, one hand crossed over the other, when they got out. He wasn't short or incredibly tall, not thin but also not hugely muscled. His extremely short hair was a non-descript brown. In fact, the only thing noticeable about him were his pale grey eyes. They watched every movement that Neil made, placid, but not missing a single thing. He held a wand in his hand. "I need to check you both. Metal detector," he said by way of explanation.

"Sure." Stephanie stepped forward, and he ran it carefully over her before giving Neil the same treatment.

He opened the back door to the SUV afterward.

"I guess we passed." Neil smiled at Stephanie.

"Yes." The man confirmed.

"I like his sense of humor." Stephanie whispered to Neil as they slid in the car.

The feel of her breath on his ear, the smell of her conditioner was too much. Neil leaned away from her. As much as he wanted to be able to be casual with her the way they used to be, he couldn't. Not now. Not yet. Maybe not ever again.

"I actually have a great sense of humor," the driver said as he took his seat behind the steering wheel. "When I'm not working. And I have great hearing all of the time." He grabbed something out of the glove compartment.

He handed two blindfolds back to Neil. "You will need to wear these until we are in the underground parking structure. Willoughby's orders."

"So we don't get to see any of the security measures?" Stephanie said, disappointment clear in her voice. "Or the house?"

"Those are my orders. Can you comply or would you like to leave?"

Stephanie took a deep breath, but she slid the blindfold on and Neil followed suit.

* * *

It was hard for Stephanie to tell how much time passed, especially with the blindfold; the world seemed to slow the moment she'd slipped it on. What felt like thirty security-filled minutes later—including an actual full pat down with a female guard—the driver removed their blindfolds and led them into an old-fashioned sitting room.

Bernard Willoughby was waiting for them, seated in a large chair which even Stephanie's inexperienced eye recognized as an antique. He rose, an unforced smile creasing his features as he extended his hand to Neil. "Neil! Good to see you again. I was certainly relieved to see you guys pull out the game in the last quarter."

Neil smiled. "Not as relieved as I was. Mr. Willoughby, I'd like you to meet Stephanie Tyler. Stephanie, this is Mr. Willoughby."

"What's this Mr. Willoughby stuff?" the man protested jovially. "I told you to call me Bernard. You too, Stephanie. Glad to meet you."

He held out his hand and Stephanie slipped hers into it. His handshake was firm and warm, and Stephanie felt a twinge of liking for the man. She hadn't expected to.

But then, she'd expected him to be thin, grave and paranoid, not heavyset and gregarious. His rugged-features had not looked handsome in the old photos taken at the time of the kidnapping, but his face had aged well and his hair was now a stately iron-gray.

"Thank you for allowing me to come," Stephanie replied, managing to cut off the "Mr. Willoughby" but unable to call him Bernard.

"My pleasure. Could I offer you a drink?"

Neil requested scotch and Stephanie asked for a glass of white wine. Willoughby poured their drinks. Stephanie was scared to even touch the fragile wine glass; it probably cost more than her entire outfit—including her not-inexpensive-purse. The glass looked as if it might break if she breathed on it. He indicated for them to sit across from him.

"You may have noted my daughter's absence. Gabrielle will be joining us later in the evening. I apologize for the delay." It was clear Willoughby wanted to learn more about Stephanie and her book before allowing her to see his daughter. He turned toward Stephanie. "Your husband was one of the finest athletes I've ever seen play."

"Thank you."

"Football's one of my favorite pastimes. I was an all-Ivy league halfback at Yale."

"Yes, I learned to enjoy it after I met Ty," Stephanie lied. She didn't want to antagonize him in even a small way.

"Moran here told me you want to do a book on my little girl."

"Yes."

"I've since read all of your other books. Didn't care much for the one you cowrote with Jalyn Williams's wife. You write well, don't get me wrong. I just didn't like the subject matter." He frowned. "It seemed unnecessarily critical. All that stuff about the wives' rules and making players play with injuries and how college players should be compensated monetarily—if a scholarship isn't compensation, I don't know what it is. But I digress. Your writing itself is fair, no preaching or slanting of the facts. I like that. If I could choose someone to write this story, it'd be you. But we've made it a point to live quiet lives since the kidnapping."

Stephanie refrained from pointing out that he had nothing to say about whether the book was written or not. And since his daughter was over eighteen, he didn't even have a say over whether she chose to do the interview or not. But considering the fact that Gabrielle hadn't left for college and had continued to live here with her father, his opinion obviously mattered a great deal to her. Stephanie would do better with his approval than not.

She said only, "It's quite a story, the kind of thing a writer can't pass up. The kidnapping and the two trials are already public. The Rodriguez case was a significant event in American judicial history. I'll touch on that, of course, but primarily I want to delve into the human issues. I want to focus on how the lives of everyone involved were changed by that event. What happened to Rodriguez after he was released from prison? What kind of price did the maid who accused an innocent man in order to help her boyfriend pay in the end? And of course, what happened with Gabrielle and your family? That's what I'm most interested in: your daughter's life since the kidnapping."

"It hasn't been at all sensational."

"No, but it's definitely been unusual. I think it would fascinate readers."

"I'm sure it would. But why should I allow that invasion of our privacy?"

"To ensure the facts are straight."

He watched her with narrowed eyes. "You're telling me that you'll write the book whether or not I allow the interview."

"Yes."

He was silent for a moment, studying her. "I'd rather you didn't. I've fought hard to keep Gabrielle from being exposed to the public."

"I realize that, and having been married to someone famous, I certainly understand. Unfortunately, your position, your wealth, the kidnapping, your ex-wife's fame—all make your daughter a public figure whether you like it or not. Even if I don't write this story, someone else is bound to. You can't keep a book from being written. But I can promise you that I won't invent anything, and I will respect your privacy as much as possible."

"And it's more possible to get the facts straight if you talk to us."

"Naturally."

Bernard sighed and opened a wooden box and extracted a cigar. He offered Neil one, then went through the ritual of snipping the end off and lighting it before he turned back to Stephanie. "I have to admit I had my mind set against the interviews. I invited you solely as a favor to Neil. However, you've interested me. I'll let you do it as long as you follow my conditions. I'll tell you anything you want to know about the kidnapping and our security precautions since then—in a general way. But I won't reveal all the specific details of the security, and I don't want you to question Gabrielle about the kidnapping itself. I will talk about what happened, but with her interviews, you'll stick to her life after the kidnapping. Do you agree?"

"Of course. I have no desire to bring up traumatic memories for your daughter, and I would think you know as much or more about the incidents as she could recall from such a young age."

"I'll be out of town for a week. I'll set up an appointment for my interview when I get back. Gabrielle can set up hers for whenever she wishes." He paused, puffing at his cigar. "I'll have Dominic—that's our head of security you met earlier—go fetch Gabrielle."

Willoughby left the room, and Neil turned to Stephanie. "You must be very excited."

"Yes." Stephanie could have danced with sheer excitement, but she contained herself. "Thanks again for arranging this. Willoughby never would have even met with me if it weren't for you."

She wanted to add that few men would have followed through with the offer after a girl had broken up with them, but she didn't want to make the situation any more uncomfortable than it already was. So Stephanie just sat there with the knowledge that Neil was really, truly, one of a kind. And she had lost him. No, she'd given him up. It made even the bright spot of this night a bit dimmer.

Neil and Stephanie sat in awkward silence until Willoughby came back and started a discussion with Neil about the next week's upcoming game. After a few minutes Stephanie heard the sound of footsteps on the marble entry. The bodyguard who had driven them in opened the door, and a young woman emerged from behind him.

"Thank you, Mr. Winter," Gabrielle looked up at him almost shyly from under her long lashes. Stephanie was intrigued. If Dominic Winter was the head of security, surely he'd been there a while. Why would she be shy with him? He was handsome in an extremely hard and remote kind of way. But probably Gabrielle was just nervous because she never met new people and here were two at once.

"You're very welcome, Ms. Willoughby." The slightest hint of a smile touched one corner of his mouth as Gabrielle swept by, and he closed the door behind her.

Gabrielle was dressed in straight-legged white pants and a crisp white blouse with a pussycat bow. Stephanie could tell at a glance that it was either custom made or professionally fitted and probably cost an outrageous sum. Gabrielle was small, the fragility of her appearance enhanced by large, liquid brown eyes, a heart-shaped face and a mass of honey-blond hair tumbling down her back. There was obviously no makeup on her golden-toned skin. The girl had to be wearing mascara, but even if she was, her extraordinarily long lashes were enough to cause a stab of envy. She seemed younger than twenty-two, more like eighteen—although Stephanie doubted you could find an eighteen-year-old today who had quite that innocence in her face. She looked as untouched and glowing as royalty from another era.

Gabrielle hesitated at the edge of the room, "Hello. I'm sorry I'm late."

Neil rose to his feet, a sort of hushed wonder on his face, and Stephanie's heart twisted with jealousy. She had to remind herself that Neil did not belong to her and that she had to get along with Gabrielle.

Fortunately, that wasn't difficult. Gabrielle was forthright and easy to talk to, which would make her good to interview. Despite her sheltered life, she was also surprisingly well-informed. Stephanie should have been ecstatic, but the strain between Neil and herself turned the evening bitter. It was a relief when, after the meal, Bernard pulled Neil away to show him a trophy case from his own days playing football.

Stephanie and Gabrielle were left alone, smiling at each other tentatively. "Would you like me to show you the house?" Gabrielle asked.

"Sounds great."

"You've seen the dining room and the sitting room. Father's study and the security core are off-limits."

"Security core?"

"It's like a panic room mixed with a bunker. You could live there for years if you needed to."

"That sounds incredibly interesting."

"I could tell you about it sometime if you want, but Father says under no circumstances are non-family members allowed to see it. Well, Mr. Winter is. But he's the head of security."

This time Stephanie was positive she saw a blush rise in Gabrielle's cheeks. There was something going on there.

"Has Mr. Winter been with your family for long?" Stephanie probed delicately. "He looks pretty young to be head of anything, much less security for someone as powerful as your father."

"He joined our team straight out of the military. His father was our former head of security, and he retired when Dominic turned thirty. So he's only had the post a few months. But it's been one Mr. Winter or the other for as long as I can remember."

"Do you get along well with Dominic?"

"He's the best." Gabrielle's face glowed. "We never had anyone that close to my age on the staff before. He eats lunch with me sometimes. And he understands my relationship with my dad. I mean, with his family it's all about honor, and with mine it's about loyalty. But it's a similar dynamic."

"So would you say you're friends?" Stephanie pressed.

"No. Dominic's dad had very strict rules about personal relationships. But I'd say we're friendly." Gabrielle led Stephanie into what was obviously a library, judging by the long study tables and the walls of bookshelves. "The library is my favorite room."

"You read a lot?"

"All the time. Aside from television and the internet, this is the way I experience the world. I never get to see anything in real life." Her soft voice was tinged with regret. "I mean, since I've been old enough to remember."

"Your father gave me permission to interview you for the book I'm writing."

"Mr. Winter told me. I doubt Dad would have even let me meet you otherwise." Gabrielle beamed at Stephanie. "He can be uptight, and I wasn't very hopeful. I'm really glad he said it was okay. I think it will be interesting talking to you. You're different from anyone else I know."

"How?"

"Your work sounds fascinating; you're so independent. And your lifestyle is glamorous."

Stephanie raised her eyebrows. "I'm pretty ordinary."

"Not to me. I've never done anything like you have. I'd be lost if I had to leave this house."

"Is that why you stay here?"

Gabrielle nodded. "Dad is scared for me to leave, so I stay partly for his sake. But, honestly, I'm scared to go somewhere else, too. I can't drive a car. I don't even know how I'd get anywhere. And once I did, I wouldn't know how to do the simple things everyone else can do."

They finished the tour of the enormous first floor and moved up the grand staircase to the second story. Gabrielle showed Stephanie her bedroom and the study next to it where she had taken schooling and music lessons from a succession of tutors. The more Stephanie saw, the more fascinated she became. Gabrielle's life really did have the ring of a twisted fairy tale.

"So how did you meet your fiancé; did he come here?"

Gabrielle nodded. "Wesley's father is an old family friend. They would stay with us for a week every summer when I was growing up. I think Wesley asked my dad for my hand because his family haven't been doing very well—financially, I mean—for a few years."

Stephanie wasn't sure how to respond to such a Victorian idea. An arranged marriage for the sake of money?

"It doesn't bother you that that might be the reason he asked?" Stephanie frowned.

Gabrielle considered the question seriously, her lovely brow wrinkling. "I'm not sure," she said finally. "I know that in the outside world, money is extremely important. And it's important to do what your family needs you to. But it's not as if Wesley wouldn't have asked otherwise. He just might have waited longer."

"But why did you say yes? Are you in love with him?"

"Wesley?" Gabrielle's eyebrows flew up,and she laughed. "I mean, I care about him, and he's nice to look at but… it's certainly not anything like it is in books or on TV. Still, he's very nice to me, and I'll get to experience more of life once we're married. And I won't have to do it all on my own. He'll be there to guide me."

"Do you really want someone else telling you what to do?" Stephanie couldn't stop herself from asking, even though it was one of her cardinal interview rules not to say anything to influence the person she was interviewing.

"I think of it like learning to swim. I really wanted to when I was little, but Dad was scared I'd drown. So at first I was only allowed in the pool if he was in there with me, holding me up. Then I could swim on my own, but I had to wear water wings. They squeezed my arms uncomfortably and kept me from diving or using correct form, but I also didn't drown."

"So Wesley is the water wings?"

"Sort of."

"But you'll have to wear them forever." Stephanie figured with someone as indoctrinated on loyalty as Gabrielle was, divorce wouldn't be an option.

"I know. But it might be the best I can do. I figure my emotions are pretty stunted because of how I've lived," Gabrielle said with astonishing candor. "What if I'm never even able to experience what others do? And I would have given up this chance."

Stephanie wished she could deny the girl's grim assessment. But how could Gabrielle know what or how deeply she could feel when she'd never had the chance?

Gabrielle turned a troubled golden-brown gaze on her. "I know it's strange. But this is the step I think I'm ready for. Wesley understands me. Other men would probably think I was too odd."

"I don't know about that." Stephanie took in the lovely young woman before her. "And there are probably a lot of them that wouldn't mind either way. You're very beautiful."

"Even if they did like me for that reason—how is that better than needing money for their family? And there's no guarantee someone else wouldn't be after the money too. I know what to expect with Wesley. And Dad will be happy if I marry Wesley. He wants so much for me to be protected after he dies, and he trusts Wesley to protect me. I don't want to displease either of them. Besides, I wouldn't know how to talk to a man like your Neil." Stephanie started to protest the girl's characterization of Neil as hers, then shut her mouth. Despite her inexperience with the outside world, Gabrielle was quite perceptive. "No, I'm better off with Wesley."

"Safer," Stephanie corrected.

"Yes. Safer." Gabrielle gave her a small smile. "I must seem very dull to you. I can't imagine you doing something so cowardly."

Gabrielle's innocent words burned through Stephanie like acid, and her mouth twisted into a wry smile. "You'd be surprised just how cowardly I am."

Chapter Seventeen

Saturday morning Stephanie went over her notes in preparation for her interview with Gabrielle. It would take a complete understanding of the timeline as well as some cleverness to ask only questions which had nothing to do with the kidnapping. But she had difficulty keeping her mind on the work at hand. Her thoughts crept back to Neil and the evening before. It had been nerve-racking being around him. She'd been far too aware of his appeal, too hungry for his touch. Being away from him was bad enough, but being around him without any closeness between them was torture. She would have begged him to take her back if he'd shown the slightest interest. But he hadn't.

Neil hated her. She was certain of that now. It had showed last night in every taut line of his body, in the way he'd avoided touching her or even looking at her. The few times she'd tried for a lighter tone or leaned in to make a joke he'd leaned away from her, as if she repulsed him. She ought to be glad. If Neil hated her, he'd have an easier time getting over the breakup. And she wanted things to be easy for him. She didn't want him to hurt as badly as she was hurting.

In the end they'd both be better off. She was safer without him in her life. God, now she sounded like Gabrielle. Stephanie frowned, but before she could turn her mind to the full implications of that thought, her phone rang. She jumped up and answered it, grateful she'd broken her 'no phone in the office' rule. It was Claire.

"Finally! I'm glad you're alive!" Claire's voice burst out. "I've been trying to get you for ages. And now I'm getting this vague sense of deja-vu." Her friend laughed. "Either you're really bad about disappearing or I'm overly dramatic."

"Or maybe a bit of both." Stephanie couldn't help but smile. "I was out of town doing interviews."

"Yep. Definitely getting deja-vu."

"Also, things haven't been great personally. I needed a bit of a break from the world."

"I totally understand. You need time. You need space. You need privacy," Claire said sympathetically before adding, "That's why I've given you a month. And now your time is up."

"That sounds ominous. Also, if you're trying to be less dramatic, it isn't working."

"Oh. I was just acknowledging that I might be overly dramatic. I have no intention of changing. There's no improving on perfection. Besides, if I was less dramatic, I'd never do this."

"Do what? Can you hold on a second, Claire?" Stephanie stood up from her desk. "Someone just knocked, and hardly anyone comes back here to my office." Except for Neil, she added silently, her heart leaping as she swung open the door. To find Claire standing there.

"You can never accuse a theater girl of not knowing how to make an entrance." Claire swept past her into the room. She turned and faced Stephanie, arms crossed. "What are you doing? Honestly, Stephanie. I tried to give you the benefit of the doubt when you missed the first couple of Pumas games and dodged my calls. But then I saw how pissed Neil was, and eventually he told Pete you broke up with him."

"Wait." Stephanie's head was spinning. "You've been going to Pumas games?"

"Yes. Pete and I are dating. Which you would know if you ever got back in touch with me."

"I thought you might have hooked up that night…" Stephanie shook her head. "But you're dating? Like dating-dating?"

"No. Like we hang out and eat dates together like old people with digestive issues." Claire rolled her eyes. "What else could I possibly mean? We are spending our nights having mind-blowing, crazy-imaginative sex. And our days… well, pretty much the same way. Do all football players have this much stamina? And if they do, then I need to ask you again—why in the hell did you break up with Neil?"

"I think I need to sit down. Talking to you is a bit like conversing with an oncoming train." Stephanie flopped onto her couch.

"You flatter me." Claire sat down across from her.

"You and Pete?" Stephanie pushed her hair back from her face. "Really?"

"Why is that so weird?"

"It's not. Pete obviously would've sold his favorite niece to get a date with you. I just never imagined you'd be into someone so…" Stephanie tried to think of the nicest way to put it. "So far from the fine arts."

"I couldn't care less! That man is the first guy I've been with since the divorce that didn't bore me to death trying to impress me with his intelligentsia bona fides. I know enough about that stuff for two people—if not more. I don't want to date my twin." Her eyes twinkled. "Twin Claires is just too much hot-fire for one couple." She winked at Stephanie.

"I'm sorry. I've been a sucky friend. Just because I'm depressed about my own mess of a love life doesn't give me an excuse to go completely AWOL when you're probably dying to share your own happiness." Stephanie couldn't help but think she'd been as happy as this herself only a few weeks ago. It seemed almost unimaginable now.

"I forgive you. We're all a bit selfish when we're in pain." Claire waved away that unfortunate fact of life. "And without you I never would've met Pete. He really is the most fun; I've never been with someone that loves to dance as much as he does!"

"But he's kind of terrible at it," Stephanie pointed out. "I danced with him at this year's opening party and I thought he'd spin me into a wall."

"I prefer to think of it as energetic. Plus, you need that kind of momentum when you're dancing to Big Band music. God, it's so exhilarating!" She gave a little shiver of excitement.

"You don't get embarrassed?"

"That a two-ton wall of hunk is obsessed with me? Not even a little bit. And he's so handy!"

"Please, I'm not sure I can take a blow-by-blow of Pete Cherneski in bed." Stephanie covered her eyes.

"I don't mean it like that. I invited him in that night when the Lyft dropped me off and he fixed my disposal for me! He didn't even need to come back the next day with his tools. Did you know they have a reset button on the bottom part under the sink?"

Stephanie laughed at the amazement on Claire's face. "I had a vague idea."

"And he has tools! Like, enough that he has one of those big red boxes like in a movie."

"A toolbox?"

"You know, I think Brayden wouldn't even have known how to open a toolbox if one wandered in off the street and bit him."

"I'm not sure anyone would know what to do if that happened." Stephanie cracked a smile. It was difficult to be despairing with Claire around. Maybe that had been part of why she hadn't called her back. She'd wanted to be sad about Neil a little longer. "Also, your ex-husband set a pretty low bar."

"I can't argue that. But Pete is great. He makes me so happy. I mean, we are very different, and who knows what will happen in the end?" She shrugged. "But I intend to get all the enjoyment I can possibly squeeze out of him. Even if we're not a forever thing."

"You're good at that. Squeezing out all you can."

"Should I be offended by that?" Claire narrowed her eyes.

"No. I mean you're brave." Stephanie sighed. "A lot braver than I am, certainly."

"Okay. Now we're down to the real subject. This is about the Neil breakup, isn't it?"

"Yes. When he got that a concussion a few weeks ago, I was sitting there in the hospital waiting to find out if he was all right, just like I'd done with Ty, and I just…" Tears welled up in Stephanie's eyes. "How can I go through all that again? How can I sit there year after year watching Neil hurt himself? I've already lost one love and I don't want to spend all my time worrying about losing another one. I can't be a football wife again."

"So you're making Neil choose between you and football?"

"No, of course not."

"That's pretty much what you just said."

"I didn't tell him he had to choose! I wouldn't even dream of asking him to pick me or the game. Neil loves football. He won't quit until he's too old and tired and broken to stay on the field. I know I can't compete. But I also can't stick around and watch him get hurt."

"Well, yeah, that's hard. But you know that football's not the real problem though, right?" Claire laid a hand on Stephanie's. "Admit it. You'd be scared if Neil were a stockbroker. You're scared of being in love. You were going along fine, having fun, but when Neil got hurt, you woke up all of a sudden and realized you were in the deep end of the pool. You're terrified of loving Neil because then you'd have something you could lose—like you lost Ty. And you don't want to risk having to endure all that pain again."

"Worse. I love Neil even more than I did Ty." Stephanie looked at Claire for a long moment, then sighed and stood up. "Okay. Maybe you're right. Maybe I am just scared of opening myself up to the possibility of getting hurt. But what difference does it make? I know I'm being selfish and cowardly and weak, just like Neil said I was. But I have to protect myself. My love for Neil is already ripping me up. If we got back together, my love for him would just get stronger. I can feel it; every day I'd get in deeper. And I don't—how could I live if I lost him?"

"Why would you lose him?"

"Someday I will."

"Well, yes." Claire rolled her eyes. "Eventually one of you will die of old age. Look, football has risks, but so do a lot of other occupations—what if he was a commercial pilot or in the military? Are you going to decide to love or not love someone based on what they do for a living?"

Stephanie frowned. "I don't want to, but it's just..."

"It's just what? Everybody dies sooner or later. What is your plan? Live the rest of your life alone so no one can hurt you? What kind of a life would that be?"

Stephanie stared at Claire, looking stunned. Finally she murmured, "A life like Gabrielle's."

"Who?"

"The girl in the Fortress."

"And you say I'm hard to talk to?" Claire raised her eyebrows.

"It's the girl I'm writing the book about. She was kidnapped as a kid and she hasn't left her house since. And now, years later, she's getting married to a man she doesn't love so that he can have her money."

"I am so confused. Isn't it usually the one that needs the money that gets married to the person they don't love? This sounds like a lose-lose proposition for our girl."

"It is! And last night I was sitting there feeling sorry for her having to live in such an empty, heartless way, when I'm doing the exact same thing!" Stephanie sank back into her chair. "I'm such an idiot. Why didn't I see it? I knew it in the back of mind—why would I have been so miserable if it was the right thing to do? I just wouldn't face it." Her breath caught as she realized the depth of what she'd done. "Oh, God, I screwed everything up irrevocably. I'll never get him back. He hates me now."

"Only you would use the word irrevocably in the middle of an emotional meltdown." Claire shook her head. "Also, that's completely ridiculous. Neil will take you back."

"No, it's true. You didn't see him; he was furious. I've never seen him like that. He said he was through with me. Then I saw him last night—he took me to the interview with Gabrielle—and he was so cold. He looked right through me and hardly said a word. He was so stiff and remote, like I was a stranger. There was a definite I-hate-you vibe."

"Didn't you tell me he was in love with you for years?"

"Yeah. I mean, I didn't know it at the time, but he would've asked me out four years ago if it weren't for Ty."

"And then you two finally get together, are blissfully happy for a couple of months and then you dump him with a lame excuse about football?"

"Yeah." Stephanie's voice got smaller.

"Well, of course he hates you!" Claire threw up her hands.

"Thanks, Claire. That really makes me feel better."

"But it's only because he actually loves you."

"Huh?"

"People are complicated. But they're also very simple. Especially men. You just have to remind him that he loves you more than he wants to sulk."

"And how do I do that? Please help me come up with a plan. I don't care what it takes—if there's any way to fix this, I have to do it."

"Well, first we'll need walkie-talkies, a bag of unmarked dollar bills and a UPS uniform."

"Really?"

"No. Not really. Come on, he's a dude. Just put on your best underwear and a pair of heels and throw a coat on top of it and go surprise him at his house."

"That seems like a better plan." Stephanie laughed.

"But I don't know, the other one did sound fun—and a UPS uniform could work."

"I think I'll go with the underwear, heels and a raincoat. I have those already."

"Good choice. Now I'm going to head out because I now know what I'm fixing Pete for dinner tonight. And I need a quick wax."

"I'm only signing off on this plan of yours if you never talk about your sex life with Pete again."

"No deal!" Claire waved. "Get used to it."

* * *

Neil curled his hand around his cup of coffee and gazed out the wide windows of his living room. He hardly noticed the view. His thoughts were turned inward, as they had been most of the night. He'd tossed and turned, now and then dozing off, only to awaken with a start and set his mind back on the treadmill.

Last evening had been vicious. Stephanie had looked gorgeous; she had sparkled and laughed with the Willoughbys, and on the drive home she had bubbled with enthusiasm over her upcoming interview with Gabrielle. Once she'd reached over and squeezed his hand and thanked him for getting her the invitation. At her touch, desire had pounded in him, hot and hard, temporarily obliterating the pain he carried inside him. He wanted her, wanted all of her: her body, her smile, her bright mind and quick tongue, her overpowering passion. Frustration had flooded him.

He wanted Stephanie so much that he ached in both mind and body. But she wouldn't let him in. It was an impossible situation. Like pushing at a stone wall. He'd never given up like this, never accepted defeat before. No matter how many times he failed at something or lost what he was striving for, ultimately he had succeeded because he wouldn't take loss as an ending. He kept on until he won, no matter how difficult or painful. He worked; he did whatever had to be done.

But this time… He was hemmed in, stymied. He couldn't force her to love him, couldn't make her take him back. There was no one to fight, to defeat, except the woman he loved, and if he did that, he'd lose her just as surely as he was losing her now.

He showered, trying to wash the previous night away, but he knew that was impossible. He would never be able to get Stephanie out of his system. He'd lost that battle long ago, before Ty died. Suddenly he froze, staring at himself in the mirror as he toweled his hair dry. He was wrong when he thought he'd never been defeated before. He had accepted defeat with Stephanie long ago. He'd given up because she was Ty's wife, and there was no way to win.

And now he saw that that was his whole problem. He expected to lose Stephanie. He had never really believed she was his—had just enjoyed their affair in a kind of stunned wonder without believing it would last. When she left, he'd accepted it as inevitable.

Why was it impossible for them to be together? The word impossible was normally just a challenge to him. But he had accepted it from Stephanie because he was accustomed to losing with her. Damn it! What was the matter with him?

Neil's eyes took on a fierce light. He wasn't going to give up. He would get Stephanie back. He tossed the towel aside and threw on his clothes, then left the house at a run.

He didn't slow down all the way to Stephanie's. He'd probably completely screwed up the suspension on his Stingray flying down his gravel drive, but he was too wound up to care. That was a problem for another day. Neil threw his car into park in front of Stephanie's house, grinding the gears on the classic engine. He hopped out and strode across the lawn, but before he reached her door, she opened it and stepped outside.

"Neil?" Her eyes widened. "Wha—"

He didn't stop, just picked her up in a fireman carry and went inside, shutting the door behind them with his foot in one smooth motion as he set her down. "I don't care where you were going or what your plans are right now. We are talking about this."

"Talking about what?" She was staring at him like he was a ghost.

"About us! I refuse to let you tear us apart because you've decided I'm going to get killed playing football." He paused, for the first time noticing her attire. "Why the hell are you wearing a raincoat? It must be ninety-five degrees out there and not a cloud in sight."

"Uh…well, it's—"

He made an impatient gesture. "Never mind." He grabbed her elbow and stalked down the short hall into the living room. "You're going to sit down and listen to me."

Stephanie perched obediently on the edge of the couch, crossing the edges of her coat together over her knees. It was a prim gesture and seemed out of place—and definitely out of character for her in the face of his current rudeness—but Neil was too preoccupied to ask her any questions.

He crossed his arms and began to pace. "I've loved you for four years now. I loved you and wanted you the whole time you were married to my best friend. I loved you all through his death and afterwards, holding back until you were ready for another relationship. And when you gave me a chance, I fell even more in love with you. It seems impossible, but somehow I desired you more and more every day. I couldn't get enough of you. I still can't." He turned to her, fixing her with his piercing black gaze, carefully emphasizing each word. "I love you. And I'm not about to give you up."

"Neil," Stephanie began, starting to rise.

"No, I want to say the whole thing." He waved her back down. He knew he was being too aggressive, which didn't help his case, really, but he wasn't going to soft pedal his feelings this time. "I won't let you do this to me. To us. At first I thought you would change your mind, that you were freaked out by my being in the same hospital that Ty was in. That it brought up some emotional flashback, and you would come to your senses. Then I finally figured out you weren't going to. So I approached Willoughby, hoping that if we were together we might talk it out. But you were so cold, and I felt so stiff and awkward… I didn't know what to say. I hated like hell the way you could turn your feelings for me on and off."

"That's not true!" Stephanie cried, flying to her feet. "You were the one who was cold and standoffish."

"I was the one who sat there all night feeling like a fool, wanting you so bad I could taste it and not knowing how to make you listen to me. How to make you love me and want me."

"Neil!" She moved closer and put a hand on his forearm. "I do love you. I do want you. The last few weeks have been horrible for me, too."

"Then why did you do it?" he thundered. "Why didn't you come back to me?" He put his other hand over hers, locking it to his forearm in an iron grip. "I couldn't sleep last night. I feel like I've barely slept at all since you left me. I lie awake wanting you all night long. I can't live this way any longer. Stephanie, I love you, and I intend to marry you, even if I have to kidnap you and take you to Vegas!"

A brilliant smile broke over Stephanie's face and her beautiful blue-grey eyes twinkled. "How romantic."

He glowered at her. "Why are you still wearing that raincoat? We're nowhere near finished with our conversation. Take it off."

"Yes, sir," Stephanie replied demurely, her fingers going to the belt of her coat. Neil started to say something else, but then she grasped the lapels and drew it down her arms, letting it drop onto the ground. She wore nothing under it but lacy black panties, a matching corset and thigh high stockings.

Neil's stood there silently, no idea what he'd been saying. He stared at her, shock quickly changing to blazing heat. "Stringer…"

"I missed you calling me that." Stephanie sauntered to him with her hands on her hips. She stopped two feet away from him, her head slightly titled at a challenging angle. "Well?"

He swallowed. "God, you're gorgeous. This wasn't—I mean, you weren't going out to see another man, were you? The guy who doesn't know how to cut an Arizona lawn, maybe?"

"What on earth are you talking about?"

"Your grass is way too short. It's going to burn. I thought maybe a new guy…"

"My lawn guy is new, but he's also in his fifties and married with three children."

"Well, he should learn to let the grass grow a little."

"I'll make sure and tell him that." Stephanie laughed.

"So you weren't going to see—"

"I was coming to your house."

"Good. I don't want to have to cut this short to go choke somebody out—" He pulled her into his arms, his mouth seeking hers desperately. She opened her lips to his tongue, twining her own around his, exploring the sweet warmth. It was a slow rediscovery which brought with it the shattering realization that he desired her more than ever. Neil pulled away only long enough to murmur, "I love you."

She didn't have to time to return his words before his mouth captured hers again and his hands began to roam her body. His fingertips massaged her hips. He caressed the smooth flesh of her thighs between the tops of her thigh-highs and her panties, teasing his senses with the different textures of skin, lace and silky stockings. His breathing was ragged as he released her and stepped back. Slowly he looked her over, his hands sliding over her in the wake of his eyes. He skimmed his fingertips along the lace where it met her cleavage, grazing her soft breasts. His thumbs came back to trace the outlines of her nipples beneath the thin lace, making them swell and harden.

Neil's hands drifted across her bare shoulders and chest. Stephanie sucked in her breath, her head falling back, her face contorting in burgeoning desire. Neil knelt and with infinite care he took off her heels, pausing to kiss the flesh exposed below her panties. He rolled down each stocking in a long caress, then stood and swept a hand down the front of the corset, popping open the fastenings. It fell from her, leaving her clad only in the seductively sheer panties.

Neil cradled her breasts in his tanned hands and bent to kiss the sensitive centers. His hands were scorching as he slid them down her body and edged under the panties. When he touched the damp warmth between her legs, he shuddered with barely restrained desire. Stephanie ran her fingers lightly down his jeans and grazed the hardness pressing against them. Neil drew in his breath sharply.

"May I undress you now?" Stephanie's eyes glinted up at him, and he nodded silently.

She rolled up his T-shirt, sliding her palms over his body as she did so. He lifted his arms and she drew the shirt off over his head, then returned her fingers to his chest. Delicately she brushed her fingertips over the flat masculine nipples and felt them tense in response. Stephanie leaned forward to outline the small buds with the tip of her tongue, delicately spiraling around them before she drew each sensitive button into the warm, moist cave of her mouth.

Neil's hands moved over her more quickly, his words incoherent. Stephanie slipped down his body, her mouth tracing the line of hair which bisected his abs and disappeared into his jeans. Her tongue dipped into the well of his navel as she knelt before him and unfastened his belt. Neil crushed her hair in his hands, his fingers digging into her scalp as she continued her liquid exploration of his abs. She sat back on her heels and lifted his feet one at a time to pull the shoes and socks from them. Neil watched her from above, entranced by the gentle, fluid movement of her breasts as she worked. At last, she pulled his pants down his legs, skimming his flesh with her fingers as she went. Stephanie removed his boxer-briefs in the same manner.

She explored his lower body as carefully as she had his chest, her fingertips fluttering over him. Neil uttered a groan of pure pleasure and reached down to pull her to her feet, but Stephanie resisted, tugging him down beside her instead. He came willingly, one arm going around her shoulders as he pressed her back onto the floor and covered her mouth with his.

He kissed her, then his lips began to trace a trail of fire down her body, consuming her breasts and stomach and the soft expanse of her inner thighs. His tongue moved insistently upon her, drawing gasps that drove him harder, further. She said his name in the merest of breaths, yet it told him all he needed to hear. He answered her with his attention, his mouth drawing more of Stephanie's moans, her hips twisting as she sought release.

"Not yet." The words seemed to be ripped from Stephanie's body. "I want to feel you."

He reached a long arm up to where his jeans lay and grabbed the condom he'd brought in the hopes that things would go this way. She rolled it on for him and Neil drew back to look at her, his eyes commanding hers not to break their gaze. Then he covered her with his body, entering her slowly. Stephanie urged him on, sinking her nails into his skin, lightly scraping them up his back and tangling her fingers in his hair.

"Don't ever send me away again," he whispered huskily.

"Never, never."

Neil surged fully into her. Stephanie matched the rhythm of her body to his pounding demand as he took her higher and higher until at last they crested in a shimmering lightstorm. Slowly, softly they came back to earth, wrapped in each other's arms. With a long, satisfied sigh Neil rolled onto his back, pulling Stephanie with him so that her head rested on his chest.

Neil's hand drifted over her hair and back. Now and again he kissed the top of her head. "I love you," he whispered. "I can't ever let you go."

Stephanie raised her head to look at him, her eyes glowing. "I love you too."

He wet his lips. "I…I've decided to retire."

"What?" Stephanie gaped.

"I'm retiring from football at the end of the season. You won't have to worry about any more injuries."

"You'd do that for me?"

"Yes," he replied simply.

Tears welled in Stephanie's eyes. "I don't deserve you."

He grinned. "I know. I'm a hell of a guy."

"I mean it!" Stephanie sat up agitatedly, brushing her hair back with her hands. "I never imagined you'd give up football for me."

"It wasn't much of a choice. You're my life."

Now the tears spilled out, trickling down her cheeks, and Neil reached up to brush them away as she spoke. "I never meant for you to choose between me and your career. I know how much you love football, how much it means to you. I'd never, ever ask that of you, and it's not necessary. You can have us both."

"What?" He asked, puzzled. "Why the sudden about-face?"

"I realized today that it wasn't ever about football. That's what I was coming over to tell you. I was just trying to protect myself. I was terrified. I couldn't face the pain of possibly losing you."

He frowned. "I don't understand."

"Of course not. Even I didn't understand why I was doing what I was doing at the time—it wasn't based on any rational thought. When I saw you lying on that field, not moving, I realized how much I loved you. It was all consuming in a way that I've never felt before, even with Ty. And I remembered the pain of losing him; how would I ever survive losing you when you meant so much more to me? You'd become my world. And I was petrified that eventually something would go wrong: you'd die or leave or stop loving me and I'd never recover. It felt like if we got any closer and I lost you, I'd lose me too. Completely. So I tried to end it before that happened. I was scared and I ran. But that's not what I want out of life. I realized that I was acting like Gabrielle. That's never been me, and I refuse to let fear turn me into somebody else. I'd rather have you and risk my heart than be safe and have nothing."

Neil raised one of her hands to his lips, kissing each finger tenderly. "I promise to take very good care of myself. I'm determined to keep you this time." He paused and added jokingly, "And you know what happens when I set my mind to something." He looked at her expectantly.

"You make it happen," Stephanie finished. "Which is good because I'm not leaving you again unless you make me."

"A highly unlikely possibility."

"So please don't give up football."

"I'll have to eventually."

"But not now, and not for me. I don't want you to be bitter and resentful."

"I could never resent you. But I promise, when the time comes, I'll do it for myself and no one else. Agreed?"

"Agreed. But not too soon."

"I guess it depends on if marriage makes me so happy and lazy that I don't want to play anymore," Neil went on.

"Marriage?"

Neil grinned widely, and Stephanie raised her eyebrows. "Do you have a candidate in mind for the bride?"

"Hmmm… well, I know what I'm looking for." Neil ticked off the traits on his fingers. "She has to be beautiful, sexy, intelligent and talented. And she has to have experience in marriage, since I have no idea what I'm doing."

"A widow, in other words?"

"Or a divorcee," he shrugged. "Fortunately I know a woman who fits the requirements, so I won't have to conduct a long search."

"Oh, really? Local talent, then?"

"Yes, and you know her, so I thought you could feel her out for me."

"I'm not sure. I'd have to check. Who might she be?"

"Claire, obviously." Neil held his arm up as if to protect his face. Stephanie slapped his chest instead. "I mean, I have to admit at first I wasn't one hundred percent sold, but then when I saw her in the sweats and little star-shaped face stickers, I knew I couldn't hide from my true feelings any longer." He laughed.

"You better watch out talking like that about Pete's new girlfriend. He's got fifty pounds on you easy. Plus he's a little bit insane."

Neil's hands went to Stephanie's shoulders and he pulled her against him. "Of course I mean you. Will you marry me, Stringer?"

"Yes, I'll marry you. Whenever you want."

"I wouldn't want to rush things. How about Monday?"

"That's not rushing?"

"You have to remember that I've already waited four years."

Stephanie laughed. "Well, we'll have to get a license first."

"As soon as we legally can, then. All right?"

"All right."

One of his hands went behind her head, holding it firmly as he kissed her. His lips moved hungrily on hers and with one quick movement he rolled them both over so that his body pressed into hers. His hand began a leisurely exploration of her body. "Neil!" Stephanie protested jokingly. "Again?"

"Mmm… I have a lot of time to make up for."

Stephanie pulled back to look at him, widening her eyes in mock innocence. "But there's a game tomorrow. You have to save something for training."

"To hell with training," he growled, and covered her mouth with a kiss that promised the future.

Turn the page for a preview of

Raging Fires

by

Candace Camp

&

Anastasia Hopcus

Coming Soon

JAKE

Jake grabbed his keys and left the house. He wasn't going to be late. That was the old Jake. This was the new Jake, the man Pops would be proud of, even if his grandfather was no longer alive to see it. New man. New team. New life.

Besides, if he was late, he'd never hear the end of it from Kelli. He could picture her, eyes narrowed with annoyance, hand on hip, which was cocked out in that way he used to think was sexy as hell. "If that isn't just like you," he murmured to himself.

He decided to take the old Jeep instead of his SUV. Kelli had always hated that car—said it was too top-heavy for someone that took corners as fast as Jake did. It seemed like a fitting good-bye to freedom. He'd just pulled out onto the street when his cell rang. No Bluetooth in this classic, so he picked it up to answer, just like you weren't supposed to. *Did he live for danger or what?*

"Jake!" It was Kelli's voice, and she sounded frantic.

His heart jumped. "What? What's wrong?" He could hear traffic noise in the background.

"My car died," she said, and he relaxed a little. She was just angry, that's all.

"Need a ride?" he asked smugly. He knew how much it burned her to have to call him for help.

"Yes." He could practically hear her teeth grinding. "I'm at the McDonald's on Thomas."

"You stopped for a burger?"

"No, I did *not* stop for a burger." Yeah, she was pissed. His lips twitched up at the corner. She went on, "Can you pick me up on your way to the Blue?"

"Gee, Kell… I don't know. It'd make me late, and I have orders to be there on time." She growled, and he laughed. "Yeah, hang on. I'll be there in ten."

He made a U-turn, still grinning, and headed the other way.

It took him a little longer than he'd said, which wasn't his fault; he hadn't known there was construction the way he came. His excuse was already in his mouth as he turned into the McDonald's lot. Then he saw her, and everything left his head.

Damn, she looked hot. She wasn't overdone, of course; that wasn't Kelli's style. But her skirt was just short enough to show off her legs, and the soft sleeveless top let you know what was beneath it without clinging tightly. Her heels weren't sky high, but they had those thin straps that looked like they might snap beneath your fingers. She was… enticing. Especially if you knew what she looked like when she took off those clothes. Used to, he was the only one that did.

He frowned, his good humor leaving him, and stepped out of the car. "You're still driving that old junker? You wouldn't have to call me for help if you'd get a decent car."

"You should talk," she shot back, nodding toward his Jeep and taking off her sunglasses so she could zap him with the full force of her glare. "And I'm regretting calling you more and more by the minute." Her mascara was smudged beneath her eyes, the lashes stuck together.

Had she been crying? Surely not. Why would you be in tears because your car wouldn't start? Whatever Kelli was, she wasn't the kind that was always crying all over you. Breaking something was more like her.

She was holding a cardboard take-out tray with two big drinks in it. He knew what they would be—diet Sprite for her, regular Coke for him—and somehow that thought made his chest tighten. Kelli leaned into his car to set down the drinks, then turned back to her car and reached in to pull out something from the other side, giving him an excellent view of her ass, which, he noted, was just as firm and round as it had been.

Apparently, his body reacted the same as it had back then, too, which annoyed the hell out of him. Jake got back into the car, and as soon as Kelli sat down, holding the jacket she had retrieved from her back seat, he slammed the Jeep into reverse and stepped on the gas.

Which sent the two large drinks sitting on the dashboard flying through the air. Before Jake could react, they were doused with soda. Kelli let out a shriek, and he stomped on the brake, stopping the car with a jolt. "What the hell! Why did you set the cups on the dashboard?"

"I didn't know you were going to peel out before I could even fasten my seat belt," she yelled back. "Look at this!" The drinks had hit her worse because the tray had been sitting on her side of the dash. Only his arm was wet, but the liquid had soaked her top and drenched her face and the front of her hair as well.

"Well, if you hadn't set them on top of the fu—"

Kelli picked up the half-empty cup in her lap and threw it in his face. Cold liquid flooded down his front, and Jake's words ended in a string of curses.

A car honked behind them, and someone shouted, "Hey! In or out, jerkwad!"

A customer walking to his car helpfully added, "Not a parking space, dude!"

Jake broke off his swearing monologue and pulled back into the empty space. Kelli shot out of the car and began sweeping ice and puddles of Coke from her clothes like they were sparks. "Damn it! Damn it! It's all over my jacket, too."

"Why the hell did you throw your soda at me?" Jake jumped out, too, wiping his face and pulling his wet shirt away from his chest.

"Because it was your fault, and you're just sitting over there, laughing."

"I was *not* laughing!"

"Okay, sitting there shouting at me, and not a drop on you. Look at this!" She brandished her jacket at him like a weapon, shaking it. "It's ruined! I can't go to the wedding like this!"

Her top clung to her wetly, outlining every curve. It was a damn good look on her, but she was right; it wouldn't work at a wedding. "Don't you have anything else you can wear?"

"No. No, Jake, I do *not* have anything else to wear. I'm not in the habit of changing clothes at McDonald's."

"You go to the gym, don't you?"

"Yes. Okay, I do have a sports bra and shorts in my trunk. You think I should get married in a sports bra and old saggy gym shorts?"

"It might start a trend." He cracked a smile. Now that he'd gotten the ice cubes out of his shirt, he'd calmed down some. And Kelli in a snit looked… well, there was no other word for it. She looked *cute*. "You know, when you think about it, this situation really is kinda funny."

Kelli gave him a death glare and swung around to pop open the trunk of her car. Every movement was a jerk—she was probably imagining that she was pulling out his fingernails—as she slung her damaged jacket into the trunk, then pulled out a small duffle bag and unzipped it, yanked out a piece of cloth, and slammed the lid of the trunk shut. She stalked toward him, holding up a scrap of gray cloth.

"This, Jake. This is what I have to wear. Aside from being, you know, *underwear*, it's a crop-top. I am not getting married with a naked stomach and a T-back bra."

"Okay, okay, calm down. Let me see what I've got." He ambled around to the back of the jeep and dug into it. "Hey!

Here. I've got a box of something. T-shirts. There are plenty. We can both change."

He straightened, holding out a fluorescent green shirt with ***Kents do it in Tents*** emblazoned across the front.

Kelli's jaw dropped. "The old t-shirts from your family reunion?" Astonishment had driven the anger from her voice. "What are you doing with t-shirts from five years ago in the back of your car?"

"Shockingly, a lot of people 'forgot' to take theirs home after the reunion was over." He shrugged. "I guess I just left them here. I don't drive the jeep much."

She came over to him and took the t-shirt, looking uncertain. "Really? We're going to get married again in matching t-shirts that say ***Kents do it in tents***?"

"You tell me." Jake plucked the gray bra from her and held it up in one hand. "Sports bra." He raised the t-shirt in his other hand. "Or matching t-shirts that make us look like a couple of jackasses."

Kelli groaned and grabbed both garments from him. "Well, at least I won't have to go bra-less beneath the jackass t-shirt."

Okay. That was an image that would mess up his mind for the rest of the afternoon. Kelli climbed into her car to change, closing her door and turning her back to him. Like he was a stranger. That was irritating as hell.

"You don't have to hide," he called. "I've seen it all before."

"Yeah, well, I'd prefer not to get arrested for indecent exposure outside McDonald's. And just because you've seen it before doesn't mean you're ever going to see it again."

"Right. Thanks for reminding me. For a minute there, I forgot we hated each other." She didn't reply; he wasn't sure she'd heard him. Probably better that way.

Jake stripped off his shirt and pulled on the hideous green one. He could barely shove his head through the opening, and it was so tight he thought it might cut off his breath. He dug through the box, pulling out shirt after shirt. Apparently they were one-size-fits-all. He hadn't been able to wear one-size-fits-all since he was fifteen. He pulled at the constricting neck, hoping to stretch it, then tugged at the hem, which barely reached the waistband of his jeans. He had visions of the shirt splitting apart like The Hulk's in the middle of the ceremony.

After a few minutes, Kelli emerged from her car wearing the baggy tee with her skirt. "At least I didn't have to wear the fugly gym shorts. I had the jacket on my lap so my skirt only got a few spots on it."

She turned around and saw him in his too-tight shirt, and she burst out laughing. "You're right. It is kinda funny."

* * *

KELLI

They were silent on the drive to the Blue Shack. The open-air Jeep was too noisy to hear anything. And anyway, what was there to say? Kelli's spirits, already low today, had severely dropped by the time they pulled into the bar's front parking lot. There were only a few cars there, one of them Gran's dinosaur Buick.

"Geez, are they still letting Gran drive around in that thing?" Jake remarked as he pulled in beside the behemoth. "She's got to be a wreck waiting to happen."

“They?” Kelli asked sarcastically. “Exactly who do you think is going to stop her? Pops was the only one she ever listened to. She’d still be hauling around empty kegs in the back if he hadn’t been so insistent that she stop. Don’t know who can possibly do anything about her now.” Kelli’s eyes filled with tears again and she looked away from Jake, blinking until they subsided.

“You have a point.” He gave her hand a quick squeeze. It was an innocent gesture, but the touch of Jake’s capable fingers still sent shivers through her. And her mind was now running through the other, decidedly *not* innocent, ways Jake had touched her. Kelli quickly pulled her hand away.

Getting out of the car, she tried to finger comb her hair into something that didn’t look like she’d tuck her finger in an electrical outlet. She remembered now why she hated Jake’s Jeep. It was like being in a wind tunnel. On the positive side, the hair on the front third of her head was no longer in wet sticky strings. It was now in dry, sticky spikes. The Jeep had no handy mirror in the visor, of course, so she bent to peer into the side rear-view mirrors. She tugged and swiped, but her hair was hopeless. Nor could she completely wipe off the mascara smudges beneath her eyes from her stupid tears earlier. As if dealing with Pops’ death hadn’t been bad enough on its own, she’d had to call her ex for help, knowing exactly how much he would enjoy her humiliation at having to ask him to rescue her.

Now here she was, looking like she just got off a rollercoaster, wearing a dorky t-shirt with her favorite skirt and heels. And she was late for her wedding. The only thing that could be worse was if she was having to re-marry the jerk she’d divorced four years ago. Oh, wait. She was.

Why had Pops left the bar to her with this requirement? Why had she agreed? Was owning this stupid bar really worth it?

Well, yes, it was. Because this stupid bar was her home, the place where she'd found a family, the place that had taken her in when she'd returned from Miami, licking her wounds. It was where her life was, and she couldn't bear to think of giving it up, even if it meant marrying Jake. She'd already done that once; this time couldn't be as bad.

She squared her shoulders and started toward the front door. Jake walked around the car and came up beside her, resting his hand lightly on her lower back like he used to do, and it felt so natural that they were almost to the door before she realized what he'd done. She glanced up at him sharply, and he seemed to become aware of it at the same time because he pulled his hand back, shifting away from her into that side-by-side-but-not-a-couple walk.

He opened the door for her, and Kelli entered the bar. She stopped so abruptly that Jake, coming in behind her, bumped into her. They stood there, frozen, staring in shock at the scene before them.

Someone had been busy draping a lot of white ribbon around the place and putting candles, flowers and white tablecloths on all the pockmarked wooden tables. A white arbor trellis stood in front of the bar. But unexpected as the decorations were, they weren't what made Kelli's eyes widen. It was the people. *All* the people.

It was supposed to be only the two of them and the justice of the peace, her bridesmaid Naomi, Jake's best man Asa Jackson, and Gran, and maybe whatever relative or friend Gran badgered into coming with her. Those few were here, all right. But there were a whole lot more people than that.

They were divided into two distinct groups. On one side of the room Gran sat at a table with her sister Lucy, and assorted cousins, aunts and uncles. Around them stood the Blue's employees, as well as a number of the bar's patrons, recognizable by their leathers, bandannas, and beards.

On the opposite side of the room were several very large men dressed in crisp pants and button-up shirts, and their dates in dresses and heels. Asa and Jason Kowalski were among them, and Kelli recognized Neil Moran, the Pumas quarterback. So this group must be Jake's new teammates.

In the center, beneath the trellis, stood a small bespectacled man in a black choir robe.

Jake turned to Kelli. "What the hell?"

"I have no idea."

"I didn't see—where were their cars?"

She shot him a look. "Yeah, because *that's* the important question."

"Sorry. I didn't know there was a proper etiquette when you find out your ex-wife slash new bride invited a hundred people to your 'small, quiet' wedding!" Jake's voice grew louder with every word until his voice was booming out like he had a bullhorn.

"*I* didn't invite them!" Kelli snapped. "And could you keep your voice down? You're not on the field calling signals!"

"Yeah, like you're being reaaallly quiet."

She realized that everyone was watching them with faces that were as astonished as Kelli felt. Being dressed like crazy people and yelling at each other was probably not a good look for a couple about to get married. She straightened her shoulders and told Jake in a studiously calm voice, "Why don't we try to at least look civilized?"

He shrugged, and they turned back to face the crowd.

"Um... hi, everyone," Kelli said. "Sorry we're a little late."

Jake lifted his hand in a half-hearted wave. "Kelli had car trouble."

Of course, he had to add that.

"All of us parked in the back lot," Asa helpfully answered Jake's original question, not even bothering to try to hide his grin.

Naomi, at barely 5'2", was still able to push her way through the crowd of burly bikers with ease. She came to a halt when she saw Kelli. Her eyebrows shot up and she hurried over. "What happened to you? You look…" She stopped, apparently rendered speechless.

"Long story," Kelli replied. "What are all these people doing here?"

"I'm sorry. It wasn't me. I swear." At least Naomi kept her voice low, but that only made everyone in the room lean in to hear better.

"Gran?" Jake and Kelli asked at the same time.

"Jinx," Naomi said. At Kelli's glare, she rushed on. "Right. Sorry. Not the time." Naomi turned her back to their audience and whispered, "It was *her*." She jerked her head toward the jock side of the room. "The one that looks like she just stepped out of one of Pops' old movies."

"The blonde with the bob?" Kelli studied the tall, sleek woman in a dress that screamed designer standing between a beefy guy and Neil Moran's wife.

Naomi nodded vigorously. "She came in about an hour ago with all this stuff." She waved her hand vaguely at the decorations. "Then she ran around putting it up—well, actually, telling these two workers where to put things. The tablecloths and flowers and candles. Even that wedding arbor thing. Do you *know* her?"

"Never saw her before in my life," Kelli replied. "What is she, the Wedding Fairy?"

"That's Pete Cherneski next to her," Jake said. "He's a linebacker. Kind of nuts."

"Yeah, well, I think she is too," Naomi told him. "I mean, she looks normal—aside from the fact that her dress probably cost more than my car—but she keeps saying weird things. I'm not sure if she's joking or not. And while she was doing the arranging, that Pete guy was over at one of the tables, and he kept pulling the tablecloth off. I mean, with the centerpiece and everything on it, and it would all fall off, and then he'd put it back on and yank it off again."

"Oh, yeah, he does magic stuff," Jake explained. "The other day, he kept showing me this thing with a fake flower where he pulls the flower out of his jacket like it's some big surprise. Only it never is because you just saw him stick it in there."

"Good grief!" Gran bellowed—no question where Jake got his voice from—and hauled herself up out of her chair. "Are you two going to stand at the door talking the whole time?" She stalked over to Jake, took his arm in a firm grip and tugged him forward. "Let's get this thing started."

"Gran, come on," Jake protested, trying to unobtrusively pull his arm from her grasp. "I can walk over there by myself."

His tone was so much that of a ten-year-old kid that Kelli had to laugh. Which was a mistake because Gran turned her attention to Kelli. "You, too." Letting go of Jake's arm, she went back to pull Kelli up beside Jake. "If you don't get going pretty soon, Aunt Lucy's going to fall asleep. She's always in bed by eight o'clock."

"All right, all right," Jake growled and grabbed Kelli's hand. They marched up to the arbor to face the justice of the peace, who was staring at them, wide-eyed and slack jawed.

Naomi took up her bridesmaid's spot near Kelli, and Asa quickly positioned himself on the other side of Jake. Asa was trying to stifle his laughter, his lips pressed firmly together, but his shoulders were shaking. Obviously a number of other people didn't even make the effort. Kelli could hear snickers all around them.

"This is worse than that time you and I fell in the pond at the mayor's fancy party," she whispered to Jake.

"Ha!" Jake let out a little reminiscent laugh. "That was crazy. And I wasn't even drunk."

"And when you came up, there was a lily pad on your head." Kelli couldn't keep from grinning at that memory. "It looked like you were wearing a cloche!"

"A what?"

"You know, one of those flapper's hats that women wore in the nineteen-twenties," Kelli explained.

"How would I possibly know that? Only you would think a dude would know what a clonche is."

"Cloche. It's not part sea-shell."

The judge cleared his throat to get their attention, and they turned to face the man.

Jake straightened, jaw set, and said, "Okay. Let's do this."

The robed man leaned in and asked in a quiet voice, "Are you two sure you're okay with this?" He glanced warily at the bikers on one side, then at the assembly of jumbo-sized men on the other. "I mean, if someone is trying to force you or… well, it's really better, you know, for a child to have a single parent than a mother and father who don't want to be together."

Kelli and Jake stared at him until his meaning sank in. "I am *not* pregnant!" Kelli hissed. "This isn't a shotgun wedding!"

Jake let out a snort of laughter, and Kelli turned to glare at him and Asa, who had finally lost his battle with laughter. "Would you two straighten up?" To be fair, Naomi was giggling too, but these guys were more obnoxious.

"I'm sorry, I'm trying," Asa got out between laughs. "It's just… oh, man." He managed to pull his face back to normal, though his lips kept twitching. "Okay. Sorry. I'm good."

The judge squared his shoulders and drew a breath to speak. At that moment, the door to the restroom hallway banged open, and a man's voice said, "Geeze, it's dark as a mine back there. Haven't you people heard of lights?" There was a yap, followed by the man's voice, "Shut up, Princess."

Asa burst into guffaws again. The justice of the peace heaved a sigh. Jake said, "Oh, God, Howard brought that freakin' dog?"

Kelli was numb to surprise by now, and she merely turned to look in the direction of the voice. Whoever the speaker was, he was too short to be seen behind the team, but there was a ripple through the group as he edged his way to the front.

"Have they showed up yet?" the disembodied voice went on. "I heard he missed the team plane once in Chicago. Move your butt, Kowalski. You're too damn big. I can't see a thing."

Jason Kowalski, who had covered his face with his hands in a vain attempt to muffle his laughter, moved aside, and the speaker finally emerged. He was short and middle-aged, and he was carrying a Louis Vuitton purse. *A purse?*

The man looked at Kelli and Jake, and his jaw dropped. "Good God, Jake. What the hell are you wearing?"

A tiny face pressed against the mesh that covered one side of the purse, and Kelli realized that the bag was actually a high fashion dog carrier. Princess, Kelli presumed. She looked like a ball of fluff with bright black eyes, and as soon as she saw Jake, she burst into a paroxysm of barking.

Asa, who had been gradually quieting down, let out a howl of laughter.

"That dog hates me," Jake muttered.

"Good judge of character," Kelli snarked.

Asa was now bent over, wrapping his arms around his torso. "You're killing me, J. I got bruised ribs, you know."

"They taped them, right?" Jake asked.

“Seriously?” Kelli asked. “You’re going to stand there and have a conversation about football in the middle of the ceremony?”

Jake shrugged. “What ceremony? We haven’t even started.”

The justice of the peace cleared his throat loudly. His face was turning an alarming shade of red, and Kelli suspected he wished he had his gavel so he could pound on something. She certainly would like to do that herself.

“Silence!” The judge finally roared, and the voices died down obediently. Asa managed to straighten nearly all the way up, though he was still hugging his ribs, and his laughs had died to shallow breaths. Princess’ owner rolled down the flap above the mesh—to hide her from view, or, more likely, to hide *Jake* from Princess’ view—and even the dog had finally stopped barking.

“Now.” The judge looked at Kelli and Jake with deep disapproval. “I assume you two have not written your own vows.”

Jake snorted, and Kelli said, “Just make it short, and let’s get this over with.”

Candace Camp is the NY Times best-selling author of over 70 novels, including A Momentary Marriage and the popular Mad Moreland series (which now encompasses a not-so-small portion of that 70). Candace wrote her first novel while in law school.

The experience taught her two things: 1. She can write even surrounded by towers of textbooks tall enough to crush her to death if there were an earthquake. 2. The only kind of tort she has any interest in is the kind that comes after the word chocolate and has an E on the end. So after Candace sold her first book, she happily gave up lawyer-ing to pursue her lifelong dream of writing.

She lives in Austin, Texas with her husband, Pete Hopcus. Her daughter is author Anastasia Hopcus.

Type the following into your browser: http://bit.ly/CCampNewsletter to join Candace's newsletter for exclusive content and to win great prizes EVERY MONTH like FREE books and gift-cards to Amazon!

Website: **http://bit.ly/CCampWebsite**

Amazon: **http://bit.ly/CCampAmazon**

BookBub: **http://bit.ly/CCampBookBub**

Goodreads: **http://bit.ly/CCampGoodreads**

Instagram: **http://bit.ly/CCampInsta**

Facebook: **http://bit.ly/CCampFB**

Twitter: **http://bit.ly/CCampTwitter**

Pinterest: **http://bit.ly/CCampPinterest**

Anastasia Hopcus wrote her first book in the 2nd grade. It was entitled 'Frederick the Friendly French Ferret' and was seven pages long. During high school she started (but never finished) several screenplays as an alternative to doing actual school work. Now she writes even though she's not trying to create a fictional world where she can escape math class.

Anastasia is the author of the YA novel *Shadow Hills.* She lives in Austin, Texas and when she isn't writing, she's watching old horror movies and playing D&D with her husband and friends...or chasing her furry, four-legged children after they've decided to eat something decidedly inedible.

You can follow her on:

Instagram: **@anastasiahopcusauthor**

Amazon: **http://bit.ly/AHopcusAmazon**

Made in the USA
Coppell, TX
12 December 2021